Books by J.S. Frankel

The Nightmare Crew

Beginnings
Law and Order
Integration

Single Titles

The Menagerie

Beginnings

ISBN # 978-1-78651-963-4

©Copyright J.S. Frankel 2016

Cover Art by Posh Gosh ©Copyright 2016

Interior text design by Claire Siemaszkiewicz

Finch Books

Published in 2016 by Finch Books, Newland House, The Point, Weaver Road, Lincoln, LN6 3QN, United Kingdom.

The Nightmare Crew

BEGINNINGS

J.S. FRANKEL

Dedication

To my wife, Akiko, and to my children, Kai and Ray,
Thank you for making my life complete.

Chapter One
Night in the City

Night time, New York City, the Bronx

Paul Wiseman scavenged around the abandoned building for two things, clothes and food. This being a New York winter—the middle of January—it was friggin' cold. He wore only a pair of cutoff jeans a size too small and a threadbare sweater over an equally threadbare T-shirt. The sneakers that covered his feet, soles worn and laces broken, weren't enough to keep out the chill of winter. Additionally, the wind whistled its way through the holes in the building and made him shiver.

Cold, miserable and hungry, he kept up his search for anything to keep the chill out. Movements—four legs… but maybe two?—made him stop and listen. Anything on four legs didn't bother him. Anything on two did. Aware of the potential for trouble should the two-legged variety find him, he kept as quiet as possible. If not the cops, then he had to watch out for gang members. Neither group was on his to-meet list.

The cement was cracked and uneven, and it caused him to trip as he awkwardly stumbled around in the darkness. He cursed as he fell over a crate and landed hard. A second later, he shut his mouth, fearful someone had heard him. Sitting up, he examined his knee. Blood seeped out of a gash and he wiped it away.

Another scratching noise made him freeze up and hold his breath. A second later, the intruder scampered out of the shadows and bolted for the door. It was a rat.

Breathing a sigh of relief, he got to his feet. *Damn, that was close!* Continuing his search, he spotted a bundle in the far corner. After getting to his feet and limping over, he hurriedly pulled the bundle open and...bingo! He found a hoodie and a pair of pants.

Yes, luck was on his side for a change. He hadn't had much lately. At the age of seventeen-plus, he'd gone through a succession of foster homes from an early age onward, had miserable experiences with all of them, and finally ended up in an orphanage. There, at least he could get a high-school education, but even so, a high-school education didn't get a person very far these days.

This was his second time taking flight from his home-not-really-a-home. St. Joseph's, one of the orphanages operating in New York City, had taken him in at the age of ten. Located in the Bronx, it had served the community for many years.

It served as a place to stay, but Paul knew his time was limited. Initially, the head of the orphanage said he could remain...until the age of sixteen. Sixteen came and went and the orphanage, which relied on donations, got a sudden influx of cash from a few decent millionaires, and the people in charge changed the policy to eighteen.

After eighteen, though, he'd age out and be on the streets. Eight months shy of that not-so-magic mark and a one-way ticket out, he'd decided that he might as well get used to the homeless life.

The first time he'd got caught was at the age of fifteen, figuring they'd boot him out soon enough. He'd made the classic mistake of staying in a coffee shop at all hours of the day and someone eventually called the cops. In turn, they called the orphanage.

Brother Max, the director of the orphanage, a huge man in his forties with a large gut and a kindly — although at times world-weary — attitude, brought him back personally and scolded him in the administrative office.

Seated in a rickety hardwood chair, Paul glanced around.

It was a dreary room with gray walls that housed a small desk, a leaky sink, a couple of file cabinets and a few chairs. It felt like a jail cell, not a whole lot different than his room.

"What's the deal here?" asked Max with an aggrieved tone in his voice. "We're trying our best for you. I admit this isn't an ideal place, but it's a whole lot better than being on the streets. You've seen the people out there. You know what it's like."

Having lived almost eight years behind these austere walls, Paul also knew what life was like there. It was a place where only the strong ruled and the kids didn't care. They knew what was going to happen to them after they turned the not-so-magic age. "If you call getting your face smashed in every week fun, cool," he said and couldn't keep the bitterness from showing. "I'd call it something else."

Max clasped his hands and tapped his forefingers together. It was his way of figuring out an answer. Paul just hoped that mention of a deity wouldn't be involved. If there was a God, then He'd made Himself absent, for reasons unknown.

In the long run, it didn't matter. What was done was done, and he'd deal. He'd *dealt* with a lot worse. He'd *dealt* with being ignored by his foster parents or beaten by them. He'd *dealt* with the other kids picking on him because he studied. He'd *dealt* with having no friends.

Most of all, he'd *dealt* with all of this crap because he had a dream of being someone and making it in this cruel and uncaring place called Earth...

Falling silent, he wondered for the umpteenth time why his parents had given him up. He didn't recall his mother at all but had a picture of his father someone had given to him when he was around five. He couldn't remember who'd given it, but it was special—a memory of home—and he always carried it with him.

It was like looking in a mirror. Both on the short and slender side of five-seven, they had the same mop of brown hair, brown eyes and a birthmark the size of a dime on the left cheek. Same looks, same hair... Paul shut the memories down, indistinct though they were. For all he knew, his parents were somewhere probably living the life of royalty, and he was here.

A gust of bitterly cold wind interrupted his trip down abandonment lane. He'd been on his own for almost a week. Social Services would probably find him sooner or later, but he was counting on the latter and not the former.

This time it would be different. He'd checked out all city maps, found the more desolate areas and memorized the places he thought were the safest. In addition, he planned on moving around as much as the inclement weather would let him. "It's a big city," he muttered. "Lots of people... They won't find me."

At first, it had been cool to come and go as he pleased and enjoy a measure of freedom. He'd spent the daylight hours ducking in and out of stores, sneaking into and sleeping in low-rent movie theaters and reading books in stores. From the way he acted, quiet and cool, keeping his head down and bothering no one, it had seemed he was invisible and he'd liked it that way — up to a point.

Deep down, though, he was lonely and hungered to be part of something, but practicality cut through the euphoria of being independent. Even if the authorities didn't find him, he had to come up with something soon. There was no way in the world he'd steal. He'd seen other bums and streetwise kids do it.

A fight he'd seen over a bottle of wine between two homeless people had sealed the deal. He'd ducked into an alley to take a leak and had seen a homeless man try to take a bottle of wine away from another homeless dude who'd been asleep. It proved to be a mistake, as the second guy had leapt up and clobbered the would-be thief. He'd then spotted Paul. "You want some?" he'd yelled, while whipping out a knife. "I'll cut you good!"

The threat gave him all the impetus he needed. Paul had taken off as fast as his feet could carry him. Catching his breath in a bookstore ten blocks away, he'd known that he was outsized and outmanned by the bigger, more experienced crowd. The streets could be most frightening, as well as unforgiving. For now, he figured if he couldn't steal, he'd have to come up with something else.

Since he wasn't any physical threat, he tried another tack—acting. Standing on various streets corners during the day, he put on his most doleful look, sat with a moldy baseball cap in front of him that he'd found in a trash can, and begged. "Spare some change, sir? Spare some change, ma'am?" he asked the passersby.

Those were the words he always used, accompanied by a soulful, lost look. Considering he looked more than a little bereft with a skinny hangdog face, a pair of limpid brown eyes and a rather cute smile, the people he hit on usually offered a few kind comments and dropped some coins or even some bills into his palm.

He thanked them, too—always politely—but he never stayed in one spot too long. The streets were dangerous, but alleyways were worse. Lots of big men, mean men— women, too—often got their marks in those places. Usually they just stole money or, at times, the victims' clothes. However, sometimes they killed their victims in order to leave no witnesses. Paul didn't feel like becoming another statistic.

Speaking of statistics, something he'd seen on television at the orphanage about ten days before he'd fled made him think New York was going through another crazy spell. Madness usually gripped the city come summertime— the heat always made people a little nuts—but this was the dead of winter. The reporters had talked of a giant bat flying overhead, something like a six-foot rodent dropping out of the sky and whacking out the criminals.

No proof, though. It wasn't as if anyone had photographic evidence. The entertainment and online channels had talked about a new sort of avenger who'd come to fight crime. "It's like something out of a comic book!" one reporter had exclaimed.

Comic books were comic books. This was reality. If the people were talking about it, the crooks weren't. Being duly concerned about the public's welfare, the statisticians claimed that crime had dropped four percent in only a few days. That may not have been much, but at least some people could walk late at night and not get toasted.

"It's all ratings," one kid had said at the time. A group of kids had clustered around the television and had watched the reports with everyone speculating on what was going on. "They just gotta get their ratings up and give people a story."

"How do you know?" Paul had asked.

The kid had turned and fixed with him with a look designed to stop any future conversation. "Like, would anyone really look that way? Get a clue, dude."

Most of the other kids had laughed. A giant bat causing terror, sure thing, and let me tell you about the alligators in the sewer...

Another blast of cold air chilled him to the marrow and brought him back to his task. He lugged his stash over to a relatively warm spot. The hoodie turned out to be old and stained, but it didn't smell too bad, and it was just his size, too. He hurriedly slipped it on and turned his attention to the pants.

Oh man, they smelled rank! Tossing them aside and continuing his search, he found a pair of boots and some socks in a corner and put them on. They fit well enough, and a feeling of warmth spread through his body. "Yeah, this'll do," he murmured, grateful to whoever had thrown these clothes away.

Now, all he had to do was to get something to eat and his evening would be complete. He quietly crept around the room, found nothing, and resigned himself to going hungry for the second night in a row. Dumpster diving meant going outside into an alleyway and no... That was a definite no.

"If this keeps up, I'll be a skeleton before long," he said aloud.

"You're gonna be dead in about two minutes," responded someone in a deep, grating voice.

When Paul pivoted, he saw that three large men stood in a row not ten feet away. A fourth man appeared out of the darkness and stood near the exit, blocking off all possibility of escape. Frightened and looking around wildly, Paul saw only one way out — and good luck getting passed the gang members.

"Crap," he whispered.

"Yeah, that sort of sums up what's left of your life," said one man who stood larger than the rest. With a face pockmarked by the scars of adolescent acne as well as battle scars he'd probably received in an untold number of fights, he added, "Got anything to say?"

Paul started to shake once the men came closer. From the way they dressed — long, black overcoats, black boots and black shirts — he knew they were Bangers. They were a group of punks who'd made their presence known a few months before with a series of violent acts against the homeless and the unlucky.

On the rare occasions when they deigned to meet the press, they always wore masks to disguise their faces as they espoused their *raison d'être*. "We're here to clear the streets and keep New York safe. We're street sweepers."

Street Sweeping — they called it their motto. Some of the more clued-out citizens thought of them as guardian angels, but in reality they were merely punks who enjoyed killing homeless people.

As for the police? Hey, this was New York, and what went on in New York stayed there. They often claimed that they were in the process of making arrests. However, thus far they'd only hauled in two of the street-sweeping scum. Either they had more important things to do or else they were falling down on the job.

Concerning their weapons of choice, the Bangers very

rarely used guns. Walking mountains didn't need guns, although they did carry an assortment of metal pipes, knives and chains. Now, the rustle of metal grating against metal resounded throughout the building and it sent another chill down his spine.

"Guys," he said, summoning up his courage, "I was just looking to keep warm, you know? It's cold outside, and — "

"And we're going to send you to a warmer place," interrupted the leader as a savage grin split his ugly face.

Looking more closely at the man, Paul noticed that he actually had his name stenciled on his coat — Louis. Now what kind of moron would advertise his name for the law to see? Oh wait, the law wasn't here and no one cared.

"Are you ready, kid?" Louis asked. He carried a metal pipe and smacked it against his palm. The sound of metal hitting flesh echoed across the room. From the way he held it, it looked as though he knew how to use it. "You deserve to be rotting in hell along with the other scum," he continued, swinging the pipe faster.

"We put a lot of 'em there," added Banger number two, who carried a length of heavy chain. He didn't have his name stenciled on his coat, but it didn't make him any less threatening. "Get ready, punk. If you want to pray, do it now."

Allowing a final prayer also set the Bangers apart from other thugs. From what the newspapers had said, the Bangers always allowed their victims one last prayer before they ripped them apart. They then wrote the prayer in blood on the ground so all could see.

Quivering now, a feeling of hopelessness along with loose bowels struck, and Paul clenched up downstairs, desperately trying to hold everything in. He only hoped that his end would be quick. Bending to one knee, he made his voice sound as quiet and humble as possible. "Guys, I didn't do anything to you. I just wanted a place to — "

His stopped speaking when he saw their implacable expressions. They weren't going to listen to him anymore than the wind would. He stayed down, but spotted a crowbar out of the corner of his eye. Oh yeah... Say hello to my little friend!

When the leader asked him again if he wanted to pray, Paul seized the crowbar and in a shocking burst of desperation, smashed the big man on the kneecap. Louis fell to the ground and howled, "You freakin' hit me!"

As the other two men stood by, shocked that a victim would actually hit back, Paul got to his feet, set his stance, took batting practice and knocked out Number Two. The other two men ran at him, but he menaced them back until he reached the door.

"Come and get some," he challenged.

Bad idea, as the other men came at him. Stunned, he dropped the crowbar and tore out of the door, the howls of the men following him into the night.

"You're dead!" they screamed. "You're freakin' dead!"

No, he wasn't—not yet. The cold air revived him, and he ran out of the building and down the alleyway. Strength wasn't his forte, but he could run, and fear and desperation fueled his flight. A metal fence at the end of the alley separated him from the safety of the street. Salvation lay ten feet away, straight up and over.

With a lunge, he jumped halfway up the fence and started to scale it, but a knife sang out of the darkness and buried itself in the back of his right leg. He screamed and fell to the ground. Closing his hands around the haft, he yanked the blade out. Blood spurted from the wound as agony lanced through his body. Try as he might to get up, he couldn't. The enemy closed in on his position, the leader limping noticeably, and Paul cowered against the fence.

"You little turd," growled Louis. "We usually get rid of the scum quickly, but in your case, we'll make an exception."

"I'm only seventeen," Paul protested. Why they were doing this to him was wrong and didn't they care? He wanted to shout it, but then realized, just like everyone else, they *didn't* care. The pack surrounded him and the assault began. Kicks to his ribs, punches to his face and body…

Covering up didn't help much. In that period known as the-moment-before-it-all-ended, he silently asked the wind to take him away. All he heard, though, was a whisper.

Abruptly, the men stopped the beating. "Did you hear that?" one of them asked nervously. "It sounded like… wings."

"Maybe it's that bat they're talkin' about on the news," another punk said with a note of fear in his voice.

"Shut your mouth," snarled Louis. "There ain't no such thing."

The whisper of the wind grew stronger, and a gale force sprang up, pushing the attackers back. It wasn't random. It was as if someone or something had thrown up an invisible column of air, hard and impenetrable. "What's goin' on here?" Louis asked with a note of fear in his voice.

His friends didn't say anything, just pointed to the sky. Following their lead, Louis looked up and screamed. The other three men screamed as well when someone wearing a black cape dropped out of nowhere to land noiselessly in front of them. Black leather pants and boots completed the picture.

This was no bat. It was a person. It was dressed much the same as the Bangers, but it looked sleeker and totally otherworldly.

"What in the hell are you?" Louis shouted. "What are you?"

The individual didn't answer. It stood stock still at first, and from his vantage point, Paul estimated the person to be around five-six. Not overly large at all, but whatever this person was, they had some veil of power capable of keeping the scum at bay.

As for this person's gender, it was impossible to tell, even though they wore their hair long. It streamed behind their head like a black waterfall, glossy and full, and shone clearly in the dim light of the streetlamps.

Quickly the Bangers forgot about their terror and went

on the offensive. Using their weapons as well as their fists, they beat on the newcomer, but the person in black simply allowed them to wail away. Their chains and pipes bounced off its hide.

Finally, in what had to be the last, desperate move of an equally desperate person, Louis pulled a pistol from his coat pocket and emptied the clip into the figure in black. He shot at point-blank range, no less than two feet away. No way could he miss…and he didn't. The person jerked around from the impact of the bullets but didn't go down. The ejected cartridges hit the concrete, each of them making a faint pinging sound.

Abruptly the gun clicked empty and it fell from Louis' suddenly-nerveless hand. "What's going on?" he screamed in fear as well as frustration. "Why won't you die?"

"Because I can't," the person answered in a very feminine voice.

A woman— It *was* a woman! Paul shrank back against the fence and watched as she went into action. In a series of moves almost too fast for his eyes to follow, she seized the enemy one by one in an iron grip around their throats and tossed them at the wall in rapid succession. They hurtled through the air, hit the bricks with a sickening thud and fell to the ground.

Seconds later, she strode over in a casual manner to where Louis was. Bending over him, she addressed him in a tone colder than ice. "Now, you shouldn't be picking on people. You know better." She waggled her finger as if to underscore her statement.

"Don't kill me," he babbled in a voice thick with fear. "Don't kill me…please."

A second later, he began mewling out of sheer stark raving terror. Through a blur of pain, Paul observed the ownage going on, and it was sweet. Call this a moment to cherish…if he lived that long.

"I'm not going to kill you," the woman said.

Louis shrank back against the brick and his rant shut off

like a faucet being twisted. "You're...not? What are you, lady?"

Her voice softened only a shade, but the iron remained as she replied, "I'm your nightmare come true. The one you don't talk about. And I'll come back if you don't stop what you're doing."

In a lightning fast move, she punched him, just once, but very hard. His head snapped around, connected with the brick, and he slithered to the ground, unconscious.

She pirouetted, and Paul got his first clear view of her. The face wasn't an adult's. She looked to be around his age and had angular, pretty features, but with very white skin, so white it resembled porcelain. Her eyes were ice blue, the color of the Arctic Ocean.

Pretty though she was, his attention wasn't on her face or body. He zeroed in on her teeth. No, not teeth... She had fangs.

Fangs...it wasn't possible. This was the twenty-first century. People like this didn't exist. His mind screamed one word—vampire.

"What's your name?" she asked.

"Paul...Paul Wiseman," he blurted out.

She cocked her head to one side and her eyes traveled up and down his body. "You're bleeding," she said in a very pleasant voice. "You should get that looked at."

She stooped down and dabbed at the blood on the ground with a long, tapered finger. In a slow, careful move, she put a spot of the blood on her small pink tongue and swished it around in her mouth. A moment later, she gave a nod of what seemed like approval. "This is AB-negative, just like mine. That's rare. I think I might like you."

"Like me?" he asked, fearful for his life. First, the Bangers had almost beaten him to death and now it looked as though he'd suffer the same fate, although it would come in a different form. "Like me as what, your dinner?"

"No, I don't work that way," she replied. The hardness in her face disappeared and a smile emerged. Her fangs retracted, and she showed small, white and even teeth. In total, she looked pretty hot, even with her bone-white skin.

How *did* she work, then? He wanted to ask her, but a second later the sound of a dog barking distracted him. A mutt, small, scrawny and half-starved, entered the alley. It ran up to the girl and started to growl. In turn, she hissed, a sharp and totally mean sound that sent the dog away howling.

"Dogs don't like me," she offered as an excuse.

Paul could only stare at the scene. This wasn't happening. It wasn't real.

"Let's go for a ride," she said, interrupting his thoughts of the weird and fantastic. "We need to talk."

In a quick move, she grabbed the collar of his hoodie and hauled him up into the sky. One second ago he'd almost been Banger meat, and now he was soaring with some vampire chick over the city.

A riot of questions ran through his half-conscious mind. It wasn't as if he didn't know his blood type — he did. But how could she possibly know what his Rh factor was without using some kind of machine for it?

Oh wait, she's a vampire, and now she's probably taking me to a quiet place so she can drink up and be on her way.

During their flight, Paul tried to talk, but only a series of choking sounds emerged from his throat. After a magnificent effort to get his vocal chords working, he managed to stammer out, "Thanks."

"If you mean thanks for saving your butt from those punks, don't worry about it," she said over the sound of the wind rushing by. "Just doing my job is all."

"Doing your job…"

He fell silent then, looking at the buildings below him. They had to be at least two hundred feet off the ground, if not more, and she could fly. Where were they going? What was happening?

It had to be a dream, but a second later reality intruded. She went into a dive and his ribs whined in pain. "Oh crap!"

gasped Paul. This was it. This was the end.

However, they landed with a gentle bump in what looked to be someone's backyard, and she released him. He fell to the ground, trying to get his breath back. Sitting up, he found that they'd landed in a small residential area. Quaint-looking wooden structures lined the road, but fortunately there was no one around at this time of night. It was biting cold and the ground was hard as rock.

This being winter, a crust of frost and snow covered everything. In addition, a sharp wind had begun to blow and he shivered. Rational thought was difficult, but the one thing he managed to get out was, "What's your name?"

"Angela," she said in a cottony voice that somehow took away the cold. "Do you like it?"

How to answer her? "Yes."

"I don't have a last name," she continued, kicking dirt off her boots and brushing a few stray specks of mud from her cape. "None of us do."

Us... Who is us? And what was up with the no-last-name business? This didn't make sense…and his mind felt as if it was taking a trip outside his body. He looked down at the ground. Blood dripped in a steady pattern from his wound, yet he felt no pain.

She cocked her head to one side as if judging him and bent down to examine his leg. "The bleeding's started again," she said. "You're going into shock. Anyway, this is our home." With a delicately-pointed finger she indicated a white wooden two-story house. "We'll fix you up. Don't worry."

"Fix me up?" Paul wondered if they were going to simply dress his wounds or carve him up like a turkey. "Am I, like…next on your hit list?"

The person called Angela offered what he took to be a kind smile. "I'm not the one you should be worried about."

Her answer wasn't the answer he'd been expecting. He wanted to tell her something else, but the pain and shock had really started to set in, and heaviness settled over his eyes, forcing them to close. Through a dim curtain, he heard her say, "Stay with me. Stay with me."

No way he could fight it, but her words rang in his ears — *Stay with me.*

If this was how he had to go out, so be it. In the last moments of consciousness, he heard her voice, soft and low, urging him to hang in there and stay with her. Then the world faded into nothingness.

Chapter Two
Meet the Crew — Part I

Remembrances, Paul had a few. He didn't dream very often, but somewhere in the dimmest recesses of his mind thoughts of his parents surfaced. Who were they? What were their jobs? Did they somehow lose their lives in an accident? Maybe they'd been called away, but for what purpose, he did not know.

When he was very small, he had the idea his parents were superheroes. It seemed like the dream of every little kid. They were working for the government, spies sent on secret assignments to save the world. It was hard to let go of this concept. In his reveries, Kodachrome-colored deeds of derring-do, battles against super-villains and fights for justice flashed in front of his eyes. Those images comforted him.

Above all, the concept of his father being more than human stood out. He may have been on the short side, but to a young child, all adults were giants. He remembered the pitch of his father's voice, high and somewhat nervous. Did superheroes get nervous? Maybe, as saving the world was a tough job.

Then there was the smell of his aftershave. It smelled like freshly fallen rain, washing away the grime and unpleasant things of the day. The sound of his feet padding along the floor, his quick movements and the timbre of his voice — these qualities indicated someone close and special, and how could his father be anything but special?

His mother, though... He struggled to recall her face and couldn't. Somewhere in his subconscious, the vision of a small room sprang up. He played with his toys there. The walls were a bright yellow, the carpet felt soft and soothing to his skin, and he remembered his father lifting him up…

Shifting now to his later years, the images became sharper, intensified and grew more unpleasant. He recalled his first days in a foster home. He was maybe five at the time. Mrs. Swanson was his first foster mother, a short and scrawny woman who constantly beat him for the slightest perceived infraction. She also hit two other foster children she was raising. "You're not grateful for my care!" she'd screamed.

If this was care, he'd wondered what punishment was but suffered in silence. A visit from Social Services revealed the truth. They'd taken him away when they'd seen the bruises and lacerations on his face and body. He hadn't known what had happened to the two other kids.

Seven now, and he had been on his fourth house. This family hadn't fed him anything but canned soup and stale bread. "We don't have enough food for you," his foster father had said.

Billings had been the man's name. They'd sat at a loaded dinner table, full of decent food, and he and his wife and two children had tucked into their steaks. Paul and Mr. Campbell's Soup became friends…for a while.

The years jumped forward. On perhaps his seventh or eighth foster home — maybe — he recalled a small apartment somewhere in New Rochelle. His foster parents had been alcoholics. They'd smacked him around frequently because he liked to read and they didn't. It had interfered with their bottle time.

When they'd hit, they had used a strap. Made of thick leather, it'd had holes drilled into it, and it had left thick and deep welts on his back and shoulders. It hadn't taken long for him to learn how to run and run fast. He'd struck back whenever possible, but there had been two of them. They had been bigger and meaner, and he hadn't been able to understand why this was happening to him. A broken arm had alerted the authorities once more. They'd come and yelled at the drunks then had taken him away.

"You'll like it," the woman from Social Services had said. She had been in charge of his case and had known of the difficulties he'd been facing. A middle-aged and kindly sort, she'd brought him to St. Joseph's Orphanage, located in the Bronx. She'd had a word with the people in charge and had left him there. "You'll be taken care of here," she'd said.

Little Paul, almost ten, had looked up at the grim gray walls and a sense of foreboding had run through him. The place looked like a prison. This wasn't going to be good… but he'd had nowhere else to go. Still, he had tried one last time and hadn't been able to keep the pleading tone from showing. "Can't I stay with a nice family for once?"

The woman's face had softened and she'd dabbed at her eyes with a handkerchief. "We'll keep trying to find your real family, Paul. Do your best."

A moment later she had been gone and there he'd stayed. He'd walked inside the doors with Brother Max, a large and kindly man who'd spoken softly and had seemed decent enough. Max had shown him to his room. "You'll be staying here for now," he'd said. "Dinner is at six."

Apparently the orphanage had believed in providing the bare minimum of creature comforts. Three unsteady-looking study desks and three cots had filled most of the space. A large closet had sat in one corner near a grimy window. A broom and dustpan had been in the opposite corner.

Peeking outside, Paul had seen a single maple tree in front of the window, the lone piece of nature in this area. Shifting his view to one side, he'd seen the driveway that the would-be adoptive parents used along with the delivery trucks. That had been all.

Emitting a sigh of frustration as well as loss, he'd turned away to stare at the room once more. It had been a room for three…but no one had entered for the longest time, so Paul had sat on the edge of one hard bed, had tried to stop the tears from coming and couldn't. He'd cried for no one wanted to listen to him and no one cared.

"We're all equal here," Max had told the kids one night. It had been their usual bull session where everyone sat around with their friends and aired their grievances. "You get equal time from us because this is what we do. We help others."

Paul had taken those words to mean no one would beat on him or call him names or make fun of him because he was a nerd and didn't fit in with others. Being equal had had to be considered a good thing. That had been all he'd really wanted.

"You've got a good head on your shoulders," one of his teachers had said after class one day. "Once you get out of here, you'll have a bright future."

Oh yes, this had indeed been a compliment. Paul had loved reading, had loved to learn and he'd figured if he couldn't compete with the other kids on the sports field, at the very least he could outdo them in the classroom. They'd respect him for being smart…or so he'd thought at the time.

A reality check had come about two weeks later. "Nerd," one of the kids had said before smacking him in the face. Paul had fallen to the ground, blood dripping from his nose. "You're just a loser who wants to make us look bad."

Talk about a mismatch. This kid had been older and bigger by five inches and fifty pounds. He'd also happened to be one of the more popular kids around and had had a lot of friends. Paul hadn't. In a dog-eat-dog environment such as this, a kid without friends hadn't been able to be very happy. What had made it worse, though, had been morons like this kid who couldn't even pass lunch hadn't liked anyone upstaging them.

In a fit of anger, Paul had gotten to his feet. Rage had outweighed reason, and even though he had been no match for his opponent, he'd lashed out and caught the punk with a sharp, snapping left. It'd rocked the other kid back on his heels. "I don't have to make you look bad," he'd said. "You got this all on your own."

It hadn't been a typical answer. Shy by nature, he'd tended to back off and take the passive approach. Still, there had been times when only a fist would do and this had been one of them.

The kid had come forward to finish the job, but Max had hustled over to break up the more-than-likely massacre. "That's enough," he'd shouted while holding back the bigger boy. Jerking his head at the door, he'd added, "Paul, go to the library. We'll talk later on."

With a nod and a faint smile of surprise as well as gratification for hitting back, Paul had left. His nose had hurt, his body as well, but he'd felt a sense of pride. He'd hit back for a change and taken satisfaction in having gotten in one shot. It hadn't helped much, as the same night the other kids had entered his room and ganged up on him just after lights out...

In an abrupt flash of neurons, the sense of total recall happened and things shifted to his most recent alleyway adventures — the taste of blood in his mouth, the agony of every muscle and nerve ending on fire, the imminence of death... It all came through and forced him to wake up. He did so, heart thudding. A shadow seemed to cross the room then his eyes swam into focus. "Where am...?" he started... and fell silent.

Swiveling his head around, he peered through the darkness. This wasn't a hospital room. Hospital rooms were white. They were sterile and impersonal and cold. This place had wooden walls, a dresser and a full-length mirror in the far corner near the window, and he lay in a comfortable bed. "Wow," he said in wonder, "I'm alive."

Continuing his inventory, he saw a small wooden night table next to the bed. An electronic clock on it showed the hour of six in the morning. He wore the same dirty clothes minus his pants. Neatly folded, they sat at the foot of the bed. Looking down at his body, there were fresh bandages on his injured leg.

A sudden stabbing pain in his ribs made him exhale a sharp breath. Lifting up his hoodie, in the dim light he made out large bruises on his torso. It was amazing he hadn't suffered any severe injuries. He reached down to touch the bandage on his leg. Someone had fixed him up, but who could have done it?

Her— It was the girl. It had to be. In a flash, he recalled the events of the night before. Death had come to him along with a savior. The girl... She was some kind of vampire... Angela. She said her name was Angela, and from the way she'd destroyed the Bangers, she seemed more like an avenging angel than one of mercy. He couldn't decide which.

On the surface it didn't seem possible, yet at the same time he wasn't lying in some alleyway bleeding to death. He was alive...but where?

Getting out of bed, Paul tested his legs, found they worked and moved stiffly over to the window. Peering out, a large backyard with a single tree in the center of it greeted him. A garage sat just outside the fence. He had to be in a house.

"Duh, thanks, Captain Obvious," he muttered.

After grabbing his pants and drawing them on, especially carefully over the bandage on his right leg, he went to the door and eased it open. He poked his head outside and swiveled his neck left then right. The hallway was dark, but he made out two other doors directly across the way. Another door was next to his.

"Hello?" he called softly.

No answer, so he crept outside and went to the first door across the hall. Gently turning the knob, the door opened and he saw a room much like his, with the exception of there being no furniture. Outside of two wooden tables roughly twelve feet by six in the center of the room with four large buckets positioned at each corner, the only other thing he saw was a transparent bag with a valve attached. It lay at the base of one of the tables.

However, Paul's attention wasn't on the bag. He stared at

the bluish liquid jumping from one bucket to the next. He also stared in wonder at the second table. Sand was leaping from each bucket in a series of McDonald's-type arches. Not a grain spilled. It was like watching something...*alive*.

"This can't be happening," he whispered.

Both elements kept jumping back and forth, but now took on other shapes. The water went first and the sand imitated it. First there was an airplane, next a bird and finally, a dolphin. At times he thought he saw a pair of eyes staring back at him from the water, but denial was not just a river in Egypt, as the joke went.

"Oh man, this...isn't real," Paul murmured. "It can't be."

Slowly, he backed out. Trying the next room, he found the door was also unlocked and it was dark inside, but he thought he saw a refrigerator in the corner. There was no other furniture, save a bed, and on it sat a figure that seemed to fill the room with his presence. He took up most of the space on the bed, and his shoulders had to be at least five feet in width. A second later, the figure got up and stood there as a monolith would, silent and impersonal, its head brushing the ceiling.

"Oh holy crap," Paul whispered as the figure shambled over. By his estimation, this thing stood at least seven feet in height. It wore a pair of clean black pants and a neatly-pressed white shirt along with heavy work shoes. That was normal.

When the creature stepped out of the shadows, though, all thoughts of normal went out of the window. The face — scarred, greenish-yellow skin, hollow dead eyes and patches of rotting flesh — made Paul think of only one word.

Zombie... This thing was a zombie. It stood there, bits of flesh dropping from its face to the floor, but it didn't seem to notice them. "I'm hungry," the thing said in a gravelly voice like a truck running along a bumpy road at high speed. "Can you get me something to eat?"

Screaming was called for in this situation, and Paul let one loose that would have rivaled anything out of a Grade-B horror flick. With a start, he leaped back and shut the door with a slam. This…was too unreal.

A touch on his shoulder made him jump and he let out another scream. "Holy crap it's…"

His voice died away when he saw Angela, her hands clasped in front of her body. "Hi," she said. "You're up."

"It's not a dream," he breathed. At this point in time, he was totally convinced he'd stepped into some kind of nightmare.

"No, I'm real," she answered, giving a tentative smile. "How are you feeling?"

"Uh, better, I guess."

After taking in a couple of deep breaths, Paul felt his heart rate slow from hyper-high to semi-normal. His body still hurt, but it felt a lot better than before. However, he wasn't thinking about his body. He was thinking about what he'd seen and more importantly, what those things were going to do. "What's going on here?"

In the dim light of the hallway, she stood out as a slender waif. In a fashion shift, she'd changed her outfit from black leather to a pair of jeans and a long-sleeved light green blouse. No shoes or socks. The floor was freezing cold, so he immediately wrote off the concept of central heating. Yet the cold didn't seem to bother her.

Her fangs were also gone, at least for the moment. Long black hair swirled around her face, and her blue eyes regarded him with a look of curiosity. A second later, the look of curiosity faded as she sniffed the air then leaned over to sniff him. Her nose wrinkled and she pulled back. "You need a shower."

At her declaration, Paul became aware of his own body odor. He reeked and reeked hard. "Oh, um, yeah, I guess I do. Where's the shower room?"

"End of the hallway," she stated in an even voice and pointed with her finger. "Leave your dirty stuff there. I'll get some fresh clothes ready for you."

Dazed and confused, he followed where she pointed,

wandered into the shower, stripped off his clothes and looked at his face in the mirror. He noticed a number of bruises and a black eye stood out, making him look like a raccoon. The tile was old and stained and the toilet looked antique with a chain to pull when the job was done. The bathtub also had a number of cracks in it, but the hot water felt good and it put him in a more positive frame of mind.

Stepping out of the shower, he found a towel had been placed on the toilet seat and he dried off. Wrapping the towel around his narrow waist, he padded back to his room and saw an old pair of black pants, a belt and a lumberjack shirt neatly folded on the bed. They were a little large, but clean clothes were clean clothes.

When he came outside after getting dressed, Angela was waiting for him. "Now that you're ready, I'm going to ask you what you think of my friends. You met them, right?" she asked.

"Friends… They're your friends?"

She shrugged. "I don't have anyone else. We talk…sort of."

Oh…this was a little too much for him to process. How could you talk to water, sand and a patched up quilt-work of a person? Angela caught hold of his arm in an iron grip and steered him back to his room. There, she flicked on the light and guided him over to the bed. He sat, wondering what was about to happen.

"Before we do the introductions, let me give you a rundown on your injuries," she began, and started reading from the list. "Those Bangers gave you a real beating. I'm surprised they didn't damage you worse."

"Who, uh, who put the bandage on me?" he asked.

"I did," she answered, and glanced at the chart again. "You were out for a few hours. From what I can figure, you have a couple of severely bruised ribs. You've also got contusions and a whole lot of lumps. Other than that, you'll make it."

"Thanks," Paul said, still somewhat dazed, but acceptance

was slowly beginning to sink in. He did ask the most obvious question, though. "Uh, do you want me to call you Angela or something else?"

"Call me Angela," she said. "Like I told you before, I don't have a last name."

No last name. She didn't have a last name and her friends probably didn't, either. But were they really alive? People weren't vampires or intelligent water or zombies. They didn't exist. He'd read the stories, seen the movies and thought it all mindless fun. At the very least, it had taken away from the grim reality of his life in the orphanage for a while.

However, now he'd come face to face with these myths that weren't myths at all, and he had no idea of how to handle it. All he thought of was Angela's most previous statement. "You don't have a last name...okay. So...next question...what were those things?"

"They're not *things*," she replied in a somewhat testy voice. "They're my friends. They just look a little different, okay?"

She didn't wait for him to reply, but her manner softened somewhat as she said, "I'll give you the basics. The water guy you saw? His name is Ooze. The sand thing—I haven't figured out if it's a he or a she yet, but we think it's a guy—is called Sandstorm. We call the big guy CF."

A water guy, a sand dune and a zombie...perhaps a werewolf was next on the list? Oh wait, maybe another creature that slithered or flew or spit acid was lurking somewhere in this place. Angela remained silent, so he posed another obvious query. "What does CF stand for?"

"Cannon fodder," she answered in a matter-of-fact tone, as if it explained everything. In fact, it made his confusion increase exponentially.

"Cannon fodder," he repeated, and wanted to say something more but a knock sounded at the door.

Angela went to open it. The zombie and a transparent bag full of water with a vaguely human shape stood there.

"Hey, we got a new recruit?" the water guy asked, staring at Paul curiously. "He looks like everyone else we see on television."

A mouth formed inside the plastic bag, and the voice, while male, sounded like it was coming from underwater. In a moment of supreme lunacy, Paul wondered what else it would sound like.

Grunts came from the zombie and a piece of its cheek dropped to the floor. After a moment, he bent over to pick it up. This whole scenario had entered the land of the weird, gone straight to the realm of odder still and was now in the process of taking a detour to planet strange, times a hundred.

"Where's Sandstorm?" Angela wanted to know.

Her question broke his train of thought. Ooze replied, "Staying in his room," and he jerked a water-filled finger behind him. "You know he's a little anti-social."

"I'm hungry," the zombie said again. "Where's the food?"

Now a pair of eyes formed in the water and they rolled around. When Ooze spoke again, he sounded more than a little aggrieved. "Where else do you think it is? It's in the kitchen. You also got a fridge in your room, but I guess you didn't notice that, either."

"It's empty."

With that reply, the zombie moved off, his feet making heavy thudding sounds as he clumped along. Angela pointed down the hallway. "Ooze, follow him and make sure he doesn't get into trouble."

"That's me," the bag of water sighed. "Call me nanny." As they disappeared from view, his groan filled the air. "Man, please do *not* disintegrate on the floor. You know how hard it is to vacuum up skin."

"Sorry…"

Angela shut the door and let out a sigh as if she'd been expecting this to happen all along. "Are you freaked out?"

Talk about an understatement! "Where am I?" Paul asked, once he'd gotten his mouth working again.

Waving her hand at the wall, she recited, "You're on the second floor of this house. We're in Allegany County, New York. This place's name is Angelica. That's where I got my name from. My maker chose it for me."

"Your maker chose it for you?"

Angela offered a curious smile. "You repeat things a lot, don't you?" Before he could answer, she continued, saying, "Suit yourself. I use the word *maker*. You could call him my father, my creator or the scientist who works in his secret laboratory. It doesn't matter what word you use. He made me. He made all of us."

Paul mulled the information over in his mind. Whoever this maker was, that could wait. "Uh, well, you have a nice name," he agreed. It seemed like the thing to say, something nice and neutral. "Uh, is this some kind of farming community?"

"It's more like a tourist spot," she answered. "I'm not really sure. I'm still in learning mode."

Confused by her reply, he started to mumble out a question, but she took his hand in hers once again. Her skin was cool and dry, and she opened the door and pulled him along the hallway. "Come with me."

With her strength, he couldn't resist. At the end of the hallway lay a set of stairs. As he walked down them, a creaking sound resounded and he made an effort to tread lightly. It didn't help.

On the first floor, the water bag—Ooze—and the zombie were sitting on a couch facing a television set. The room was filled with antique furniture. It was dark as the drapes were drawn. However, lights that must have come from a nineteenth-century bar lit the room in a cheerful yellow glow.

From his position on the couch, Ooze offered a smile which stood out in the liquid. Nothing else floated inside the bag—its brains had to be part of the water. Thinking and talking water—this was going to take some getting used to.

The zombie guy exuded a vaguely mossy smell as it munched on something pink, the size of a hamburger. While Paul had seen enough zombie movies to know what they liked to eat, he decided not to ask. Some things just weren't worth knowing.

Their journey continued past the living room and through a large and fully stocked kitchen which housed three freezers that wouldn't have looked out of place in a restaurant, a dinner table with chairs and two ceiling-high cabinets.

"We're almost there," Angela said.

She stopped at the second cabinet. It had three drawers. She twisted the handle on the middle drawer. Immediately, the cabinet's front slid aside and Paul's jaw dropped as he viewed a series of steps leading down. "What is…?"

"Secret passage," she said in an offhand manner. Reaching inside, she flicked on a light switch and motioned for him to follow her. "Down here."

"What is this?" Paul asked in another moment of wondering what movie set he'd walked onto. With tentative steps, he descended the staircase and came face to face with something out of a mad scientist's finest fantasy.

"Take a look," she said, once they had reached the bottom of the stairs and she'd flicked a switch. Unlike the lights upstairs, here, a series of light bulbs strategically strung across the ceiling illuminated everything in a sickly yellow glow.

It had probably been a cellar once, but now it had been turned into a laboratory. Roughly fifty feet by fifty feet square, it housed an impressive array of equipment. Four chambers stood at the wall opposite the door. Cables and pipes linked to a generator fed into them. Oval-shaped, they had to be at least eight feet in height and around four feet in diameter. All of them had cracks in the sides and were charred a deep black.

In the center of the room, a desktop computer, beakers full of chemicals and assorted medical equipment lay on a table. Another table next to it held a jumble of circuit boards and wires. As for the rest, the only other things that stood out were a large refrigerator in the far right corner and a cot next to it.

A figure lay on the cot, encased in a form-fitting transparent plastic cover. Paul walked over to get a better look. The person inside was a rather smallish man who appeared to be in his seventies. With sallow skin and nondescript features, he could have been anyone. However, given the situation, Paul knew this guy wasn't just anyone's kindly old uncle.

Angela walked over and took up a position next to Paul. She gazed at the body and bowed her head. In a tone that indicated loss, she said, "He was our maker."

Okay, go with the dead scenario. "Your maker," Paul repeated and silently vowed to stop echoing what she said. It was dumb. He fell silent as the totality of the situation hit him. Obviously, this man had created these things. And now he was dead and these monsters were free to roam and hurt and kill.

However, it didn't answer the question of why they hadn't killed him. As he contemplated the intransigence of life, Angela touched his arm, which caused him to jump. "Relax," she said. "I just need to ask you a question."

Right. Don't enrage the vampire chick. "Sorry, I…uh… Go ahead."

"Did you have a place to stay before?" she asked. "What I mean to say is…did you have a family?"

"No," he answered, feeling the truth might prolong his life. "I, uh, don't have parents. I was living in an orphanage."

In a quick move, she leaned over to look him in the eye. He felt the warmth of her breath on his face. "I know what an orphanage is. I guess it wasn't much fun there, was it?"

"No, not really," Paul admitted. Oddly enough, right now he felt no fear, only curiosity.

Angela gave a slight shrug and waved her hand toward the chambers. "I don't know about other places to live. I only know here. I woke up a month ago. My friends woke up about a week after me. They're still getting acclimated. Ooze is pretty up to speed, Sandstorm doesn't talk very much, and CF…" She shook her head, apparently in sympathy for him.

Call this scenario beyond strange. He had the feeling the oddities would keep on coming. "Um, you woke up?" he asked. "You mean" — he pointed at the chambers — "you were made in those things and this guy" — he waved at the corpse — "made you in them?"

"Yes, that's right," said Angela and cocked her head to one side as if considering all the angles. "Before I give you more details, let me ask you a question. Do you need a place to stay?"

It didn't take him more than a millisecond to say, "Yes." He needed food, shelter, and even though this situation was totally freaky, acceptance had started to creep in.

She smiled. "So you need a place to stay, and we need someone to talk to. That's really all we want, too."

"Okay," he said, his mind somewhat calmer, "tell me your story."

Angela led him out of the door. "Where do I start?"

Chapter Three
Meet the Crew — Part II

Back in the living room, Ooze and CF sat on a sofa watching television, with the former focusing on the screen and the latter staring into space. "I guess Sandstorm isn't going to join us?" Angela asked.

"Nah," Ooze replied, flicking through the channels at light speed.

Click, click went the remote, and the images whizzed by so fast they became a blur. Either he had attention deficit disorder or he could process information much faster than the average homo sapiens. Paul figured it had to be the latter.

"Is that your answer?" asked Angela with a tinge of impatience.

Ooze's head didn't move a fraction of an inch. "Like I said, he's still feeling anti-social. You would, too, if you couldn't talk."

Paul wondered how the sand thing could communicate then decided not to ask. The zombie was still eating and stared at nothing while the water-bag finally stopped channel-surfing and settled on a news program that was in the process of giving out the day's events.

From the way the broadcasters spoke and their animated expressions, it seemed something new and unusual was about to happen or had already happened. With a note of mounting excitement in his voice, Ooze said, "Hey, I think we finally made the evening edition."

Sure enough, a recap began of the previous night's happenings with the beaten and bruised Bangers being hauled away. The voiceover continued with Louis, his face bloody and swollen and almost unrecognizable, yelling, "*A vampire, man, I'm tellin' ya. It was a vampire...*"

The police escorted him and his friends to their cruisers and took them away. A reporter, young, blonde and serious-looking, intoned, "*And that seems to be the story so far. From the information we've obtained, it seems a vampire, a young woman, attacked these men tonight and they're being taken away for treatment then questioning...*"

They conveniently left out the fact the Bangers were going to kill me, Paul thought. Ooze turned around and a smile formed on his face. "Hey, Angela, that was you?"

She nodded. "It was."

"Lookin' good for a first time," he replied. "That's the ticket right there. Own the scum. That's the way things are done here!"

He turned back to watching the news. The zombie continued to chomp away and as he ate, his smell gradually disappeared. This was off the chain!

Paul started to relax, although he remained wary. The front door was close. If he had to run, then he'd motor on out as fast as he could. Screw the cold weather. He was gone. *Oh wait.* The girl could fly. It wouldn't be too difficult for her to catch him, and he'd already seen what she could do in terms of fighting prowess.

The camera then cut to the broadcast booth. "*And in another item,*" the newscaster said, "*a teenager is still missing from St. Joseph's Orphanage. Paul Wiseman, seventeen, apparently ran away five days ago. If anyone in New York State knows of his whereabouts, please call this number.*"

A picture of Paul's face appeared on the screen along with his vital statistics. "*He is not considered dangerous, but the authorities are concerned...*"

Ooze turned around and a look of surprise appeared on his watery face. "Hey, that's a nice mug shot. You ran away?"

Paul nodded. "I didn't like it there very much."

The water-bag shifted and it looked as if he was shrugging. "Congratulations on surviving the mean streets. Don't worry. You can bunk with us. Angela needs someone to talk to."

Angela's face suffused a bright pink. She mumbled something incoherent then indicated with a wave of her hand for Paul to take a seat on the couch. As he did so, he caught sight of the zombie. He'd finished eating, and the body-rot seemed to halt in its tracks and reverse itself. It was like watching time-lapse photography, only faster.

Angela cleared her throat. "Hey," she said.

Startled by the miracle of science then her voice, Paul swiveled his gaze to meet hers. Her eyes held no malice in them, only honesty, and he started to feel a little calmer. "So, you're here and you want the whole story?"

"You said you were going to tell me."

Angela sat down beside him and folded her hands in her lap. "Like I told you downstairs, I woke up about a month ago. I was created — *we* were created — by that man you saw. I don't even know his name, but he gave us names and life and powers. He downloaded essential facts and data into us. That's all I know."

"You knew to come to New York?"

She tapped the side of her head. "I have knowledge, but I don't have any experience. There's a difference, you know. But I've got powers and I wanted to see what I could do."

"Powers," Paul echoed and vowed once more to stop repeating things. He'd seen her fly, and she was ridiculously strong. Additionally, he remembered the gunshots. Bullets didn't slow her down for a moment. "I saw you take care of those punks…but…what can you all do?"

A face not unlike a smiley emoticon formed on the bag. "See this?" he asked, pointing to his bag. "It's not really a bag. It's a containment suit, which is just a fancy name for a bag, anyway. With it, I can walk like you do, but I travel faster in water."

The vision of the bucket trick returned, big time. "Wait…

so you can actually go through water?"

Ooze laughed. "In case you haven't noticed, I *am* water. Be like water. You know who said that? Bruce Lee did. I become whatever shape I want, and I can control water. Sandstorm does the same thing, except he travels on land and even through the air if the wind's blowing hard enough. It's all done on a molecular level. It's got something to do with atomic structures and being attuned to the particular chemicals and all that."

Another brief chuckle burbled out. "The guys in lab coats always use twenty-dollar words. My maker downloaded most of his knowledge in me, but I'm still learning how to do what he did. Anyway, I like to keep things simple. I don't know the science behind it. It's in me, so I just do it."

An instant later, he contorted his body into the shape of Rodin's The Thinker, a statue of a baseball player at bat, and a starfish. "It's impressive — or am I wrong?"

"Yeah, it's impressive," answered Paul, feeling amazed. What other miracles of science were out there?

Ooze resumed his semi-humanoid shape and said, "I can't really hold these shapes for too long. I'm still learning. I can walk in my suit, but it's a little difficult, you know? This suit just wasn't made for walking.

"Still—" He paused. "If you really want to see me get around, just dump me in a lake or river and I go where the current takes me. Or I can go against it, if I want. I'm pretty self-sufficient. I don't eat. I don't need to breathe. All I need is a container, like what I'm wearing right now. If this suit gets damaged, just toss me in a garbage bag. I'll make do."

Pointing his finger at the zombie, he added with a note of admiration, "CF isn't much of a talker, just like our dirt buddy. But he's a doer, and that's important."

"What does he do?" Paul asked.

"I lift things," CF answered.

He got up, and with his thumb and forefinger only, he lifted the sofa and put it down. He then went over to a cabinet in the far corner and did the same thing, lifting it as a child would a toy. Ooze's voice held a certain note of triumph mixed with awe. "That weighs over three hundred pounds with all the clothes and stuff that's in there, and he's just using two fingers. You don't want to see what he can really do if he has to."

He swiveled his gaze to the giant. "Careful, CF. Do it gently," he counseled with a mildly chiding tone. "This is your home, too, remember? You don't want to be breaking stuff."

"I got it." The zombie lowered the cabinet. "And now I'm hungry again."

"You're always hungry," snapped Ooze, frowning now. "Kitchen's over there. Get something to eat and come back."

As the massive zombie creature lumbered into the kitchen, a smile replaced the frown. "CF isn't what you'd call overly bright, but he's really strong. I just wish he wouldn't rot away so much."

"Rot…" Paul breathed.

A laugh burbled out from the water. "You saw what happened before, didn't you? Don't pretend you didn't."

Fumbling for the right words, Paul got out, "Yeah, I saw it, and—"

"You're having a hard time believing it, am I right?" Ooze interjected, his voice wavering between sarcasm and bluntness. "Well, believe it. If he doesn't eat, he starts to decay. That's the deal. When we woke up, it started to happen. I wanted to start a pool on which body part would drop off first, but Angela thought it was too cruel. Anyway, that's why he was made."

"Made for what?"

Ooze shrugged. The movement sent his body rolling and undulating in waves. "He's cannon fodder. You know what that means, don't you?"

Paul recalled Angela mentioning the term. "Uh…"

"He's designed to take the first hit and keep taking it. That's his job."

Take the first hit… It sounded like they were soldiers.

"We were made for a reason," Angela cut in as she swept her hair behind her ears. "I can't really explain it, but it's like I have my maker's voice in my head sometimes. It's saying he gave us powers for a reason. He wanted us to be special."

Special didn't cover the half of it. "Uh, don't take this the wrong way," Paul began, "but are you really a vampire?"

Angela looked at him, her eyes guileless. "I can fly and control the wind to a certain degree," she said. "I'm strong. I know that. But that's all I can do. I don't shape shift. I can't control wolves or rats or peoples' thinking. I know what a vampire is because of my download, but I'm different. Besides, I've never tried human blood before."

Her reply about not having tried human blood sent Paul's heart racing. Was he going to be first on the list? He wiped away the sweat from his forehead. She seemed to notice his sudden fear and raised her hands. "Calm down. I'm not interested in drinking human blood."

To hear her say so was a relief and his heart gradually slowed to its normal rate. "But, you guys…eat?"

"I don't," Ooze cut in. "I'm water. I float, I drift and I swim. CF eats synthetic food that our maker made for us. We have a pretty large supply…"

He stopped speaking as a resounding crash emanated from the kitchen followed by, "I dropped something."

"Great," Ooze muttered as he flowed off the couch and headed to the kitchen. "If he doesn't eat everything in sight, we won't have to go shopping for a few more years."

Warning given, he disappeared through the door. Angela chewed her lip. "I don't know much about my powers outside of what I can already do," she continued. "I know that I can't be hurt by bullets. Those guys with the knives and pipes, they didn't hurt me, either."

Paul had already seen the zombie regenerate, so what other miracles were in store? "So…let me get this straight. You've both got powers of regeneration and you can't be hurt." He thought fast. "Don't take this the wrong way, but you're a vampire, sort of. Can you go out in sunlight?"

Angela nodded. "I can, but I don't like it."

"Why don't you?"

She stopped chewing her lip and the icy glare returned to her eyes. "People out there stare. The first time I went out for a flight, I landed in a town about thirty miles from here. People asked me if I was sick. I didn't know what they meant, but they started to make jokes. I understood then just how different I was. And you saw the way those punks looked at me, didn't you?"

An image of their terror-stricken faces flashed across in front of Paul's eyes. "Yeah, I did," he replied.

A look of distinct discomfort replaced the one of uncertainty. "Ooze can't go out and it's sort of obvious about CF because of what he is. Sandstorm likes to stay inside, anyway. The upshot is, we stay here and we keep the drapes closed at all times. We keep a low profile."

Keeping a low profile was one thing, but what if someone delivered food or came around to check on the electricity? Putting the question to Angela, she offered a shrug. "I have makeup in my room that makes me look more" – her voice faltered – "more human. The house was registered in my name. I pay the bills in cash and keep the receipts." She swept her hand toward the large cabinet. "We've got enough."

She ran her fingers through her hair in a quick, nervous gesture. "Anyway, I only go out at night because that's the only time I can fly. That's the way things work for me. I'm still strong during the day, but no flying."

"Uh-huh," Paul said, filing this information away.

"At first, I just flew around this area and learned where everything was," continued Angela, and she ticked off the places she'd been to on her fingers. "I saw the river, the other houses and the highway. Then I branched out. When I found you last night, that was my first time in downtown Manhattan."

In the movies, the mad scientists made clones and

creatures. They created the creatures to take over the world, kill and maim, and usually their creations rebelled or escaped by the end of the flick. However, celluloid wasn't reality. This was.

"Um, can I look at the lab again?" he asked.

Angela got up and pulled him up with her. "Yeah, sure, you can look." A rumble came from her stomach and she wavered on her feet. "That's low blood sugar working or in my case, low platelet count. I need to eat. My stash is downstairs. And something inside me says we should bury our maker. Can you help me?"

"Sure," he answered as she led the way downstairs.

Once there, she went to the refrigerator and opened it. A massive assortment of tiny bottles filled with red fluid lined the shelves. "This is my dinner," she said. A transparent injection gun sat on the work table. She fitted one of the bottles onto it, twisted it, and the fluid emptied into the gun. "It's ready now."

After rolling up her sleeve, Angela stabbed herself in the arm. Immediately, the fluid emptied from the gun and her veins stood out as the blood coursed through them. Giving a satisfied "ah" sound, she put the gun down.

One second later, she stretched out in a movement and gave another grunt of satisfaction. "Yeah, the strength's coming back."

As if to prove it, she did a backflip and showed off some lightning-fast martial arts moves. "That feels good. It'll keep me going for about twelve hours. It's synthetic blood."

Paul watched this with the rapt attention of a baby watching fire. He came back to the here and now when Angela snapped her fingers. "When I came out of the chamber, I saw his body dressed in his suit," she said. "He was already inside the plastic covering, but it was open. I shut it. Now," she added as she went over to the corpse, "it's time to bury him."

In a tender gesture, she placed her hand on the corpse's shoulder as perhaps a final farewell then lifted the body effortlessly in her arms. "Go to the far end of the room to the last chamber on the right," she instructed. "There's a red button on the wall. Do you see it?"

He walked over and sure enough, there it was. "Yeah, I see it."

"Push it."

Doing as she requested, a door slid open to reveal a sarcophagus with its lid open. "I know that I'm supposed to put our maker in there," Angela said from behind him. "He wanted to be near us. Move, please."

He did, and she gently placed the body inside. After doing so, she pushed the red button and the door slid shut with a soft click. Bowing her head, her shoulders began to heave and seconds later she began to sob and tears streamed down her face. "I never knew his name. All I know is he wanted to be buried like this."

Out of respect, Paul bowed his head as well. They remained silent for a time, and finally he straightened up and headed over to look at the laptop. Turning it on, the screen remained black. The power worked, but the computer appeared to be broken.

"It doesn't work," Angela said as she joined him and closed the lid. "Ooze is trying to fix it. He'll come down later to take a look and see what he can do."

She turned her attention to the work table and searched around. "There it is," she said, and pulled out a file from under a pile of wiring and circuit boards. Opening it up and handing it over, she added, "This is what I wanted you to see. When I woke up and got to know the place, I found this file."

Reading through it, Paul tried to make sense of things, but all he saw were incredibly long and difficult chemical equations, none of which made any sense. In frustration, he closed the file and placed it on the table next to the laptop.

Angela wiped her eyes. "If you can make any sense of that, go ahead. I haven't read over that information yet."

Her answer surprised him. "I thought this was part of

your download or whatever you call it," he said. "Why didn't you?"

For only the second time since they'd met, Angela's voice carried a note of uncertainty and she worried her hands together. "Our maker didn't give me that kind of information. Like I said, I just got the essentials. I know my name, I know when I was created and I have basic knowledge of this place and New York City—of the language and the people.

"But this is..." her voice shook. "I was scared to," she finally admitted and wiped her eyes. "I wasn't sure I should know. But since you're here, I guess you can read it."

She gestured to the cot and Paul sat down after grabbing the file. Reopening it, he skipped past the formulas and found one page he could understand. It had the heading of *XSPU*...it stood for *Extraordinary Soldiers Protection Unit*.

The first paragraph caught his eye immediately.

Developed for the battlefield or urban combat, the XSPU will ensure safety of mortal soldiers, ensure the acquired targets will be dealt with in an extremely prejudicial manner, and in the long run, will save lives.

The report went on to list the ways in which the XSPU could be streamlined, enlarged and also enhanced. Full of numerous and detailed technical terms, most of the information went over Paul's head, but after rereading it, he got the basic idea and the concept made his heart begin to hammer. This...was beyond cutting edge. It was radical... dangerous. He closed the file and placed it on the table.

"So, what's it all about?" Angela asked.

A bead of sweat traced its way down his face and he swiped it away. This kind of information blew anything considered normal off the books forever. Taking in a deep breath and letting it out, he said, "You're soldiers. It seems this guy created you as weapons."

Angela's mouth dropped open. "That's...that's not what I feel," she stumbled out. "I know I'm supposed to go and help others. I don't know why, but that's what I do. That's why I helped you. There's got to be a mistake."

Paul shook his head. When faced with the truth, you could either deny it or accept it. He'd already accepted the truth of where he was and who he was with. "There's no mistake. I read over the info and what it says here is that you're all war machines."

Chapter Four
Pounding the Pavement

Angela's face turned even whiter. "This isn't true," she whispered. "I'm not a weapon. I'm not."

As if in shock, her legs started to shake and with a series of unsteady steps, she tottered over to the chair by the worktable and sat down. With trembling lips, she heaved in a series of deep breaths. Finally, she got herself under control. "This is all wrong."

"What do you remember?" Paul asked, fascinated by the idea of someone stepping out of a chamber fully grown — almost — and up to speed on most things. Being born with full adult knowledge took the difficulty of growing up out of the equation. In a way, he could relate. It would have saved him a number of years of agony.

Angela related her afterbirth in a somber voice. "The first thing I saw was the chambers. I...I knew where everything was, where my room was and where my clothes were. It was as if someone was guiding me."

It made sense. She had downloaded knowledge, so it was like operating on auto-pilot. After listening to her explanation, Paul went back to the page he'd been perusing. It listed the specifics of each individual. They were only a few lines, and he read them out.

"*Subject — Angela — abilities include the powers of flight, enhanced strength and regenerative abilities. Objective — Aerial reconnaissance and pacification of violent extremists.*

"*Subject — Cannon Fodder — abilities include the powers of super strength and regenerative abilities. Limited intelligence makes subject easy to control. Objective — Ground-based pacification of violent extremists.*

"Subject – Ooze – abilities include the power to control water. High intelligence is essential for this subject. Objective – Reconnaissance via waterways. It may be used as a water-based source to pacify violent extremists.

"Subject – Sandstorm – abilities include the power to control sand and perhaps larger Earth-based objects. High intelligence is also essential for this subject. Objective – Reconnaissance via the land. It may be used a land-based source to hinder the vision of violent extremists while the other task force members complete their duties."

Once he'd finished, Angela's head whipped around, meekness now gone. Instead, anger mixed with confusion resounded in every word she spoke. "This is all wrong! I'm supposed to protect the city. This is what I do. That's what I was doing last night."

A number of adjectives ran through Paul's mind about her performance last night and all of them fit. Spectacular, amazing…no, she had been beyond totally awesome. Beautiful when in motion, fast and fluid, hot and terrifying at the same time, she'd taken down the scum as if they were children's blocks to be kicked around.

Yet…the file told a different story. According to the information, though, she'd been initially created to do something else.

Created… How could anyone do that? Paul kept going through the file, but after the initial explanation, all he saw was more formulas detailing various chemical combinations, telomeres and cell division. Talk about cutting edge stuff! He'd training in basic chemistry, but all of this went way over his head.

It also didn't answer the question of how the scientist managed to build the chambers without anyone noticing. He didn't expect Angela to offer an explanation and she didn't. All she did was wait patiently with her hands folded in her lap, but after twenty minutes she got up and said, "If you can figure it out, fine. I'm no expert."

"I thought you had downloaded information."

Angela waved her hand, as if dismissing the question. "Just the basics," she said. "I know who I am. I'm self-aware like you. Right now, I'm tired. I'm going to pass out upstairs."

Paul looked up and rubbed his eyes. Even though it was early in the morning, he still felt dragged out from the events of last night and looking at all the figures had made his head hurt. "How, um, do you sleep?"

Immediately he felt foolish for asking such a dumb question, but she didn't seem to mind. "In a bed," she replied in an even tone. "Just because I'm different doesn't mean I don't sleep. My room is next to yours, by the way. I'll talk to you later on."

With a sharp move, she pivoted on her heel and strode out of the room. Paul stared after her retreating back, cursed softly under his breath for acting like a mental midget and went through the file until his head spun. He found no mention of the maker's name, but found another name scribbled at the bottom of the last page—R-Allan. Maybe that was the old guy's name.

Grabbing a pad and pencil from an adjacent table, he noted the name down then stuffed the paper in his pocket. On the subject of creation, the scientist had used stem cells from an unknown donor and somehow had infused them with these abilities. Another notation in the file spoke of multiple failures until he'd hit upon the right combination.

Someone knocked on the door. Spinning around to see who it was, he saw Ooze leaning against the aperture. "Angela said she was talking to you about our maker," he said as he moved laboriously over to where Paul sat. "I'm going to take another look at the computer. I think the hard drive is damaged but not gone. I might be able to repair it. If I can fix it, I can pull some information out."

"I thought this was part of your download." There it was again, the catch-all 'part-of-your-download' explanation. Paul felt idiotic for asking, but he didn't know what else to say.

Ooze chuckled. "When I said before that I got my maker's knowledge, I didn't mean I got everything. There's a lot I still don't know. I know I'm synthetic. I have information about this area, same as my buddies do. I know something about the science behind all of this, and I can process information faster than most people, but that's about it. What I don't know is what she doesn't know, and that's our maker's name. I just woke up a short time ago, remember?" He pointed toward the chambers then inclined his body toward the stool.

Hint received, Paul got up and as he did so, a yawn escaped his lips. You couldn't fake tired.

Whistling a tune, which sounded like someone singing underwater, Ooze parked himself at the computer and waved his hand at the door. "Yeah, I'd say you're pretty out of it. Better get some rest."

It seemed like a plan. "Maybe I'll crash for a bit," Paul mumbled.

Making his way upstairs to the kitchen, a rumble in his stomach reminded him that he hadn't eaten anything in the past twenty-four hours plus. Opening the fridge, he found nothing but a half-eaten jar of blueberry jam. The freezer held a loaf of bread and he put in inside the fridge to thaw out.

While doing so, he saw a multitude of plastic packets all neatly lined up on the shelves, filling up most of the space. Taking one out, he read the contents and a little bile came up in his mouth. "Synthetic brains…fifty percent sugar… fifty percent protein…and he eats…?"

Immediately, any thoughts of having food disappeared from his mind. "That's just…gross," he said, and shut the door.

A sudden lassitude filled him, and his injured ribs started to hurt. Later—he'd think about what to do later. Wearily he wended his way up to his room and passed out in bed.

* * * *

A sudden cramp in his leg woke him. Sitting up to massage the knot away, he glanced at the clock on the night table. It read six a.m. Had he been out the whole day and night? Apparently so, but his internal body clock said things were moving into a more regular rhythm.

His breath came out in faintly whitish puffs, and he huddled under the covers. A few seconds later, though, he got out of bed. The floor was icy and he hopped around on it until he got used to the cold. Moving was better than staying in bed, anyway. When he passed by his companion's rooms, Paul saw that Ooze and Sandstorm were going through their usual acrobatics routines while CF sat on his bed, staring into space. What was he thinking? Did he ever sleep or did he just sit and contemplate his navel?

The board under his feet made a creaking sound as he took a step, and the zombie turned his head. "Good morning," he grated. "I'm hungry, but Ooze didn't get me food." Something fell from his face and hit the floor with a soft splat. He bent over to pick it up.

Paul stood dumbstruck for a moment and CF's lower jaw sagged. After watching CF put it back into place, Paul said, "Hang on. I'll get you something."

Downstairs, he grabbed two packets from the fridge, hesitated, then took another package. Returning to CF's room, he handed over the food. The giant carefully tore open the packets with his thumb and forefinger and started to munch on the brain-burgers. "These are good," he grated, while giving a number of satisfied grunts as he worked his way through the edibles.

For him, saying anything over one syllable for the most part didn't figure in his mental makeup. "Uh, do you need help or something?" Obvious question, but right now subtlety had gone into left field.

"I'm fine here," replied CF, his mouth full. "These help me to think." Once again, his skin began to knit and a light

50

of understanding shone in his eyes.

Paul recalled the cell decay from the files and reasoned that maybe the synthetic brains helped replace the cell loss in the big guy's mind. He also remembered reading in school that the brain ran on sugar, so this had to be the ultimate fix. As he turned to leave, CF asked, "What will you do today?"

"Oh, uh, I thought I'd look around and check out the area," replied Paul, thinking fast. It was a bit surprising to hear the question come from the zombie, but maybe he'd just had his first individual thought.

CF nodded, a slow, heavy movement, and resumed staring out into space. Apparently, conversation wasn't his forte. Paul did wonder about the question, though, but didn't think it was a good idea to go out and meet the neighbors, just in case they'd seen his picture on television. The last thing he needed was for the authorities to show up on the doorstep. Still, if he stayed inside too much longer, say hello to cabin fever. At this early hour of the day, he doubted anyone would be out.

There wasn't too much in the way of furniture outside of the basics, but he came upon a small chest at the back of the living room. It held some clothes, probably those of the late scientist. They were the same size as the old clothes he had on now, so quickly changing, he balled up the dirty clothes and put them next to the dresser. After rummaging around in the bottom drawer, he found a light jacket and donned that as well.

Stepping outside, he closed the door and inhaled, but not too deeply, as his ribs still ached. The weather was crisp and clear and a light sifting of snow lay on the ground. A slight breeze lifted his spirits and he went down a neatly laid out front walk to the street.

Turning around to get a better look at the house, he noted its white color along with the peeling paint, the quaint Georgian-style appearance like something out of the old South, and the somewhat dilapidated garage with a sagging roof. All in all, the place looked old, yet somehow held a certain charm. And it was home, at least for now.

When he lifted up the door, he saw that a large blue van sat alone and unloved. There was nothing else inside the garage with the exception of a dirty carpet covering most of the floor and a few crates. A coating of dust sat on everything, and Paul shivered in the chilly air.

Since there was nothing else to see, he left, but as he did, his foot kicked against something on the floor. Lifting the carpet up, he found a door with a lock on it. A slow smile spread across his face. It was probably another entrance to the secret lab downstairs. He replaced the carpet, walked outside then shut the door.

Checking his bearings, he noted that the house lay at the end of a quiet street a good distance away from the same style houses. A number of empty lots sat between his new residence — Thirty East Main — and the other houses. If this scientist had wanted privacy, he couldn't have chosen a better location.

After filing the address away, Paul began to walk down the road. A few stray stones crunched under his heels and a light sifting of snow covered the ground. Turning a corner onto the main street, he saw a number of restaurants, souvenir stores and antique shops.

His muscles yelped as he moved, but he ignored the pain and focused on the positives. He had a place to stay, food to eat — not much, but he'd figure something out — and his new acquaintances? Well, they were…different.

Angela was pretty hot, though, and he wondered if she knew more than she was saying. Downloaded knowledge… super powers…this was like a myth come to life. Better than myth — this was reality! Staying in a house inhabited by fantasy figures got him stoked. No one would believe him, but all the same, this was pretty off the chain.

Stately trees lined the road and led into a forest area on both sides of the road. He kept walking, and eventually he arrived at a crossroad. A sign told a creek lay to the left. If he walked to his right, he'd eventually end up on the highway. "Let's try the creek," he said to the air, and walked down the road. No traffic came his way, and he eventually got to the bottom of the path. Another sign on a pole told him this was Angelica Creek, a tributary of the Genesee River.

The creek wasn't overly large and was bracketed by a steep river bank with patches of ice on it. Stepping carefully down to the bottom to survey the area, it was quiet here, and the cold nipped at his face and hands. He wondered what kind of place this was, how many people lived here, what they did, if they had families...

Families...he would have to think of that and shut the concept down. It didn't work, though, and his mood turned sour. He trudged on, his idea of having a decent morning shot to hell.

Turning his eyes on the creek, Paul realized that someone had decided to use it as their own personal dumping ground. A bicycle and what looked to be a small fridge stuck their noses out of the water, and the sight repelled him. He'd seen enough garbage in the Bronx. This kind of place, though, didn't deserve all this trash and in spite of the cold air, a distinctly foul smell came from the water.

"Well, that's that for now," he said, tired from his sightseeing sojourn, and walked back.

Once he'd reached the house, he was about to go in when a voice stopped him. "Excuse me, young man."

Surprised, he turned around. Who else would be up at this time of day? An old woman wearing a threadbare coat, a woolen cap and galoshes stood in front of him. A small Corgi stood at the end of the leash and tugged on it, whining. "Be still," she scolded the dog and peered through myopic eyes. "My name's Mrs. Porter. Are you related to Mr. Bolson?"

Bolson...the old guy's name was Bolson. Thinking quickly, Paul nodded. "Yes ma'am, I'm his nephew. I'm just visiting for a few days."

The dog panted and whined. It pulled again on the

leash and scrabbled to get away. She sighed, apparently embarrassed at her dog's lack of manners and when she spoke, it sounded like someone who was used to endlessly disciplining her pet. "Yes, Peter, we're going soon."

Instead of leaving, though, Mrs. Porter continued to stare at him, seemingly filing away every detail. He felt the power of her gaze but didn't move. Her dog kept whining and she yanked sharply on the leash, which caused the dog to yelp. It stopped and crouched down, growling softly.

"I thought you were new here," she said, and nodded with satisfaction as if she'd solved the case of the century. "I know the people in this town. I've lived here all my life. I haven't seen Mr. Bolson around lately. He bought this place about two years ago and always kept to himself."

"Oh, is that right?"

"It most certainly is." She nodded. "He bought the place and had some workmen come in to fix it up. Not from around here, no, he brought them in from other towns and cities. He couldn't give the locals a chance to get some pay in."

She continued to ramble on about how the noise kept some of the "honest folk" as she put it, awake at night. Bolson had trucks deliver parts — "plastic things and wiring and cables," she said — and usually kept to himself.

Paul desperately wished he could come up with an excuse to dash back inside the house, but knew he couldn't. He'd seen looks like this in the orphanage and in the foster homes. The looks meant the people were sizing him up, weighing what kind of character he was and what they could get away with. The looks were ones of suspicion, dislike and indifference all rolled into one.

No, he couldn't leave, not yet, for she'd get suspicious and might tell someone. That could lead to trouble. With a massive mental effort, he forced himself to put on a cheery smile. "My uncle and I, er, haven't seen each other for a long time. He likes to sit and chat."

"He's not under the weather, is he? I notice the shades in

54

his house were drawn."

Wow, this lady was nosy! In fact, Paul wanted to say Dr. Bolson was a little more than under the weather, but in a burst of inspiration he came out with, "Yes ma'am, actually, he's had, er, a bad cold and he needs his rest. I'm helping him around the house. Like I said, we talk a lot."

"I see."

If she did, then her eyes betrayed her, as something sparked in them. It looked like suspicion. "Well, I'll be going now…" he said and started to turn away.

In a surprisingly quick move, her hand shot out to snag his sleeve and she squinted at him. "Your face is all bruised up. What happened?"

How about I got my butt kicked a couple of days ago by a group of homicidal maniacs? A second later, he checked his thoughts. She probably wouldn't appreciate the response. "Slipped on the carpet, fell down the stairs."

Dumb answer, but it seemed to satisfy her as she lifted her shoulders in a gentle shrug. "Well, you're young. You'll get over it. I hope you enjoy your stay here."

"Thank you, ma'am," he said. "I'll try."

Then she was gone, yanking on her poor dog's leash as she went. Paul walked inside and locked the door, breathing heavily. That had been close. He was not only a fugitive, but if anyone saw him with…

"Did you go out?"

The voice startled him. Angela stood at the staircase, dressed in a pair of dark blue pajamas. Arms folded across her chest, the expression on her face resembled a volcano about to erupt. "In case you hadn't noticed, we're supposed to keep a low profile here."

Embarrassed at being called out, Paul felt the heat rush to his face. He'd screwed up and he had to own it. "Sorry," he began, "I was just trying to figure out where everything was, and…"

Angela waved off his response. "And someone saw you. I have pretty decent hearing and I heard you talking to some old lady. Remember, we go out at night. At least, *I* do." She uncrossed her arms and the severe expression faded. "Did you eat breakfast?"

"Not yet," he replied. "There's just some bread in the fridge. That, and some jam. I, uh, don't have any money for food, and—"

She interrupted, "You need to eat."

Pivoting on her heel, she walked away and into the kitchen. While she was gone, he thought about what Mrs. Porter had said. Workmen coming in, delivering parts, secrecy...this had to be kept a secret...

"Food's ready," Angela said as she reemerged from the kitchen carrying a plate with a slice of bread covered in jam. She proffered the plate. "Here you are."

Paul took it and bit into the bread. It was stale and the jam had no taste, but like the lady said, he needed to eat. A clump of bread lodged in his throat and made him gag. With an effort, he forced it down.

"It tastes good?" she asked.

"Don't worry about it," he lied, but put the plate down. He'd eat later on.

Angela nodded and went over to the large cabinet in the living room. Opening a drawer and reaching inside, she pulled out a large wad of bills. "I guess this is enough," she said as she returned to his position and handed over the money.

When counted, it came to over five thousand dollars. "It's, uh... Yeah, it'll do," Paul said, impressed at the amount of money he held. She'd mentioned having enough money to pay the bills, but this? Totally ridiculous. He'd never seen this much cash before, much less held it. He was used to getting a few dollars here and there from the Brothers at the orphanage to buy books and they were always used books.

"Our maker wanted us to have this," continued Angela as she pulled open the bottom drawer.

The sight of the sea of greenbacks almost made Paul's heart stop. The doctor had taken a lot more than equipment from his company. Continuing to gaze at the drawer, Paul saw it had been packed with new bills, all hundreds, and he gave up counting after five seconds. "I think that's more than enough."

Angela shut the drawer, took a seat on the couch, and waved him over. He sat next to her, feeling uncomfortable. This was an awkward moment in time. He'd never spoken to any girl as long as this and didn't know what to say. "Um, I guess I could get some food from a supermarket later on."

"You're not going to buy it here," she stated with an air of certainty. As if to underscore her statement, she pointed to the front door. "Too many people might see you. Secrecy, remember?"

So, if he had to remain cooped up, what would he do? As if reading his mind, Angela said, "Listen, I'm going to go on patrol tonight. We can go together, if you want."

It sounded good, but with no superpowers, he thought that he'd just get in the way. Crisis management in terms of gang control wasn't his forte. "I don't know what I can do to help."

A tiny grin crossed her face. "I have an idea."

* * * *

Midnight, back in the Bronx, and this was most definitely a *déjà vu* moment. This spot was only a couple of blocks from where he'd almost met eternity the first time. During the day, he'd gone over the notes while Ooze worked. The water-bag man shuttled back and forth between working on the computer and mixing chemicals. He worked with a quiet diligence, and rarely spoke except to ask for help holding some vials and adding in some chemicals. Paul tried to stifle his feelings of frustration at not being able to understand things entirely, and finally Ooze let out a grunt. "Hey," he said.

Paul looked up from his file. "What is it?"

"These things take time, and I'm not a technician. Have a little patience, will ya?"

Patience was the one thing needed, but this stuff went way beyond anything traditionally taught in chemistry class or perhaps anywhere else. The only thing Paul did understand was Bolson—Dr. Bolson—had managed to infuse a single stem cell with the necessary powers to allow these people to do what they did. It didn't explain why CF was decomposing nor did it explain why Angela could do what she could do. He just had to accept it as fact.

Finally, after his brain shut down, he excused himself and went back to his room. Lying in bed, he started to nod off, spiraled down into a world of black.

Minutes—or perhaps hours—later, he felt a hand shake him gently. When he opened his eyes, he saw Angela. "Hey, if you're ready, let's get going," she said. "It's almost eleven." She held some fresh clothes in her hands. "Get dressed. I'll wait outside."

After dressing warmly in a pair of pants and a couple of shirts under his jacket, Paul opened his bedroom door and met her outside. "Um…what do we do now?" he asked.

She grabbed his hand and pulled him downstairs. "I've got this. C'mon."

In the backyard, the sounds of the night, mainly quiet punctuated by the hoots of an owl and the flutter of a bat's wings, came through. The neighborhood was quiet and still and she looked up at the sky. "It's clear tonight. The stars… They're pretty."

Following her lead, he turned his gaze to the night sky and the stars shone out, a brilliant white that seemed to beckon him. "Hang on," Angela said. After looping her arm around his waist, she took off.

A second later they were well over two hundred feet above the ground. Paul thought he should be terrified, but he felt her arm, iron-hard yet gentle, supporting his weight and went with it. "Pretty cool," he said and his voice shook, but only for a moment.

"Yeah, flying is pretty decent," she replied. "It's…like freedom from what I am."

She sounded somewhat subdued, almost sad, but he decided not to ask her about it, not yet. She'd mentioned something about other peoples' reactions — negative ones.

Instead, he turned his attention to the night sky, felt the wind whip by his face, smelled the cleanness of the air and thought, yeah, flying… I'm actually flying!

They were moving fast, and soon the concrete jungle known as New York appeared. Angela dove for the ground and landed in an alleyway. Paul let out a breath and actually felt stoked about being here. "That was a rush — the flying, I mean."

"Good, get ready for more thrills," she replied as she took a step back. "Hang around here for a bit. I'll be watching."

Before he could get a word out, she leapt up into the air as straight as an arrow. Paul stared at her quickly vanishing figure and scuffed his toe in the dirt, pissed off that she'd ditched him.

"Hang around for a bit," he muttered then inhaled sharply as the truth hit home. Oh crap, she was using him for bait! "Thanks a lot."

Bait — he'd been set up and dangled like a worm on a hook over shark-infested water. All he needed now was for the killers from the deep to smell the blood and it didn't take long for trouble to arrive. Three Bangers men dressed in their usual garb strolled by the alley.

A second later — after looking around to see if the coast was clear — they entered and mean smiles crossed their faces. Immediately, the leader — he stood a good six inches taller than the other two men and was built like a pro wrestler — waved to the entrance and his compadres formed a wall, blocking off any chance of escape. Paul looked behind him. A concrete wall around twenty feet high lay at the other end. He was trapped.

"What've we got here?" the leader asked.

"Looks like a punk who should be at home," another

member chimed in and began to chortle. "It's a school night. Do you know where your children are?"

His voice trailed off, and the third member of the group—a squat, fat slob with a tattoo of a cross on his cheek—nudged him. "What's up?" he asked. "You know this kid or something?"

Scumbag number two stared at Paul and began to nod. "Yeah, I do! I heard about it from Louis."

The leader cut him off with a smack to his face. "Louis is bugged out. You know what I'm saying? *I'm* runnin' things now."

"But I saw his face on the news…"

He didn't get another word out as Angela silently dropped down behind scumbags two and three and clanged their heads together. Bone smashed against bone with a resounding crack and they sagged to the pavement. The leader backed up against the wall, shaking his head at the sight of a fanged woman coming at him. In spite of his overwhelming size, right now he resembled a frightened child trying to hide from the boogeyman—or woman, in this case.

"No, no, keep away!" he yelled.

"Too late," she replied and decked him with a swift right hook. Once he crashed to the ground, Angela turned around with an ear-to-ear grin. "Hey, that went well. I'd chalk this up to a successful mission. Glad you stuck around."

Paul didn't see any reason to be overly joyful. In fact, he was downright pissed off and crossed his arms over his chest in a gesture of moral outrage. "Thanks for setting me up. I've already gotten my ass kicked once."

"Did you think I'd let them hurt you?" she asked.

"You tell me."

After a moment's hesitation, she took his hand in hers. He didn't shy away, simply stayed there, surprised at her warmth—and strength. "I told you," she said in her soft voice, "I'm here to protect the city. And that means you too, okay?"

Her tone sounded sincere enough, but Paul didn't feel comfortable being a potential target. Recalling the first time he'd been rescued, he asked, "Why did you pick me?"

Angela released his hand and regarded him with a slight smile. "If you mean when you were jumped the first time, I was flying overhead doing reconnaissance. I saw you. You needed help. I gave it. And," she hesitated, "I think you're cute."

Tapping the side of her head, she added, "Downloaded knowledge, remember? I know what people are supposed to look like. I've got my own conception of cute and you're it."

"Oh…"

Her answer got him all flustered, and in spite of the cold, he felt the blood rush to his face. Averting his gaze, he scuffed the ground with his toe, wondering how to provide a suitable answer. His stomach then did the talking by rumbling loudly, which made him feel even more embarrassed. "Um, well, thanks. I guess I need to eat."

Flipping her hair back, she scanned the immediate area and pointed to a convenience store across the street. "Go ahead," she said. "I'll wait and watch for trouble."

It was bright inside the store. Paul kept his head down in order to avoid being recognized by the security cameras and avoided making eye contact with the few other late-night shoppers. He'd taken two hundred dollars with him in order to buy food. Grabbing a basket, he loaded it up with some eggs, bread, pasta, and other essentials, and after paying for it, walked outside. A donut shop a few steps down the street caught his attention and he headed in its direction.

A millisecond later, Angela joined him. "What are you doing?"

"I need a donut," he said, thinking of the ensuing sugar rush. He hadn't eaten a donut or anything sweet since…he couldn't remember. Store cameras or no, it was worth the risk. "C'mon."

Doubt reigned on her face, but she shrugged. "Okay, but after that, we go back to work."

"I guess I have to get used to being cannon fodder," he quipped, which elicited a giggle from her.

The Donut Hole was a small place, and only a few people sat in the booths, nursing coffee and chowing down on donuts. The booths were leather-lined set-ups, curved for maximum customer potential, and each booth had an old mini jukebox on it with earphones for some privacy.

Paul gazed at the music machines and smiled at the retro idea, wondering if anyone actually used them. He ordered a chocolate donut and hot chocolate, and carried his tray back to the booth where Angela sat.

As he sat down, the patrons began to do the stop-and-nudge-each-other-and-stare routine. Not all of them, but he heard the whispers of "Weird", "Strange", "Freaky" and more.

Angela also heard them and began to fidget. Paul noticed her discomfiture and asked, "What's wrong?"

"They're staring," she muttered and turned her head away.

Craning his neck around, he observed the stare crowd doing the goggle-eye act. "Well, first of all, you're not wearing a coat and it *is* the middle of winter."

"I don't get cold," she answered.

That figured. "Second," he continued, "they're being jerks. Just pretend it's a Goth look you've got on."

"What's Goth?" she asked, blinking her eyes as if suddenly confused by the term.

Apparently her download didn't account for modern trends. "Uh, it's a fashion choice," he said. "You wear black leather or ripped up black clothes, white makeup and have piercings — that kind of thing."

In voice full of doubt, she said, "It doesn't sound very fun. This is comfortable. I like it."

Yeah, well, you had to wear what made you feel good, Paul reasoned. He was grateful he had warm clothes, even if they were about thirty years out of date. As for his treat, the donut was stale and the hot chocolate tasted like lukewarm mud, but it was a lot better than the garbage at the orphanage. Little things like this meant a lot. Angela stared at the cracked Formica and said nothing.

Racking his brain for something clever or pithy or cool to say, nothing surfaced. *Chalk this up to being dullsville time.* He then recalled what she'd said on the flight over. "What did you mean before when you said freedom from what you are?"

Angela bit her lip, and her usual cool and in-charge demeanor seemed to evaporate. "I'm not human," she said in a low voice. "Not entirely."

Her eyes flicked back and forth, locking onto each customer, but they'd had their fun and were too engrossed in their own lives to bother looking around.

"I was created," she continued. "I don't know what else to do with my life. This" — she swept her hand at the window, which meant going on patrol — "is all I do, I guess. I get to do that and spend time with my housemates."

An air of pathos permeated each word. Paul didn't have any set answer. "Uh, well, I don't have parents, either." He stole a look at the streets. A young couple walked by hand in hand and an idea occurred to him. She'd said he was cute, so…"But, um, if you want to know more about what people do, we could go on a date."

"A date," she repeated and a series of fine lines furrowed her brow. "You mean, with other people?"

She really *didn't* have any experience, he realized. Then again, he'd also never been on a date in his life. "Well, not with a group or anything like that. It just means, um-m," he stammered out, "being around other people. But we'd be with each other."

Angela sat back in her seat, a thoughtful expression on her face. "That means…you like me?"

It sounded really innocent, like a little girl being told she could have double helpings of ice cream. In a way, Paul could relate. He'd never had a double helping of anything. "Yeah, I do."

She suddenly smiled, revealing her white, even teeth... and no fangs. "Okay, let's go out."

A look of curiosity settled over her face as she caught sight of the jukebox. "What is this for?" she asked.

"You put money in. It plays music."

Wonder shone in her eyes and she whispered, "I've never listened to it before. I mean I've heard it, and I know what the word means, but I've never really listened."

"Now's your chance," he said and dug three quarters out of his pocket. "Put these in the slot and press any button you want. Then you put the earphones in your ears and listen."

Hesitantly, she put the money in the slot, but after pushing one of the buttons, a spark leapt out and she quickly jerked her hand back. "Ouch, that hurt!" she exclaimed and shook her finger.

"Are you okay?" Paul leaned over for a closer look. The flesh had turned a slight brown, he noticed, and it had been only a tiny spark...

"It jolted me," said Angela, shaking her finger.

A waitress, middle-aged with a mop of dyed-red hair, immediately hustled over. Manner all sympathetic, she said, "Oh, I'm so sorry, miss. Are you okay?"

Angela nodded, but kept her gaze averted. The waitress, flustered by this turn of events, shook her head. "I'm sorry," she repeated. "The machine's broken. A few other people told us they got a shock from it, so we stuck a sign there, but someone must have taken it off."

Not wishing to draw attention to their position, he kept his hand covering the side of his face. "She'll be fine, ma'am."

After the waitress left, he murmured, "I guess that means no sticking your finger in an electrical socket."

His comment earned him a rueful chuckle. As he looked on, the damaged flesh on her finger quickly reverted to its normal white color. "Can we leave now?" she asked.

"Yeah, okay," Paul said, and they went to the cashier to pay up.

At the counter, flicking his gaze off to the left, two men sat in a booth in the far corner of the shop. They wore black suits, sunglasses and laced up shiny dress shoes. Talk about obvious! They had to be some kind of government agents. In their thirties, they both had short black hair, but that was where the resemblance ended.

One of them was massive, almost as wide as he was tall, but not fat. Under the suit there had to be a lot of muscle. A large mug of coffee sat in front of him.

In contrast, his partner was a tall, extremely lean man with a pale hatchet face and tiny, roving eyes. He picked up a donut from a mound that practically spilled from his plate and chewed it with a look of delight on his face.

"That's gross," the larger man said.

"It's not," answered his partner. "I'm hungry. I need the sugar."

As they spoke, it all sounded most casual, but both men shifted their heads every so often in a watchful, observant manner. They didn't move very much, but from the way they scanned everything, it seemed as though they were categorizing and filing away every single detail of this place.

Like something out of a movie—a very bad one—it seemed staged and yet creepy at the same time. If they wanted to stand out and have others look at them, they were doing a very good job of it. For some reason, Paul had the feeling they were looking at him.

Why, though? He could understand the police searching or someone from the orphanage or Social Services, but those guys looked like government agents.

Still, they hadn't made any threatening moves. In fact, the taller man chose that moment to deliberately look out of the window as if the inhabitants of the donut shop were of no interest to him.

The bad feeling persisted, though. "We should hurry,"

Paul suggested, but a second later, his bowels twisted and he clenched up downstairs. "I, uh, I gotta go. Be right back. Wait for me outside."

Angela didn't say anything. After a quick nod, she took the bags of groceries from him and strode out of the restaurant. He ran inside the bathroom and entered a stall. While going, he heard the clicking sound of dress shoes. It was one of them—one of the agents!

He had to get away, but how? He waited, heart beginning to pound then the sound of the door opening and closing made him breathe out a quiet sigh of relief. After finishing his business, he flushed the toilet and cautiously poked his head out of the door. The room was empty, and he spotted a window on the wall large enough for him to squeeze out of. A radiator sat beneath it, hissing out steam.

After he'd carefully climbed on top of the radiator, Paul opened the window then slipped out of it and fell into a trash-filled alley. No one was around, and after getting up and brushing himself off, he ran across the street then ducked into another alley to take up a spot behind a huge dumpster.

Three seconds later, the two men emerged from the donut shop and looked up and down the block. Once again, they didn't talk to each other. They simply scanned the area. Then they crossed the street and walked unconcernedly over to the alley where Paul was standing.

Now, paranoia really took hold. *The men in black... They're here.* He took in a series of shallow breaths. Lesson one in the secret agent's manual—how not to be seen. Breathing quietly, he cautiously peered out from behind the dumpster.

"You always have to go there, don't you?" the massive man said in a tone that indicated he thought the shop and its denizens beneath him. "You've been there every single night for the last two weeks. That place is a dump."

Skinny dude offered a tiny shrug from his narrow shoulders. "I like the donuts. They're good, and I get hungry..."

A black van pulled up the curb near them. A shadow flew overhead — Angela moving out of harm's way. The door opened and someone got out. Paul stole a look at the new arrival. An enormously fat man maybe six feet in height and around three hundred pounds stood in front of the two agents. The fat man held an equally enormous sandwich, dripping sauce and other edibles. Also clad in black, he chewed on his meal, ripping out chunks of bread and meat and chomping on them with gusto.

Taking in a deep breath, Paul flattened his back against the wall and did his best to listen in on their conversation. His heart pounded and the cold speared him, but he ignored both. This was important.

"Mr. Finger, Mr. Hand, have either of you spotted anyone we should know about?" the fat man asked between bites.

Finger…Hand…Paul thought about the old joke he heard at the orphanage. 'John broke his finger today, but on the other hand, he was fine.' Thinking about it, it was a dumb joke and why did he have to remember it now?

A loud throat-clearing noise by the fat man startled him back to alertness. He squinted and noticed the fat guy had a perfectly round head like a basketball. What got his attention, though, were the man's eyes. They lit up the darkness, a cold green. "Well," he prompted, "do you have any information?"

The thickset man bobbed his head. "Yes, sir, but we…lost the target."

"You lost the target," the fat man replied in a most withering tone after chewing and swallowing. "You lost it."

Silence hung in the air until finally the agent or whoever he was said, "Yes, sir, we lost it." He hung his head. "We're sorry, sir."

"Wonderful, is there any more good news?"

The hatchet-faced man spoke up. "There's another problem."

"And that would be…what?" The brick said nothing, so the fat man shifted his gaze to the thin man, ingested the rest of his meal in a single bite, and let out a loud belch. "Mr. Hand, would you mind telling me what the problem is?"

Mr. Hand obediently piped up, "They want more money."

Who are they? Paul listened, breathing very shallowly now, and he strained to catch the information.

"I should have known they'd get greedy," said the fat man. He sighed as if he'd been expecting this all along and brushed the crumbs from his suit. "How much more do they want?"

"Double," said Mr. Finger.

"Double," the fat dude echoed and offered a brief shrug. "Then pay them double. I want a little terror on these streets and the Bangers are the ones to do it."

"Yes Mr. Simpson, sir," said the two men in unison.

His name was Simpson. Mr. Simpson gave a curt nod, and in a move that contrasted sharply with his bulk, he swiveled gracefully on the ball of one foot and entered the van. It drove off in a whirl of dust and the two men melted into the shadows.

After waiting a few seconds just to be on the safe side, Paul cautiously edged out from the alley. A group of late night party people walked by in an unconcerned manner, laughing and talking, and he wondered what to do next.

Turning to his left, he stopped short when he found Angela lounging against the wall, arms folded across her chest, and the grocery bags dangling from one finger. She'd landed without a sound, but he was pretty sure she'd been listening in the whole time. "Did you get what those guys said?" he asked.

"Yeah, I was up on the roof. My hearing's pretty decent. Who's this Simpson guy?"

"I don't know."

Angela took his hand in hers and pulled him into the shadows of the alleyway. A growl from one of the denizens greeted them. It was a dog, mangy and skinny. Its hackles rose and it bared its fangs. "What's going on?" Paul whispered, wondering if the dog would attack.

"I told you, dogs don't like me," she said.

Her fangs came out and she hissed at the animal. It immediately backed away, whimpering then took off with its tail between its legs. "I guess you're not going to be a veterinarian," he commented.

Angela chuckled and after retracting her fangs, offered a wintry smile. "I'll have to find another line of work. C'mon, patrol's over."

After scanning the area, she put her arm around his waist after watching him pick up the bags. "Hang on," she whispered, and a second later they were aloft. The ride back to the house didn't take overly long, but Paul's mind wasn't on the flight. It was on the two men he'd seen and the guy who was probably their leader, Simpson. And this Simpson guy was connected to the Bangers.

While putting away the groceries, Paul mulled over what he'd observed only a short time ago. He knew that Finger, Hand and the fat man, along with the gang-bangers, weren't into being good Samaritans. Now he had something to work on. Who said that doing homework was boring?

Chapter Five
Rave to the Grave

Simpson…it was a common enough name, but without a frame of reference, where did one start? Without a computer, Paul had no way to check, but Ooze came around his room the next afternoon.

"I got things working," he said.

With a wave of his pseudopod to indicate *follow me,* Ooze led the way downstairs and straight into the laboratory. "The computer's already on," he said as they went. "I got the Internet working, but as for the files—if our maker hid any—that's going to take a little longer."

"Do you mind if I play around with it?"

"Have a party. By the way, the password is *Angela.*"

After sitting down and cracking his knuckles, Paul got to work. He checked out the FBI first. Their files were encrypted. Obviously, they weren't exactly going to advertise their presence as doing something possibly illegal.

Same deal with the CIA and NSA. Even their information sites said any attempt to hack them would be traced back to the server. The expression of *keep a low profile* echoed in his mind. He did not want to be in anyone's gun sights.

Trying another tack and returning to his initial question, he typed in Simpson — FBI and surprisingly got a response. A news article from roughly two years ago popped up.

Agent Thurmond Simpson, forty-two, was fired from his position as an agent of the Los Angeles branch of the FBI for excessive violence demonstrated toward criminal suspects…

It seemed pretty amazing he'd avoided a jail sentence. Either everyone in the agency liked him or else he had a very good lawyer.

Further checking revealed no new information, so Paul decided to check on the names of Hand and Finger. Nothing appeared onscreen. Were they ex-FBI or CIA or NSA or ex-military? It didn't really matter where they'd come from, as they had some kind of training. At the very least, though, he knew their rendezvous point—the donut shop—and he filed that information away upstairs.

His leg itched. When he scratched it, he felt something in his pocket. It was the paper he'd written the name on earlier. He thought of the now-dead maker...Bolson, typed in his name...and the screen came up blank. There was no connection, no name and no link. It was as if he'd never existed.

Frustrated, he muttered to the air, "Okay, so where do I go next?"

A tap on his shoulder made him look around. It was Sandstorm. He rapidly formed the letters and the word came out as *Rallan. No hyphen needed,* he added.

"You can understand English?" Paul asked and then realized he was talking to dirt. This was somehow even weirder than talking to water.

Sandstorm whipped his granular body through the air and quickly formed a series of words. *'I can't speak, but I can understand. Our maker also gave me knowledge. I don't know everything, just what's been downloaded into me. I know about this area, my fellow creations and Rallan. That's all.'*

"Oh...okay, that's cool," Paul said. "Um, dumb question, but why don't you talk—I mean, sign—to the others?"

'I'm not much into social relationships. I like staying in my room. Nothing personal... I just like my own company. See you later.'

A second later, he slithered out of the room and disappeared up the stairs, leaving nary a grain of sand behind. "Thanks," Paul called out then entered the name on the computer. Immediately one company listing came up — Rallan, Inc.

"Who are you guys?" he muttered.

According to the site it was located in Los Angeles. A biogenetic fruit company, it was in the business of mixing genes of various fruits and vegetables to create a hardier breed of food. It had been in business for the last five years, was listed in the stock exchange and had received glowing reviews as an up-and-coming leader in its field.

"Boring...no dirt?" he murmured and clicked another icon. Lots of pretty pictures emerged, mostly of purple apples, green turnips, and pink carrots. After that, there wasn't much else.

After reading through page after page of reviews, his eyes grew tired and he shut off the computer. The only connection he had was that Simpson used to work in Los Angeles and Rallan was located in the same city. Had Simpson been working for them? Did Bolson work for the same company? No idea...but he'd left Los Angeles and there had to be a reason...

"Hey, are you done here?"

Startled, Paul looked up to find Ooze standing in front of him with an enigmatic expression on his watery face. "I just spoke to Sandstorm. Actually, he signed to me. He said he got you a name. Did you find anything?" he asked.

Paul shook his head. "Maybe your maker, uh, worked for a company out in LA," he answered. "But I'm not sure. I'm also worried about this computer being traced. They can do that, right?"

Ooze gave a simulation of a nod, which meant his body bobbed forward and the water inside the containment suit sloshed back and forth. "They could if they knew the IP address. I rerouted it."

Call that good news, and Ooze went on to say, "At least you found something. I've been searching my own memory, but I just got bupkis. I'll check on any hidden files, if I can. You didn't see any additional discs, did you?"

He shooed Paul of the chair and parked his butt on it. Tapping the keys quickly, lightly, almost reverently, he burbled out the lyrics to "Under the Sea, but then said, "I heard you're going on a date."

Surprised, Paul stammered out, "Angela told you?"

Ooze bobbed back and forth again. "Yeah, she seemed—I don't know—excited. Don't get angry or anything. It's just that we—I mean CF and me—can't get out and we know she can. We'd scare the neighbors. You, you're human, and Angela looks pretty."

"She is," replied Paul, suddenly feeling acutely embarrassed at how everyone knew where he was going.

His reply earned him a watery chuckle. "That's what I figured you'd say." Ooze got up from the chair and planted a squishy hand on Paul's shoulder. "Listen…our maker gave me the basic knowledge of human relationships. I know what I look like. Sandstorm isn't much of a talker as you've probably figured out by now, and as for CF? Well, he's—"

"He's a zombie."

"Yeah, what you said." Ooze turned around and went back to his seat. "But Angela's been okay to us and she seems to like you."

More than a little mortified, Paul used his foot to scuff the floor and mumbled, "How do you know that?"

His innocent act didn't fool Ooze for a second, though, as a knowing expression formed on his watery face and he laughed again. "I was here when she brought you in, bud. She was real careful with you. She put the bandages on you and stayed with you just before you woke up. And you're both about the same age."

The shadow he'd seen… It had been her. A flush of gratitude swept over him, but at the same time, did being the same age make two people compatible? He was almost eighteen, and as for Angela, she was less than a month old. It was a big difference.

Ooze interrupted his thoughts by burbling, "Anyway,

like I said, you two make a nice couple. It's not like I can have a relationship or anything. I mean, I'm sentient. I can think, you know? But try talking to tap water. It doesn't work. Still…Angela…she's special. She was made special. So be nice to her, okay?"

Taking advice from a bag full of water—he didn't know whether to be chagrined or offended. In the end, he just said, "Thanks."

Walking upstairs, he remembered the door in the garage and resolved to ask Ooze about it next time. The sound of a vacuum cleaner interrupted his thoughts, and running through the kitchen, he found the zombie lifting the sofas and other furniture effortlessly while he ran the machine over the surface. "You're cleaning?" Paul asked over the roar.

"I want to," CF answered in a noncommittal manner. He seemed to be very conscientious about his duties and didn't miss a spot. "I don't know why. I just have to clean. I can do your room, if you want me to."

When in doubt about the weird, embrace it. "That would be great. Thanks."

CF nodded and switched off the vacuum. Seconds passed as he traced the cord from the end of the vacuum to the wall socket then he put the dots together, took out the plug and lumbered upstairs.

Paul stared after him in disbelief. He was living in a house alongside a zombie with a cleanliness fetish. Now he'd seen everything. A second later, he took that thought back. There was a lot he hadn't seen and right now he wasn't sure he wanted to.

The room was dark as usual and smelled more than a little musty, so he went over to the window, reached through the drapes and cracked the window open a few inches. A cold draft entered and soon aired out the room. Maybe a little sunlight would be a good idea, but as he put his hand on the fabric, a voice out of the gloom said, "No."

Jumping from the suddenness of the voice, he turned

around to see Angela standing beside him. Talk about silent and possibly deadly… He'd never even heard her footsteps. "You get that we're still keeping a low profile, right?" she asked.

"Yeah, you're right," he answered and vowed not to mess up. "Ooze is still working on the computer and—"

"I know," she interrupted. Pausing a moment, when she spoke again her tone seemed a little warmer. "Since CF is making the place neat and tidy and we're all busy, I just wanted to ask you what I should wear tonight. If we're going to go out, do I need special clothes?"

Now he'd become a fashion expert…not. Grabbing the remote, he turned on the television and flipped through the channels until he happened upon a video show. Loud rock music was playing in the background with skinny guys and pretty girls dancing around up close to the camera. "Check out those fashions for the girls," he said. "There should be something."

Wordlessly, Angela took a seat on the couch and gazed at the screen, her body immobile. She seemed to be engrossed in the show, so he decided to catch a nap upstairs until it was time. As he mounted the first step, above the roar of the vacuum he heard the usual refrain from the zombie. "Is there any food in the fridge?"

Sighing, Paul wondered why the doctor hadn't given CF more brain cells.

* * * *

When Paul landed in downtown Manhattan at roughly ten-thirty in the evening, Times Square was awash in a neon glow. It had all the noise, action and humanity New York had to offer. Paul had been to Manhattan before on trips from the orphanage, but they'd only been to museums and only in the daytime.

Now, a veritable Babel of languages and accents came all at once, simultaneously dizzying and intoxicating. English,

Japanese, Korean, Spanish, they all fought for supremacy. The smells of food also came through clearly, cold or not cold. Kielbasa, tacos, the aroma of hamburgers, hot dogs, the sour stench of cheap beer — this was how people lived.

As for the crowds, he found it difficult to get his bearings at first. He was used to going solo or, more recently, with Angela. Now, though, people jostled and shoved and pushed their way along the jam-packed streets, everyone in a good mood in spite of the weather.

Angela stared wide-eyed at the bright lights and the incredible array of shops hawking everything from souvenir T-shirts to food to hunting knives. When she saw a group of teenage girls dressed in the latest fashions — high heels, short skirts, fluffy jackets and teased and gelled hair — she whispered, "How do I compare?"

"You look better," he answered.

After taking a step back, he had to admit it — she was hot. No cape, but she had on a pair of stylish black jeans and a black blouse with puffy sleeves and a frilly collar like something out of a Victorian romance novel. High stiletto heels completed the picture.

"These were in my clothes closet when I woke up," she whispered in a voice like silk. In a quick move, she twirled around, somewhat unsteadily. "I saw that move on television. Is it correct?"

Paul's voice suddenly went missing and only returned when she smacked him on the arm — gently. "Well?" she asked, gazing at him.

"Uh…" The iciness in her eyes had disappeared, replaced by a soft blue glow. They were — his mind searched for the word — mesmerizing. "Yeah, you look great."

He meant it, and she squeezed his hand tightly. Not enough to hurt, but he felt the power in her grip. "What do we do?" she asked then stumbled. "Ouch," she commented. "These shoes hurt."

Suddenly, he felt clueless, and as he wondered what to say, a group approached them with one young woman pointing in their direction. Dressed goth-style to the max—black leather pants and shirts with lace trimmings for the girls and metal studs for the guys—they all wore white makeup and heavy black eyeliner. When they saw Angela, though, they stopped dead in their tracks.

"Hey, that's a rad look for you," one of the girls said with admiration. She looked to be in her early twenties although it was hard to tell under all the makeup. "You into styling like us?"

Angela looked confused for a moment, but recovered nicely and said, "It's my usual fashion choice."

Approving nods came her way. The girl who'd spoken fished around in her leather shoulder bag and pulled out a card. "We're going to a rave later, so if you wanna join us, you'll fit right in."

"Uh…thanks," said Angela as she pocketed the card. "We might do that."

"Bring your boyfriend," the girl laughed. "He's sorta cute."

The group left, and Paul stared after them. "Well, you are kind of cute," Angela said, breaking his spell. "She got that much right."

"Are we really going later?" he asked. Dates were one thing, but he'd seen how other people looked at her. Still, they *were* out—together—so why not?

Angela shrugged. "At least they didn't comment on how white I looked." She scanned the area then a smile lit up her face. Grabbing his hand, she said, "C'mon."

"And your plan is…what?"

She pointed to a store sign. "There," she said. "That's where I want to go."

It was a music store, and she hauled him over to it. "We can listen to music."

There's a first time for everything, he considered as they walked inside. A brightly lit place, teenagers of all shapes and colors roamed the aisles while chatting about the latest pop idol. They took up positions in the various listening areas in order to get their music fix on.

"We listen to this, right?" Angela asked while towing him over to a section entitled Easy Listening. "Is this good?"

"I don't know. It kind of depends on what you think is good."

An expression of annoyance settled over her face, accompanied by scrunched eyebrows and a frown. "I told you before that I know what the term means. You're the one with experience, remember?"

Without having anything in the way of experience concerning the Top-Ten in rock oldies, Paul figured he wasn't going to be of much help. All of this music came from way before his time. "Uh, well, listen to it and you tell me."

People swirled around them, some of them giving Angela looks of either curiosity or disgust. The curiosity came from the wide eyes, the tugs on their partners' sleeves and the surreptitious finger pointing. The looks of disgust were indicated by a sneer or a shake of the head, invariably both. In order to avoid any potential trouble, Paul steered Angela away from the stares. "Put these on," he said, pointing at the headphones.

Her hands, usually so graceful, fumbled with the headphones, and he took them from her and gently placed them gently around her ears. Soon, her body started swaying to the beat. "This is good," she shouted.

"Calm down," he whispered as he caught sight of some of the patrons staring and giggling. "Keep a low profile, right?"

"Oh...sorry," she shouted again.

Paul didn't know whether to do a face palm or make a joke. He decided to do neither action. Instead, he buried his head in the section and started to look for a name he recognized. Everything seemed to come from an ancient era when men wore wide-breasted suits, fedoras and bow ties.

Angela continued to listen and her head began to bob

more wildly, her hair flying out like a rocker going crazy on stage. Curious onlookers began to stare and point. Whispers of "What's she on?" drifted over.

He didn't know what they were talking about until a girl about his age gasped and gestured wildly to the guy she was with. She pointed again at Angela…who was floating two feet above the floor.

"Oh crap," he blurted out and tugged on her arm.

Angela ripped off the headphones. "I was listening to someone named Frank Sinatra. What's going on?"

"Look at your feet," he whispered fiercely.

After doing so, she let out a self-conscious giggle and dropped to the ground. "Sorry."

By now a small crowd had gathered and the guy whose girlfriend had alerted him seconds ago, a big and burly young dude in his late teens with a tough looking swarthy face asked, "Is uh, like, this for a movie, man?"

"Yeah, it's a movie," Paul answered, thinking fast. What else could he say? "It's a movie, you're all extras, and the director will talk to you soon."

If his answer was designed to placate the teen, it didn't work. Mr. Tough Teen strode over in tough-guy mode, flexing his arms and rolling his shoulders. His girlfriend tried to hold him back, but he shook her off with the comment of, "I'm just gonna ask a question."

Stopping in front of Angela, he waved his hand around her body. In consternation, she stepped back. "What are you doing?" she asked.

He offered a smirk as if he'd solved the trick of the century. "I don't see no wires, man," he stated. "What is this, some kind of a gag? And what's with the girl's face? Either she doesn't like sunlight or she's got some kind of a skin problem."

At that moment, Paul wished in the worst way they hadn't gone to the store, but they had. From the way this jackass set his stance and tensed his body, it appeared as though he didn't know what kind of trouble he was courting.

Worse, Angela's hands curled slowly into fists and the look in her eyes went from mild to barely contained wild. "I don't have a problem," she said in a tight voice. The tightness, though, seemed like a thin veneer. Under it, rage lurked. "But it seems you do."

This moron had absolutely no idea of who he was messing with, and Paul tugged on Angela's arm. "Let's leave, okay? It's not worth it."

"She can make it worth it to me," the large teen said with a smirk. "If she's a freak, then maybe the news guys will want to interview her." He waved his hand in the direction of the door. "Go and play somewhere else, punk."

Paul didn't think twice. He shoved the guy, but it was like a fly pushing an elephant in its side. "Punk's asking for a beating," the teen said as his smirk morphed into an evil smile. "Now it's my turn."

Bunching up his fist, he reared back to deliver a haymaker. The punch never connected, as Angela grabbed the teen's ham hock of a fist in mid-punch and began to crush it. The bones in his hand made an audible cracking sound, and his eyes started to pop. With a gurgle of pain, he sank to his knees. "Gah…"

"You'll have to rephrase that," Angela said, her voice low. In spite of her quiet and almost calm manner, the intensity lacing each word cut through the noise in the shop and the howls from everyone else.

As she spoke, her fangs came out and the blue in her eyes grew deeper and icier. "You know, I never used to get angry when I first came here except at the punks who preyed on the weak. But when you called me a freak, and after seeing jerks like you pick on others, guess what? That really pisses me off."

Once everyone saw the fangs they stopped baying for blood and fell silent. A millisecond later, someone screamed out, "Vampire!"

Then all hell broke loose with the patrons making a mad dash for the door, stumbling over each other in a frantic race to be first out of the exit. Angela kept tightening her grip and the teen, now in tears and on his knees, begged for her to stop. "I'm sorry. I'm sorry!" he screamed.

She let go and he fell to the floor clasping his ruined hand and moaning piteously. "My fingers... You broke my freakin' fingers!"

"You're lucky I didn't break another body part." She turned to Paul. "Let's get out of here."

They made their way out of the door and Paul pulled her over to the safety of a side street. "That was...intense," he said, breathing hard.

Angela muttered something in a dark voice about idiots not being leashed up properly. "We should do something else," she declared.

"Uh, like what?" he asked. They'd already pushed their luck, he felt, and she wanted to stick around? "Maybe we should go back..."

She was already fishing around in her pocket and brought out the card. "Let's try here," she said. "It's nearby."

The card read *Gothikz: Rave Joint* and gave the address. Suddenly, Paul got a very bad feeling about all this. "This really isn't the best thing —"

"We're going," she interrupted, and took his hand.

The club was located only a few blocks away. There, they spotted the same girl who'd given Angela the invitation. She waved hello and said to the bouncer, "They're with us."

"C'mon," she urged, "get raving," and pointed the way inside.

As they entered, heads turned in their direction, but Paul's attention was on the décor. Black predominated, with black walls, tables and even black lights. Only one shiny silver bar interrupted the planned darkness. Their girl guide cut out and Paul wondered what to do next.

The place didn't seem to be overly crowded. The sounds of Electro, Industrial and New Wave music assaulted his ears. Everyone had the Goth look going big time, and in the center of the room a group of people were dancing to the heavy beat. Angela shouted above the din, "Is this supposed to be cool?"

Why is she asking me? What do I know about cool? "Uh, it's a style," he answered, trying not to sound too lame.

"Let's dance," she said, and towed him to where the bodies were swaying. Paul didn't know the first thing about dancing and did his best imitation of digging ditches and baling hay which he felt made him look and feel more ridiculous as time went by.

On the other hand, Angela seemed to have picked up on the rhythm right away as she started moving her hips in time to the music, a look of near rapture on her face. The other dancers looked on with admiration and he noticed her eyes were half-closed in an almost sensual way. Then she pulled him close, and awkward as he felt at first, he began to sense the rhythms of her body.

Along with sensing things, his heart also began to race and this, he thought, was the ultimate, the one and only moment that…

"Hold it!" a voice called out and the lights suddenly came on, blinding him.

Squinting, he looked to see where the voice had come from, and a police officer, burly and mean-looking, stood at the entrance. His hand hovered near his gun holster, and his fingers twitched as if aching to draw and fire. "There was a report of an assault at a music store," he said and ordered, "Get down on the ground now!"

Immediately, the patrons stood off to the side, murmuring and pointing fingers. Hands on her hips, Angela eyed the police officer coolly. "How about I say no?"

He blinked. "Miss, I'm going to ask you nicely to get down on the ground." His fingers twitched faster and he repeated his request.

Paul's first and only thought was that this was not going to end well. This place probably had security cameras, same as in the music store. He figured they'd already captured him on tape, but he still pulled his jacket over his face.

"Angela, we don't want more trouble," he warned then cursed himself for mentioning her name.

"There won't be any trouble if this man moves aside," she said and marched in the cop's direction.

The cop muttered something and brought out a Taser instead of his gun. Turning it on, he thrust it against her right shoulder and a blue arc of electricity surged over her body. She stiffened at the shock then staggered. Then he jammed the Taser hard against her shoulder, cutting through her blouse. A few drops of blood oozed out. "Hey, what is *wrong* with you?" she exclaimed.

However, she soon recovered enough to rip the weapon from his clasp. With her free hand, she grabbed his collar and effortlessly heaved him over her shoulder. He sailed through the air and landed with a crash at the back of the club. The patrons screamed and ducked for cover, while the cop reached for his pistol. Angela whirled around.

"Don't even try it," she warned.

Slowly he withdrew his hand. "What are you?" he asked weakly.

"Believe it or not, we're on your side," she said before turning around. Staring at the Taser with a look of disdain, she crushed it. "That really hurt," she muttered.

A crowd of restless, shifting and curious people had formed a wall in front of the store. For a moment, the wall held, but when Angela turned her gaze on them, something fierce and totally unearthly, murmurs of surprise and fear broke out among the would-be righteous. "Move," she said in a voice filled with quiet menace.

"You're bleeding," one man said, pointing at her.

"Yeah, and it hurts, too," she answered. "If you don't want more of the same, get out of my way."

Without so much as making a sound, the crowd moved aside. Heaving in a deep breath, she grabbed Paul by his shoulder and towed him past the waiting line of the curious. Just as they cleared the pack, she stumbled. "I hate these shoes!" she cried, and kicked them off.

"Wear boots next time," he said and, after stealing a look behind him, added, "Oh crap!"

"What is it?"

"The natives are restless," he said, jerking his thumb over his shoulder. "Run!"

The shouts and screams began and they began running in earnest, chased by a mob. Many of them were armed with garbage can lids while others carried sticks and metal bars. Where they got this stuff was beyond him, but he didn't have time to figure it out.

"This wasn't my idea of a date," he panted.

Angela threw him a cross look. "Don't blame me. It was my first time," she replied then added, "Grab onto me!"

As he obediently put his arms around her waist, she leapt into the air. Their journey was accompanied by cries from the crowd below. Sirens wailed and the sounds of "She's up there. She's up there," rang out from the street.

Paul turned his attention to his impromptu chauffeur. Her face wore a look of pain. "Can you make it?" he asked.

"I...think I need to sit down," she said as they flew unsteadily. Their flight plan got more and more erratic until Angela finally seemed to run out of gas. She descended and landed awkwardly, sprawled out on the gravel. Paul went tumbling end over end until he slammed to a stop against a wall. His ribs, formerly on the mend, protested and he let out a cry of pain.

"Ahh...that wasn't fun," he groaned. If almost getting punched out and landing hard on gravel was someone's idea of fun, forget about it. There were other, better ways of having a good time.

"Sorry about the landing," Angela said in a rueful tone. She sat up and examined her body all over then got to her feet. "Wearing shoes hurts. How do girls walk in them?"

Since no clever answer came to mind, he said nothing. Angela rubbed the injured area on her shoulder and shook her head. "First I get called a freak then I get hurt. I wasn't expecting the policeman to shock me."

As she spoke, her wound began to heal. In seconds, it was gone.

"I wasn't expecting to get into a fight, either," Paul replied, still surprised at the healing factor she had.

His initial shock of the almost-fight and near escape had worn off. Now, as he wondered if his face was going to be on the midnight news flash, she broke through his reverie to ask, "Did the date really stink?"

The way she asked, innocent along with a slightly sarcastic tone, made him chuckle. "It was...different," he decided to say.

Angela came over to put her hands on his shoulders. "You have a funny way of phrasing things." She seemed to brighten and her voice got a note of lightness in it. "You handled yourself pretty well at the music store."

"I almost got my head kicked in."

"No, I meant you sticking up for me."

Her fingers gently kneaded his shoulders, which helped to take away some of the soreness. It also sent a warm feeling through his body. Was she coming on to him? If she was, then this was the best come-on he'd ever had. No, check that, it was the *only* come-on he'd ever had.

The massage continued, and her fingers traveled to his shoulders then to his upper back, her face close to his. Her breath smelled warm and sweet, and it took away from the chill of the night. It also made him a whole lot better about having come here. "I, uh, didn't do that much," he began, ashamed of being weak.

"You were afraid?"

It hurt to say so, but, "Yes. In case you hadn't noticed, I don't have special powers or super strength..."

He stopped talking when she put a finger to his lips. "Sometimes you have to take a chance," she finally said. "I know it sounds funny to say this, because I can't really be hurt, but if you give up before you start, then you've already lost. Fear is natural. At least, that's what my download tells me. You can't give in to it."

While he was digesting her words, she said, "C'mon," and in a graceful move, she rose and pulled him up with her. Once they faced each other, she said, "I, uh, have a question for you."

"Okay."

She bit her lip. "You said that you didn't have parents. Do you miss them?"

Surprised by her question—and a little embarrassed as well—Paul mumbled something about every kid wanting to know who their parents were. Mulling the options over, he reached into his pocket and pulled out his one half-a-family picture. "I don't remember my mother, just my father. This is what he looked like," he said. "I haven't seen him in about thirteen years."

Angela stared at the picture. "Yeah, you look a lot like him." She touched his hand in a gentle manner. "Do you want to?"

Disturbed at his feelings toward her as well as the mention of not having anyone as a real guardian around, he hastily tucked the picture away. "Yeah, I want to, but…"

A river of dryness coated his throat and he almost choked. It was a kind of split personality thing with him. Part of him wanted to know why his father had given him up. The other part told him that maybe he was better off not knowing.

"At least you had parents," Angela said, interrupting his thoughts as she stared out at the bright lights. "I wouldn't know what that means. I was made from someone's cell. That isn't a parent. That's a lab specimen." As if embarrassed by her admission, she cleared her throat. "Thanks for taking me here tonight. I had a pretty good time."

She'd listened to music someone born in the nineteen-fifties would have listened to, trashed a punk and knocked a cop out. And he'd almost gotten his face beaten in…again. Still, it had been fun—sort of.

"You did?" he asked.

Angela nodded, but a plaintive tone in her voice emerged. "Well, yeah. I mean…it wasn't so great when they started yelling 'vampire' at me. I know I'm not human, not really. I know that."

"That's okay." In a situation like this, what would — or should — someone say? She'd saved his life at least twice, looked great and he liked her attitude. Tough but gentle… he could learn from that. "I mean, you're human to me."

Her eyes flickered up to meet his, wavered, then she averted her gaze. "I've, uh, never been out with anyone before. You're…fun."

Compliments were like finding money on the street — rare and valuable. It made him feel good, sort of hot all over, and Paul decided it wasn't from the excitement. "Thanks. You're pretty cool, too."

A clock struck eleven, ending their mutual admiration session. "We should go home," she said. "C'mon."

In a slow, rather deliberate, move, she put her arm around his waist and hugged him tightly. They rose into the air, and this time her flight path was sure and steady. During the twenty-minute flight home, Paul concentrated on keeping his breathing steady. Angela tilted her head… her cheek brushed his…and oh, what a feeling that was!

Arriving home at around half-past-eleven, they landed in the backyard and Angela offered a shy smile. "We should do that again," she said in a very quiet voice. "I want to do it again."

Flustered yet stoked by her attention, he twirled his toe on the hard ground. First date or not, he decided to pop the all-important question. "Mind if, I, um…kiss you before we go in?"

Her mouth opened then shut with an audible snapping sound, and she ducked her head. "Is this what people do on dates?" she whispered.

"If they like each other, yeah, they kiss and all that." Not to mention this might be his first kiss ever.

Angela didn't say anything for a few moments. She stood there, silent and small, staring at the ground. "I…don't know," she finally said.

Rejection hit and hit hard. Paul's heart had been beating fast. Hoping against all hope was his wish for his first kiss — but it was not to be.

"Oh," he managed to get out and didn't try to hide his disappointment.

"It's nothing against you," Angela said as she picked her head up. Perhaps she understood what the downcast look on his face meant as she hurriedly added, "I've never had a date before. I didn't know if you were supposed to… You know…"

Her voice trailed off and as he looked at her, her face suffused a deep red. Confusion as well as uncertainty ruled, and to cover his disappointment and social screw-up, he cleared his throat. "Uh, it's okay. But…I still want to go out with you again…when you're not kicking someone's ass, I mean."

His comment must have pleased her, as she gave him a flashing smile. No more wallflower look from her. "Yeah, okay, we could do that," she said. She offered her hand and he took it, feeling its warmth and strength.

"I guess this means we like each other," said Paul, stating the obvious.

"It does," she agreed. "It does."

If ever there was a moment for elation, then this was it. There would be a next time. He exulted in that moment, but a gust of wintery cold came along and chilled him. Thanks a lot, winter, and nodding at the door, he said, "Maybe we should go inside?"

"Okay."

Hand in hand they entered, but Paul's mood of positivity faded when he saw his water and sand housemates sitting on the couch. The former wore a worried expression on his face, while the latter had shaped his body into the form of a question mark. "What's going on?" Angela asked.

Ooze pointed at the door. "CF is gone."

Chapter Six
The Search

A moment of strained silence filled the room then Angela asked the most obvious question. "What do you mean, gone?"

"It means what it's supposed to mean," Ooze snapped back. Sarcasm on full display, he pointed at the door. "How else do you want me to phrase it? Gone means gone, as in left, as in he isn't here. The horse is out of the barn, Elvis has left the building… You want me to continue?"

Angela sat down on a nearby chair, suddenly deflated. "This…is not good," she said.

She would have to mention the obvious.

"So, where would he go?" Paul asked.

Eyebrows formed on Ooze's face and they arched up to the top of his containment suit. "You're asking me that? Why don't you ask me something I *do* know, which isn't much? Just because I'm the resident genius around here courtesy of our maker, doesn't mean I'm a mind reader. And in case you haven't noticed, our large friend doesn't have a whole lot up there to begin with."

Angela leapt off the couch. She pointed at the ceiling and mimed the movements he used to go from bucket to bucket. "We're not asking you to perform water tricks or have fun with your chemistry set downstairs," she erupted. "CF's out there — among people — and he could be anywhere by now. You know he gets hungry. You know what will happen if he walks up to someone and asks for food."

This wasn't how the Paul wanted the conversation to go, much less the rest of the evening. He'd also been wondering the same thing, but before he could ask, Angela yelled, "If he can't get the synthetic stuff he eats, then he'll take the first thing he can get."

A more than slightly sick feeling started in the pit of Paul's stomach and started to spread to his upper chest. "I'm going to take a guess here and say that means people," he said. "It does, doesn't it?"

"That's pretty likely," said Angela as she swiveled her gaze to Ooze. Her spine arched like an angry cat's and her wrath went nuclear. "You should have stopped him. There is such a thing as saying no, isn't there?" Stabbing her forefinger at Sandstorm, she stated, "And you could have done something, too."

Sandstorm formed the words *like what* then collapsed into a pile. Ooze folded his arms across his chest and leaned forward until his ever-shifting suit was one inch away from her. "Don't get angry with him or me, either. It's not like I could have done anything, you know?" He sounded petulant at first then his voice rose and matched hers in tones of anger.

"You know CF. On the rare occasion he gets an idea in his head, he goes and does it. You can't really reason with him. I mean, if he gets pissed at me, all he has to do is toss me against the wall. You got that? I go splat and that's it. Unless you've got another containment suit handy or a garbage bag, I can't hold my form in the open for more than a couple of minutes. When I'm in water, I can control it, but I can't control me while I'm in the air very well. I'm still working on it. So what was I supposed to do?"

They continued to hurl abuse at each other, and while they did, Paul picked up the remote and flicked on the television set. Immediately, he dropped it. "Oh…crap," he said.

Ooze and Angela stopped raving long enough to ask simultaneously, "What is it?"

Wordlessly, Paul pointed at the screen. A reporter stood outside a very familiar place — the music store in Manhattan. Dozens of people hovered in the background throwing up peace signs, taking selfies and generally going for their fifteen minutes.

"And this is the scene at the Disco Forever Music Store in Times Square," the reporter, a chubby man in his forties wearing a bad toupee intoned. Clad in a trench coat, he brushed back a lock of his dark hair and the whole top of his head wiggled. That prompted a burst of laughter from the crowd. His face turned red, but he continued to speak breathlessly into his microphone.

"It seems as though the rumors about a vampire woman were true. According to numerous eyewitnesses, she and an unknown male companion who appeared to be in his teens entered the store at around ten forty-five p.m. and started an altercation for reasons unknown."

The camera then cut to security footage and sure enough, it showed Angela wrecking the punk's hand. Her face wore a stony expression.

"A bystander, Jamie Morton, nineteen, had his hand crushed," the reporter stated in a breathless manner when the camera focused on him again. *"He is expected to make a full recovery."*

The picture changed to a shot of the punk, a large bandage wrapped around his hand. Pale and shaking, he was led away to an ambulance by a paramedic. Seconds later, the camera went back to the first scene just in time to see the reporter shove a few would-be television stars out of range.

"Additionally, we have eyewitnesses at the Gothikz rave club who have told us the pair entered their establishment at around eleven and that they heard the name 'Angela' uttered by the male accomplice," he said with all the gravity of a police officer reading out an arrested criminal's rights.

"When a police officer tried to talk to this person, she flung him to the back of the club. Although we have no information on the current whereabouts of the duo, we are asking citizens to call the police if they spot the pair. She is described as being of medium height, long black hair, having extremely pallid skin and blue eyes. She was also described as being inhumanly strong and should be approached with caution…"

"Pallid," Angela repeated. Her voice grew dark. "Am I that pale?"

"Flour white," said Ooze sourly. It sounded like someone had filtered lemon water into his suit. "You make paper look tan."

More details emerged from the television. *"The male accomplice is short and is estimated to be approximately five-seven and one hundred and fifty pounds with brown hair, a big nose and brown eyes. He has been described as having birdlike features and is considered dangerous as well..."*

"So I look like a robin," Paul muttered. "Thanks a lot."

Ooze uttered a wet sound of disgust and shut off the television. "That's just great," he snorted as he tossed the remote to the far end of the couch. "Now you're both fugitives. Whatever happened to keeping a low profile and protecting people?"

"I was protecting Paul," answered Angela, her voice icy. In a swift move, she pushed her face an inch away from Ooze's and her fangs came out. For a moment it seemed as if she was ready and willing to bite through the suit. "And that punk was asking for it," she added.

Ooze didn't back off. Smarminess on full display, he responded with, "What about the cop? Was he asking for it, too? No, don't answer. I already know."

Answer given, he pulled back and hung his head on the couch, muttering something incoherent. Paul made a push for peace and got between the two of them. "Both of you want to cool it? We're in enough trouble."

With an hmphing sound, Angela turned away, but a second later, she swiveled back with her mouth forming a rather cute pout. Her body lost its tense posture and she nodded a few times.

"Sorry," she said to Ooze. "I was out of line. And I was wrong to do what I did, even though that jerk deserved it."

"No problem," he replied. "It's all good."

Since the apologies had been made, Paul asked, "Does CF have basic knowledge of this area?"

Angela walked over to the window, drew the drapes back an inch, cautiously peered out, and then let the cloth hang. "He knows the layout, but he's never been outside before or met anyone before. If he did, you know what would happen."

Let's hear it for mayhem, Paul realized. Someone would call the police, then the army then they'd have search teams combing the area for anything not human. He didn't want to think of what his new girlfriend would do to them.

"Okay, let's search," he said. "I need a map of this place." Looking at the pile of dirt, he had an idea. "Um, Sandstorm, can you form a map?"

Immediately, the pile of dirt swirled into a map of the area, using his body like an Etch-A-Sketch. A surprisingly detailed picture emerged. Ooze studied it and gave a few grunts.

"We're here," he said," as an X appeared on Sandstorm's body indicating the house. "The river is about a mile away. You've been there, right?"

Paul nodded. "Yeah, there's nothing but empty land around it."

"Right," Ooze nodded, his body bobbing back and forth. "So either's he's at the river or else he decided to hit the highway. My guess is he won't go where people are, so he may just be hiding in a field."

Sandstorm turned himself into a pile and remained on the couch while Ooze moved over to the cabinet. After searching in a drawer, he found a flashlight and brought it over. "This should work."

"Thanks," Paul said as he took the flashlight, tested it, nodded at the bright light coming out and headed to the door. "Sandstorm, can you help us search?"

No, he signed. *I think that I'm going to stay here. You'll be fine on your own.*

Angela snorted with disgust at her housemate's recalcitrance. "Thanks for nothing." Turning to Paul, she said, "I've got air patrol. I can cover more distance that way. You take the ground."

"How, uh, do we stay in touch?"

"If I find him, I'll come and get you. If you find him, yell my name once. I'll find you. Is that simple enough?"

It sounded like a plan. By now it was after midnight, the weather outside had dropped to below zero, and a harsh wind had also sprung up. Walking along the dark road, Paul hugged himself in order to keep warm and cursed his bad luck. His first date had been nothing short of a disaster, but the fact Angela wanted to go out again…that made up for a lot.

Now he was picking his way along a country road and hoping a wild animal wouldn't pop out and eat him or a car wouldn't come along and cream him. Hugging the side of the road, he kept watch, but fortunately, he encountered neither animal nor mechanical interference and he used the flashlight to light the way.

Ominous looking shadows sprang up in the glare of the white light, but outside of a few cats running away he saw nothing else. Occasionally, he shone the beam on the trees which lined both sides of the road, but only the wind was present, that, and the cold. "CF," he called out. "It's Paul. Can you hear me?"

There was no answer and he continued to a fork in the road. Go right or go left? If I was a zombie, would I take the road or the rural route? Decisions, there were always decisions…

After thinking about it, he took the road to the left, went down the hill and slipped on a patch of ice and slid down to the bottom. Bumpy though the ride down was, he didn't cry out. Keep a low profile, he remembered as he tumbled end over end and finally came to a rest against a log.

Now he could groan and did so as he slowly got to his feet.

"That…hurt," he muttered.

Brushing the dirt off his body, he stiffly walked over to the river bank. While the river continued to flow, even in this weather, the smell of refuse hit him. He'd smelled it earlier on, but for some reason it stank worse tonight.

"Let's hear it for the tourists," he said aloud. No one was around, and he wondered why people would just toss their crap away wherever they felt like it. The Bronx wasn't overly clean, but he'd always swept out his room at the orphanage. It was an old place, but spotless.

Not here, though. Maybe the visitors had done it or maybe the locals decided to use this place as their own personal dumping grounds. Some more garbage had been tossed into the water along with bags of old food and other unmentionables.

The wind returned, colder now, and it knifed through his jacket. Shivering, he called out the zombie's name again, but all he heard was the echo of his own voice. *Keep moving*, he urged himself. *Keep moving*, and he shuffled down the river bank.

While searching, he wondered if anyone who'd been in the store in New York had gotten his picture. The security cameras certainly had caught all the action as it showed the cop sailing across the room. Angela had a right to protect herself, but taking on a cop? If she had been designed to protect people, this did not bode well for the future of law enforcement.

Another spear of cold wind hit. Between the rocks and patches of ice and the fast-dropping temperature, it was only a matter of time before the cold got to him. "CF!" he called out between chattering teeth. "Are you here?"

Picking his way along the river's edge, he came to a small dam. There, he saw a monstrous figure in the middle of the river.

It was CF. The cold didn't seem to bother him as he reached into the water and effortlessly hauled out a tire and a rusty bicycle, and tossed them onto the river bank. One item after another—an old mini-fridge, a bumper from a car and a large number of beer bottles—flew out of the water to land on the river bank.

Seconds later, the zombie turned around and shambled back to the bank where he began to crush the larger objects into small, compact bundles of steel and wire. He laid them side by side on the river bank and stood there, staring off into space.

"Hey," Paul said as he walked over. His teeth wouldn't stop chattering. At the same time, his blood felt stopped up in his veins, so he stamped his feet in order to get the circulation going. "What are you doing?"

"Cleaning," replied the zombie. He didn't seem surprised at Paul's arrival. In fact, like every other time he'd been spoken to, he acted totally blasé. In a slow and careful move, he pulled a rubber bag from his pocket and began to load the bottles inside. "I like clean places."

Looking more closely, Paul could see that it wasn't a garbage bag. It was a containment suit. CF finished up and hefted the bag over his shoulder.

"Why are you here?" he suddenly asked.

For a moment, Paul couldn't find the right words and fumbled a response between numb lips. "Hey, we got worried about you. Angela and I went out to the city, and, uh, Ooze said you left, so we were, you know, concerned, and we started looking." Excuse given, he waited and shivered.

CF nodded, and like most everything else he did, it was a slow and laborious movement. It seemed as if very little air went through the windmills of his mind. "You went out to help…people," he said.

"Yeah, that's right." Paul didn't mention anything about the date. "We went and helped people."

The zombie offered another nod and started up the side of the riverbank. "That's good. My way to help is to clean. I know I have to."

At least one person wasn't freezing his butt off in this scenario. The massive zombie began to tramp along the road and Paul followed him, thinking over what he'd just heard. Angela and Ooze knew what to do, but it seemed as though

CF had been given a very simple program to follow — clean-up detail. Simple or not, though, it was effective, and the river did look a lot better.

"Uh, dumb question," he began, "but how come you decided to start making things all nice and neat all of a sudden?"

CF continued to shamble along and didn't speak for a time.

"I don't know," he finally said. "A voice in my head said that I have to keep the house and this place clean. I don't know the voice, but it said that I had to do it." He stopped in his tracks, breathing evenly. "Did I do a good job?"

In spite of his half-frozen condition, Paul couldn't help but to smile. "Yeah, you did a great job. Let's go home."

Back at the house, Angela had already arrived and was sitting with Ooze on the couch. When Paul entered, shivering and the color leeched from his face, Angela walked over to him. "Now you look like me," she whispered into his ear, her voice husky and low. "C'mon. You need to get warm."

She pulled him over to the sofa, searched through the cabinet, and brought out a couple of blankets. After wrapping them around him, Paul started to nod off. Before passing out, though, he heard Ooze say, "CF, I don't mind if you're going to tidy up, but use some trash bags next time, will you?"

* * * *

Early the next morning, Paul started awake and remembered the search from the previous evening. No way would he ever go out at midnight again, not without warmer clothes, at any rate. Sitting up in bed, he breathed out a cold plume of air. When he tried to move, he felt stiff and sore all over. As he put his feet on the cold floor and stood up, every muscle in his body protested. *Don't hurt us,* they seemed to say, but sorry, he had to get moving.

Shucking his clothes, he padded over to the shower room.

As he cleaned up, he thought about the previous night. Seeing Angela in action, her moves lightning fast, her manner fearless — this was his kind of person.

Almost getting kissed was the icing on the cake. He only hoped the next date would be better, but a little less painful and a lot more romantic.

The house was quiet. Since the inhabitants were asleep or at least at rest, he crept downstairs, hauled some fresh clothes out of the dresser, and donning them, felt like a new day had dawned.

It had, actually, as he peeked out of the drapes and found that morning had come. Frost lined the window, but he saw a few cars drive by and some of the town's inhabitants passed by without giving the house a second glance.

Should he risk going out for a quick walk? He wanted to, wanted to shout out that he'd found a maybe girlfriend, had the coolest people ever to stay with and...

"Keep a low profile," he whispered and shut the drapes.

Sighing, he made himself a quick breakfast of toast and tea then decided to go to the lab and see if Ooze had pulled anything out of the computer. Paul figured if he had more Internet access, he might be able to find a link between the mysterious doctor and the company. Right now, it was all guesswork.

Downstairs, a pile of metal and wiring sat on one end of the worktable. Some chemicals in beakers, all colors of the rainbow, sat on the other end. A note was on the keyboard of the laptop. Written in a shaky hand, it said —

I managed to find two files on the computer. There may be more, but right now I have to go slowly. I'll keep working on it. Don't touch the stuff on the worktable. I'm working on something for us. And don't use the laptop too much. The cooling fan is busted and it overheats really fast. — Ooze

Paul smiled at the note, fired up the computer and got to work. Soon the documents appeared and he scanned them intently. No other sounds came to disturb him. He wondered if CF ever slept and made a note to ask him about that one day. Eat and clean up, that was his job. It was simple, but at least he was good at it.

Ooze…he was the genius here, straight up, no lie. Paul was sure he knew more than he let on. He had the expertise, and who knew what he'd come up with next?

As for the patrols and the adventures, few as they'd been, fun didn't totally describe them. For the first time in his life, life was fun. Going out and saving the city, kicking the butts of those who deserved to get their butts trashed? Call it totally awesome.

Finally, his thoughts drifted to Angela. Having a relationship had never been on the menu before, but it would be now.

Since time was of the essence, Paul resolved to spend no more than thirty minutes each day following leads. The first file he saw had the information on Bolson. His full name was Walter Eric Bolson, age sixty-eight, according to the latest in the files. That was two years ago. Graduated *summa cum laude* in chemistry, biology and he had another degree in advanced medicine pertaining to cellular makeup.

He'd worked for a number of universities in his younger days, researching the merits of stem cells for curing various diseases, but had spent the last fifteen years doing research for Rallan, Inc.

"And what were you doing there?" Paul muttered as he read over the second file.

This one had to do with the war machines. As before, it detailed their duties on the battlefield…but Bolson had put in his own notes.

March 25, 2013. There were many failures at first. The cell integrity of the subjects did not hold. They did not exhibit a full range of their powers. There was a shortage of intelligence or motor skills or both.

The director of operations, Thurmond Simpson, is an aggressive and arrogant man. He demands results, but at the same time he realizes that failures are inevitable. He has met with the owner

*of the company on numerous occasions and has spoken on my
behalf when I asked for more time.*

*July 1, 2013. Simpson continues to push me. In turn, I push
myself and through continued effort, I have achieved a measure
of success. At first, I thought my success with the four subjects
would be appreciated.*
I was wrong.

A number of half-finished sentences appeared, but they
didn't make any sense, so Paul skimmed down to the
bottom of the file where Bolson had written his final entry.
*September 17, 2013. I have grown increasingly dissatisfied with
the way things are being run at Rallan. Thurmond Simpson had
grown extremely cruel and arrogant. The owner of the company,
Andres Peterson, is no different. Both of them want to use my
creations in a manner contrary to what I intended them for.
When I objected to the usage for warfare, they threatened to fire
me then have me imprisoned.*

It figured. Bolson had a conscience and the two other men
didn't...
*I know now that my time is short. I am ill and do not have
very much time left. I am still in the process of creating life,
but I intend for this new kind of life to help all mankind...not
eliminate it. I have managed to procure some of the materials
needed in order to help me realize my vision...*

After reading through the transcript, incomplete though it
was, Paul felt a sense of vindication. There *was* a connection
after all! Bolson had rabbited from the LA branch and the
company sent out Simpson and his goons to try and get
him back.

With a sudden stab of insight, Paul realized the agents
hadn't been trying to catch him. They'd been searching
for Angela and by extension, the three other creations.
Wondering if there were any more links he could use as
evidence just in case the cops caught him, he went back to

the computer and checked on the downloads.

One other file popped up. Entitled *Cellular Decay in Subjects,* it had a number of graphs and chemical equations filling the pages. After scrolling down to the bottom of the third page, he was just about to read it when the computer began to make an audible clicking sound and the screen began to waver, become indistinct…then the file vanished. Only a black screen remained.

A knock at the door made him turn around. Ooze stood in the doorway, and the water inside him began to bubble once he saw the black screen.

"Again?" he asked.

"Yeah, it, um, just happened. I'm sorry. I didn't use it that long…"

Ooze waved off his reply and spoke in a mild tone as if he'd been expecting this to happen all along. "Don't worry. The thing is old and has a lot of mileage on it. Let me at the computer, will ya?"

After switching positions, Ooze pulled out a disc from the drawer, opened the side slot on the computer, and slid the disc in. "This is my repair disc. It helps with rebooting the hard drive, but the computer's jury-rigged at best. This is going to take some time, so you might as well crash for a bit."

As Paul headed for the doorway, Ooze called out, "Oh, one of the files I managed to download had some information that can help if you and Angela go crime-busting again. I don't think Sandstorm is the help-a-person-out kind of guy. Don't ask me why."

Everyone was different. "Uh, what's that you said about some information helping us out?" asked Paul as he swept his hand at the pile of metal and wire then pointed at the chemicals. "Is this it?"

Ooze slid over. "Yep, that's it. The chemicals are us, at least, what Bolson made us from, along with stem cells. He passed most of his knowledge on to me, so I'm trying to, uh," his voice briefly caught and he rubbed his hand around his head, "figure a few things out."

A moment later, he sounded more confident. "Now, we come to the best part," he stated and tapped a few of the pieces of metal and wire with a loving pseudopod. "I'm going to make communication devices. I need a few hours. I'll rig something up."

It sounded like a good plan, but all the same, Paul wondered what would happen if they both got into trouble. After voicing his concerns, a smile formed on Ooze's face. "Not to worry, bud. I'll come and pick you up. You saw the van in the garage, didn't you?"

"Uh, yeah, I did." The memory of the secret door flashed back. "Uh, while I was in there I saw a door in the floor. What is that?"

Ooze's eyes widened. "I don't know. I'll have a look at it later on. Anyway, we've got more important things to think about." He rubbed his hands together and made the motion of handling a steering wheel. "It's patrol time."

After seeing the gesture, a very uncomfortable thought ran through Paul's head. "You mean…you're going to drive?"

Said smile faded, replaced by a frown on the water-bag's face. "It's downloaded. I'll get the hang of it. Don't worry. Angela can drive, too, but she's better off flying, anyway. Still," he reached up to rub his head in a very human-like gesture, "if you need backup and a lot of muscle, CF and I will be there."

Immediately the thought in Paul's head transitioned from uncomfortable to downright bad. CF had been hauling out garbage in plain sight, and now they were going to let him out in a densely populated city? "I'm not sure if—"

"It's going to work?" Ooze finished while giving a gesture that approximated a shrug. "Yeah, I'm not sure, either, but you might need backup one of these days and I'm also getting cabin fever—or CF is. Sandstorm isn't going to help us, but we could use CF's muscle, just in case. Whatever, he'll be in the van, so it's not going to be a big deal. Besides, we're supposed to protect the city, right?"

There was no way to answer the question without sounding silly, so Paul simply said, "We can try."

Chapter Seven
Making it Count

Nights were for fun, and in this case, fun meant taking on the bad guys and beating them at their own game. After getting dressed — Paul found a pair of black pants along with a black shirt — he had a word with Sandstorm. If the crooks were out in force, then they needed all the bodies they could throw at them.

As usual, the sand-man was making shapes on the table in his room. In a quick series of transitions, a plane, a steam train, and a Mobius-like pattern appeared, all at light speed and all seemingly without any effort. Sandstorm finally stopped practicing and formed the question, *'What do you want?'*

"Uh, we're going out on a mission tonight, and we thought you might, you know, want to come along." Paul tried to sound as friendly as possible, and wondered if the sand being actually understood the concept.

'You need me to come along as what?'

"As back-up," he replied, still fighting the idea of communicating with usually inanimate objects. He'd only recently gotten over the weirdness of speaking to a zombie and sentient water. Communicating with sand was going to take a bit more time.

The grains of dirt swirled around for a few seconds before forming the sentence, *'You have CF and Ooze. What do you need with me?'*

What was up with this guy's attitude? "You could set up a kind of smokescreen or something," he said after fumbling with a few ideas. "You know, blind the opposition, confuse them and throw dirt in their eyes…stuff like that." He wasn't a tactician…but if they had the abilities, he figured they should use them.

More time passed while Sandstorm shifted his form back and forth as if making up his mind about going. *'Enjoy yourself,'* he indicated, and formed the image of a hand waving goodbye. *'I'll stay here.'*

More than a little pissed at Sandstorm's attitude, Paul started to toss of a smart-ass reply then, deciding that it would do no good, walked out of the room and found the trio waiting downstairs in the living room. As usual, CF stared into space as if pondering the merits of dusting or vacuuming. A few bits of flesh hung from his fingers and Paul ran to the kitchen to get a couple of brain packets. Returning, he handed them over and CF's eyes lit up. "Thanks," he said as he tore them open.

Ooze got up from the comfort of the couch. "Let me guess, our dirt friend wants to play in his own sandbox?" he asked.

"It seems to be that way."

Angela blew out a deep breath and pointed at the door. "Forget about him. Let's get going. I'll take point."

This time they drove back to the Bronx—Morris Park, to be exact. It was a low-rent district full of hard-working families, but it also had a high crime rate and drug trafficking. Angela flew on ahead, roughly fifty yards in front and around twenty feet overhead. She'd tricked out the edges of her cape with some kind of glowing material in order to provide a beacon. It billowed out behind her, framing her against the darkness. Ooze had rigged up two-way communicators for everyone that fit neatly into their ears, and she called out directions from up top.

Paul sat in the back of the van and tried not to be terrified by the way Ooze drove. It could be summed up in two words—fast and erratic. Just before they'd left, he wondered how they'd get away without being seen, but the water-bag assured him it was all good. "This van has special glass," he said. "We can see out, but they can't see in. And the glass is shatter-proof, too."

Now, though, Paul felt the only thing about to be shattered was his spine, as another jolt sent him into the wall. Even CF had a mildly scared expression on his face. "Are we there yet?" he enquired.

"No," Paul said as he prayed for guidance, "Not there yet."

He banged on the window that separated him from the front seat. "I thought you knew how to drive!"

"Knowledge, not experience," the answer came just before the vehicle swerved to the right side of the road and almost took out a telephone pole.

Fortunately, they met with no accidents and finally, with a screech of the brakes, they arrived at their destination. Paul opened the door and sat bent over, trying not to heave. His heart hammered almost uncontrollably in his chest and he thanked whatever gods existed that they'd made it.

It was almost pitch black out. A wind started to rise, and snow began to sift down from the heavens.

"Well, we're here," Ooze called out in a cheerful voice from the front. He got out and ambled over holding a small bag in his hand. "How was my driving?"

"No comment," Paul replied, still sucking in air.

CF piped up in a plaintive voice with the comment of, "I'm hungry."

"You ate before you left," Ooze said with a pained expression on his face. "You should be grateful you don't have to go like humans do."

Angela lit gracefully in front of him. "So, what's the plan?" she asked.

A few seconds passed before Paul realized that everyone was looking expectantly at him. "Um...you're asking me?"

Nods came his way, and Angela cut in. "If we're going to fight crime, then we have to take on the scum. We find them. So what's the game plan?"

In a word, this was asking for trouble. She may have been

bulletproof, but he wasn't. Scanning the area, a number of homeless people off in the distance shuffled by, many of them pushing shopping carts loaded with their meager belongings.

Closed and shuttered shops, many of them old and battle-scarred by time and neglect, lined both sides of the street. A few men wearing heavy coats lurked in the doorways, but they were blowing on their fingers and stamping their feet in order to keep warm. They weren't a threat.

After thinking things through, Paul came to a decision and snapped his fingers. "If we're going to catch anyone," he said, "then we should go to where the, uh, bad guys would wait and do their business." He realized that he sounded worse than amateurish. He sounded downright naïve. "Um, are there any warehouses around here?"

"If you mean you want directions, ask and ye shall receive," Ooze said in an absurdly cheerful voice. He turned to the side, and a second later, a very detailed map formed on his body.

"Neat trick," Paul said in admiration while staying inside the van where it was semi-warm. "I thought only Sandstorm could do something like that."

"You're not the only one who's got special powers of cartography," laughed Ooze, and pointed to an X that had sprung up. "We're here," he said, and pointed to the X. "If you're talking about bad, then we should go…here," he added, and flicked his thumb at another spot on the map that lay roughly eight blocks away. A number of statistics appeared on his body listing recent assaults and murders. The numbers went over a hundred, enough to intimidate even the most veteran of police officers.

"Let's do this," Paul said after testing the wind with his hand. It was cold and only going to get colder. He set out, Angela followed him on foot and Ooze said he and CF would stay in the van.

Five minutes later, Paul and Angela reached their destination. While most of the warehouses were still operating — they were surrounded by chain-link fences with secure locks on them — many of them had been abandoned. There were no fences, and many were in a severe state of disrepair with broken windows and no doors.

A few figures skulked in the shadows. "Homeless people," he muttered, realizing if his situation had gone any differently, he'd be in the boat as the rest of the homeless crew — and maybe worse.

Angela suddenly let out a soft grunt and staggered. Reaching out quickly, she steadied herself against a fence. "Is something wrong?" Paul asked. Her face looked paler than usual.

With a mild curse, she shook her head. "I forgot my shot." After taking in a deep breath and letting it out in a whoosh of air, a reassuring smile emerged. "I'll make it. See you soon."

With a quick leap, she soared aloft, leaving him to the mercy of the streets once more. "Guess who the cannon fodder is now," Paul muttered as he paced back and forth. Swinging his arms to get the blood flowing, it began to snow harder and the wind increased in intensity, whipping against his face and body and chilling him.

"Why am I doing this?" he asked the air as doubt began to well up in him. For a second, he doubted his ability to lead and grew doubly scared at the prospect of getting his butt kicked yet again. Still, Angela's words about not giving up rang in his head. Now he had to make things count.

The weather didn't want to cooperate as it grew more frigid by the second. The glare of the street lamps was partially obscured by the swirling snow. He strained his ears to make out the sounds of feet clumping through the slush and sleet. Maybe he'd get lucky and no one would show. This was the worst kind of weather around. He could go home and get warm…

A second later, though, he squelched the thought. Bad weather brought out the cockroaches as five large men suddenly appeared out of the shadows. From the way they dressed, they were Bangers. At least they had some sense to dress warmly when they went out to kill someone. Paul shivered and hoped his allies were ready to rock.

"All alone here, kid?" asked one of them in a pseudo-friendly voice.

The voice sounded familiar, and looking up, the scarred face of Louis stood out against the gloom. A heavy and dangerous looking pipe dangled from one hand, but once he got within range, he twirled it around in a pair of thick fingers like a cheerleader with her baton. He nodded twice as if recalling the previous meeting's events and a slow, mean smile began to trace itself across his face. "Hey, I remember you."

"Weren't you in jail?"

"I got out early for good behavior. So who're you waiting for?"

"For my friends," Paul replied. It wasn't exactly a lie. "Piss off," he added, finding his backbone.

The other Bangers laughed, but there was no humor in their response. Louis smirked and his smile got meaner still. "You got a death wish, you know that?"

Sneaking a look over his shoulder, Paul saw the door to the warehouse was ajar. Whirling around, he rocketed over to the door, ran inside, and slammed the door shut, locking it. A second later, the sound of heavy fists thudding on the door started, followed by shouts of outrage. "You little scum sucker. You're dead. You're dead!"

He sucked in a series of deep breaths and scanned the area. A number of crates and mounds of garbage filled the open space. The air smelled foul, but there wasn't much choice in the matter.

"What are you doing here?" a voice asked.

Startled by the voice, Paul spun around and saw a man standing not two feet away. The man was tall and slight and wore various patched-up clothes along with a ripped-up coat that might have looked respectable ten years ago. Behind him stood a woman and a little girl, also wearing old and mismatched clothes. They had the look of the homeless on them—faces smudged with dirt and a lost look in their eyes. To their rear was a series of crates arranged to look like a makeshift home.

Let's hear it for the economy.

"You should get out of here," Paul warned while pointing to the rear of the place. There didn't seem to be a door, but he spotted some holes in the wall large enough for a person to squeeze through. "Lots of bad guys are coming."

"It's cold and we need a place to stay," objected the man as he planted his feet. "This building's abandoned." He squinted at Paul. "You're not a cop."

"That's obvious."

Confusion painted the man's face. "So if you're not a cop, what are you doing here?"

This wasn't the time to write a novel. "Look, I'm hiding out, okay?" Paul said as a sense of urgency overtook him. "That's all you have to know, all right?"

"Hiding…" Now the man's confusion turned into panic. His daughter—she looked no more than five—began to whimper and her mother hushed her and stroked her hair. The man shook his head in disbelief. "You're hiding from the police? What do the police want with us?"

"It's not the police."

"But we didn't do anything…"

"Shut it, okay?"

The banging on the door began in earnest. Sweeping his arm toward the rear of the warehouse, Paul whispered as urgently as possible, "Hide. Just hide and my friends will take care of things."

Bewilderment crossed the man's face, but he grabbed his wife and child and ducked behind some crates in the far corner only seconds before the door burst in. Paul took off in the opposite direction, hoping to lead the scum away, and found refuge behind a number of rusty pipes.

"Find him," Louis said. "But don't wreck him. That's my job."

The sound of footsteps echoed in the open space. The place was large, but a person couldn't stay hidden forever. "Angela," he whispered and hoped that she was listening. "I'm inside the warehouse. Are you coming?"

Static sounded in his earpiece and Paul's heart sank. She'd picked a fine time to bug out and leave him on his own. Maybe she was out of range or maybe she'd gone somewhere else to deal with trouble. "Angela," he whispered again in as loud a voice as he dared. Silence greeted him, and with a sense of inevitability, he knew his luck was about to run out.

It did ten seconds later when his nerve broke and he made a dash for the door. Two large men caught him by the arms and tossed him into a pile of garbage. "Well, kid, it seems as though you're about to meet your maker. You got any last words?" Louis asked as he strode over.

"Not really," Paul replied, "just that you're scum."

The scum didn't appreciate being called scum as a sneer formed on his face. Instead of lashing out, though, he waggled his thick finger like a parent about to scold a truant child.

"You know," he said in an almost conversational tone, "if you were a few inches taller and a couple of years older, you could be part of this cause of ours. You know how to get in and out of places and it looks like you know the city. We need smart kids like you in our ranks."

Paul figured this jerk was just trying to scare him before the beating began. If so, he was doing a good job, but this was too good an opportunity to pass up. "You need a lot more than smart kids to help you. You're so dumb your dog probably teaches you tricks."

The other Bangers chuckled at the lame joke. Louis didn't find it funny at all. In fact, his eyes narrowed, so Paul, sure his time was up, added, "You're proof that evolution can go in reverse."

This time, the other men howled with laughter. Louis, though, snorted and spit a wad of gunk on the ground.

"Guess what, kid. I'm not amused. Get ready to meet Hell."

Paul shut his eyes, waiting for the impact, but a second later, a voice called out, "Hold it!"

Risking a peek, two familiar figures approached — Mr. Finger and Mr. Hand. They nodded at the Bangers who'd been waiting for the blood to flow. "Your job is done here," Mr. Finger said and jerked his thumb at the door. "You can go."

"Suppose we want to watch?" asked one of the punks with a hopeful note in his voice. "I mean, is that against the rules or something?"

The corners of Hand's mouth twitched upwards in a smile, a mean one. "I don't see why not."

"Don't I get a say in this?" Paul put in, hoping for leniency. It was a given this situation was not going to end well and right now the cavalry wasn't anywhere near to riding over the hill.

A snort of derision came from Hand and he waved at the wall. The gang members obediently went over to stand by it. Finger knelt down and whispered, "Yeah, you get a say — just before we tear you a new one, kid. This is your one chance. We want to find your buddies. You know what I'm talking about. You know who they are and what they were made for."

Scared beyond fear, Paul summoned up his ballpower long enough to ask, "What did they do to you? They're innocent, man. They're just people."

Both men laughed, their voices echoing off the walls. "Innocent, the kid says," Finger offered and dropped his voice to a hoarse whisper. "No one is innocent," he stated with quiet menace. "They're killers. They were made to be killers, and we want them back. It's as simple as that, so tell us where they are and we'll only destroy one kidney."

Hand leaned over, and his words rattled like ice in a glass. "What my partner said times two. If you tell us where you're hiding them, it'll be just one kidney. You can live with that, right?"

Paul summoned up his courage. "Screw you."

It wasn't the answer they were looking for, as they proceeded to take turns laying in a shot here and there, each one deliberately. They took their time and waited about ten seconds to let the pain receptors kick in. Just as the immediate pain faded, they delivered fresh blows, and that meant a whole new level of agony.

Unlike the tactics of the gang members which was to use their weapons and smash anything moving, Finger and Hand used only their fists or palms. However, they knew how to hit, and more precisely, where. Paul felt that every organ inside him was being slowly crushed and wondered why help wasn't coming. It would do no good to wonder. He was on his own and maybe it was better this way…

"That's enough," a voice said.

Immediately, the beating stopped. Paul lifted his head. Simpson stood in front of him like an obscene Buddha, licking an ice cream cone. In the middle of winter, he had to eat ice cream. He also seemed to enjoy it, as rumbles of contentment emanated from his enormous belly. A second later, a loud belch resounded through the warehouse.

The sight was so ludicrous that Paul almost laughed, but it hurt to breathe. Out of the corner of his eye, he saw the homeless family steal into the night and felt a sense of relief. At least they'd made it out alive. The relief vanished when Simpson ingested the last of the cone, wiped his face with the back of his hand, and began to speak.

"You're going to talk, sooner or later," he said.

A few crumbs still clung to the sides of his fleshy mouth and his breath smelled foul. Paul wanted to recoil, but the underlings had taken hold of his arms and there was no way to get out of their grasp. "What do you want?" he asked. "I didn't do anything."

"No, but you *are* going to do something for us," Simpson began. "You're going to tell us where your friends are."

"We've been asking him the same question, sir," Hand interjected. His face resembled an angry axe, ready to carve something up. "He doesn't want to give us the information."

"Looks like he ain't going to answer," one of the Bangers called out, chortling with delight.

Simpson waved his hand for silence and didn't deign to look at the gang members. "We asked you to do a job for us and you've done it," he called out in a tone which dared anyone to contradict him. "Stay where you are and wait until we need your assistance."

The amateur hit crew looked disappointed, but they stood still like good and obedient droids, eyes bright and mouths hung open like expectant puppies. They were expecting blood and soon there would be blood.

Simpson turned his gaze around, and Paul felt the man's beady eyes bore into him like an insect into a tree. Green was usually a friendly color. In the dimness of the building, he saw only emptiness. "I..." he coughed as a spasm of pain hit his stomach like a knife, "I got nothing."

An almost benevolent smile appeared on the fleshy man's face. "Is that really all you can say? This is your chance to do your country a favor. Tell us where at least one of them is hiding and we may let you live."

Determination overrode fear. "No," Paul said. He knew then and there his time had run out, but no way in the world would he let on where his friends' whereabouts were. He owed them that much.

Simpson sighed. "You honestly think they're people? Open your eyes, son. They're product. They're demo models and we want them back. Look at it this way. You're young. What? Maybe eighteen? You have a full life ahead of you, but you won't see your next birthday if this keeps up. In fact, you won't see tomorrow, so tell me where they are."

A familiar and welcome voice called out, "One of them is here."

Paul twisted his neck just in time to see Angela stride over with a look of fury on her face. She grabbed Finger and Hand by their necks and effortlessly lifted them off the ground. In a swift move, she tossed them away. Simpson's jowls began to quiver and he backed off.

"Get her!" he yelled to the gang members.

With a shout they ran over, their weapons held high. Curses poured from their mouths as they mounted their attack. Like savages, they swung wildly and stabbed their weapons at her, but she took everything they offered and in reply, hammered them to the floor. Once they were down, she swayed and panted out, "You got anything else?" she asked as she swiveled to face the fat man. "If you do, then bring it."

Simpson reached into this pocket and brought out a Taser. "I've got this," he said, and in shocking burst of speed, ran over and jammed it into her stomach.

Unlike the cop's Taser, this model was larger and seemed to emit a more potent charge, as a blue crackle of electricity leapt out to cover her body. She screamed and her body twitched in a spasm of agony.

"Like that?" he asked with a sadistic grin. "I've got more."

To prove it, he reached into his other pocket and took out a switchblade. Depressing the trigger, a five-inch blade sprang out and he shoved it into her left shoulder up to the hilt. Blood poured out and she continued to shriek as he twisted the blade. The force of his thrust caused her to fall to the ground, her limbs jerking around wildly.

"Where are the other three?" Simpson shouted.

"Leave her alone!" Paul yelled. In a surge of courage even he didn't know he possessed, he ran over to Simpson and kicked the Taser out of his hands. Angela closed her hands around the switchblade's haft and pulled it out, emitting a cry of agony as she did so. More blood spilled and its heavy scent filled the air.

"You little fool," Simpson spat. "You have no idea of who you're messing with."

"A fat loser," answered Paul as he threw a punch at the fat man's jaw. It connected, but it was like hitting a brick wall. Lard or not, there was an awful lot of muscle on this guy.

Since punching didn't work, he tried kicking him—right in the nutsack. This brought an immediate result as Simpson bellowed with rage and covered up his bruised equipment. Paul yelled, "Did you feel that?"

The two henchmen ran over to pull him back. "You're going to feel this, kid," Hand said, and kneed him in the stomach.

The air left Paul's lungs immediately. Body wracked with agony, he wished he had the strength to stop them...

A second later, half the wall caved in. CF stood there, his monstrous hands curled into even more monstrous fists. Behind him, a group of homeless people stood waving and pointing. "Zombies, man. We got zombies!" one of them screamed.

With a look of fear in his eyes, Simpson backed away at CF's entrance. He motioned to his men as well as the Bangers. "Get him!" he cried in a voice thick with dread. "You morons, what are you waiting for?"

Neither side moved until Paul yelled out, "Get them!"

Simpson's men moved first and came at the zombie full speed. Something clicked in CF's head as he lumbered forward and smashed all the men to the ground. Hand and Finger tried using their Tasers then their guns, but although they managed to connect, nothing much happened. CF took the shots and the electricity and swatted everyone aside with an angry roar.

"Move out!" Simpson ordered and waved his hand at the door. "Everyone, we're leaving now!"

For a fat man, he moved quickly, and his bulk disappeared through the entrance, following by his two underlings. Only the Bangers remained in a semi-conscious heap, and they stared blindly at the massive zombie who stood surveying the room. "What...what are you gonna do?" Louis whispered in fear.

Angela was moving very slowly, her limps still twitching from the electrical shock she'd received. Blood covered her torso and her eyes were shut. Louis then switched his gaze to CF.

"Are you gonna kill us?" he asked.

The zombie ignored the question. A second later, he began to slowly and carefully pile all the undamaged crates on top of each other. That job done, he picked up some garbage from the floor and went over to deposit it in the pile. "You don't have a bag, do you?"

Paul's eyes bugged out. "You're doing that *now*?" he asked, unable to believe what he was seeing. "Forget the garbage! We have to move. Get her out of here."

CF nodded. "I can clean up later." With a slight squishing sound, his right pinky finger dropped off and he bent over to pick it up. Depositing it in his pocket, he went over to Angela, lifted her in his meaty hands, and walked out of the building, past the ever-increasing band of onlookers, and deposited her inside the van.

A man who looked to be in his fifties, dreadlocked and toothless and wearing a torn pink jacket, put his hands up to the side of his head.

"Oh man," he breathed as he rocked his head from side to side, "is this some kind of joke?"

"No joke," Paul managed to spit out as he staggered past him and threw himself on the floor of the van. "Happy Halloween," he yelled at the crowd.

With a yank, he pulled the door shut and smacked the wall. "Go!" he cried.

Ooze took off at high speed. This time, his driving seemed a bit surer. "No one seems to be following us," he called out. "How's she doing?"

"She's still bleeding," Paul said as he looked at Angela. He put his hands on her wound and tried to stem the flow of blood, but it just kept coming and the air in the van quickly grew thick with the smell. A moan came from her and he felt a stab of fear. She'd always seemed so indestructible and now…

"She needs her shot," Ooze yelled while driving well

above the speed limit. "I don't know how long she can last."

Angela stirred and lifted her arm briefly before letting it drop. "Sorry..." she whispered. "No strength...the electricity makes me...weak. I didn't help...too weak..."

"You'll be fine," Paul said while trying to control his fear. No, she wouldn't be fine, and his fear segued into panic. Her eyes began to flutter. Death was a real possibility here. She needed to drink...

Thinking fast, he took off his jacket. "Here, bite me," he said. "We're the same blood type, remember?"

"I..." She looked at him, eyes pleading for help, but her voice came out determined. "I can't. You might die."

Seconds counted. "You'll die if you don't drink." After rolling up his sleeve, he offered his arm. "Hurry," he said, steeling himself for the pain.

With a look of need in her eyes, Angela's fangs came out and she grabbed his arm. When the actual point of contact between enamel and flesh came, it wasn't as bad as he'd thought it would be. He'd already been trashed by the opposition, so what was one more scar — or ten?

Her fangs sunk into his wrist and a feeling of coldness began to spread from his arm throughout his body. Was this how it was? The coldness kept spreading, but then it changed to one of warmth and it felt as if someone was kissing him. Talk about a connection... He was literally into her and she into him.

It was impossible, but the emotion of being connected to her — and *in* her — could not be denied. He heard the sound of his blood being sucked out. Now the warmth vanished and fatigue flowed through every muscle fiber of his being. Paul slumped to the floor, his face inches away from hers. "Take... You can take as much as you want," he sighed.

"We're heading onto the highway!" Ooze cried and hung a sharp left.

Paul felt as if he was floating. As his consciousness began to fade. His eyesight did as well and the world turned white.

In the farthest recesses of his mind, he wondered if sex

was this good. It would be great to try it one day, but right now, this was different and better than he'd ever imagined it would be. "Keep…going," he managed to get out as his consciousness began to fade.

A second later, she pulled away and retracted her fangs. Her eyes closed, but a smile was on her bloody lips. Paul's eyes began to close as well. If he had to die, then this was the way to go.

Chapter Eight
The Awful Truth

Dreams were never about the real thing. They were only what you wished them to be. That was something Paul had read in a book long ago.

Reality decided to intrude and the events of his life rushed back in a series of kaleidoscopic images. The first days of St. Joe's, listening to the drone of the teachers and enduring a rain of spitballs from the other jerks in the classroom. The teachers who'd ignored his pleas for a little fairness, they were there, too.

Of course, there had been the rotten food, barely edible. He'd learned to wolf it down and nod his head as if it were the most nourishing swill ever. He hadn't been able to wait to leave the lunch table in order to toss it up.

Finally, there had been the punch-ups before or after class. Usually bloody one-sided affairs, the teachers — with the exception of Max — had never seemed to notice Paul's bruises and cuts. No one had professed to having seen a thing. What happened in St. Joe's had stayed there. As far as Paul was concerned, if there was a hell, he had a list of prime candidates on the A-train going straight down.

"Fight me," one of the kids had said during recess. Twelve at the time, this kid, large, fat and redheaded, had been taunting him from day one. Paul had already gotten beaten up more times than he could count and of course, no one had ever stood by him. Why should they, when the entertainment was free and on a daily basis?

Laughing and hooting, the other kids had crowded around and formed a circle. The kid who'd made the challenge was a lot bigger and tougher. Once again, Paul had known he was out of his league. All he'd wanted to do was to read his book and not be bothered, but it seemed that life wasn't going to go his way—again.

The redheaded kid had smacked him in the face. Paul had leapt up, taken out the bar of soap from his pants that he'd hidden in a sock and had whipped it around in a sharp, snapping motion. It'd caught the kid on his jaw and put him down. "Leave me alone. Why don't you leave me alone?" Paul had cried, and jumped on the other kid, pummeling him.

"Holy crap," one of the onlookers had whispered.

Soon, a cheer had started, and perhaps the home team would actually have gotten a victory for once. Unfortunately, the shouts had brought the teachers out. They'd broken up the fight, and he'd gotten sent to detention.

Bad luck sucked. Even when he'd won, he'd lost, and two days later, retribution had come from the fat kid's friends who'd proceeded to trap Paul in a locker room and had beat him black and blue. He'd known better than to complain. No one would have listened to the king outcast of all the orphans.

When they'd gotten done, he'd staggered out of the room and made his way back to his room, blood streaming from a torn lip and numerous cuts to his face. Justice, he'd thought, was a notion reserved for strong people and comic book heroes, and he'd wondered why no one would ever take his side…

Then he was fourteen. Sitting in the administrative office, he'd spoken to a prospective adoptive family. He'd done this dance four times before, and each time he'd been turned down for various reasons. They didn't like his attitude. He'd been too old. He hadn't been old enough. He wasn't what they were looking for.

After hearing the last excuse, he'd wondered what adoptive parents wanted. This place wasn't a pet store. You couldn't get the perfect breed all the time. Why couldn't people accept him for who he was?

Mr. and Mrs. Wilson had seemed nice enough. They'd spoken to him in soft voices and asked him a few questions. After twenty minutes, they'd asked to speak to Brother Jonas, another administrator, alone. Paul had sat outside on the hard wooden bench, twiddled his thumbs and had listened as the three individuals discussed his fate.

Another kid had wandered over and nodded in the direction of the door. "They're talking about you?"

"Yeah," Paul had answered. What else could he say?

The kid, short, blond, and extremely rotund, had offered a shrug. "Hope you make it. This place stinks."

He'd waddled off, and in all the time since he'd been there, no one had ever bothered offering a decent word outside of the staff. Brother Jonas had stuck his head outside and asked Paul to go to his room. "We'll talk later," he'd said.

'We'll talk later' meant that Brother Jonas had made an appearance an hour after the Wilson's had left the building. "They" — he'd hesitated — "decided to go with another child. I'm sorry, but these things happen. You'll always have a place here."

Alone in his room afterward, Paul had gone to the window to look out on the grayness of the city and had wished that someone — anyone, as long as they were decent — would take him in. Risk came with adoption and he'd known that foster homes sucked in general. He'd been through them.

However, had this orphanage been so wonderful? He'd gotten his education, his three lousy meals a day and his ass kicked on a weekly basis. The only difference between this place and a potential family had been that there was more food here. Outside of that, they'd both stunk, but he'd told no one his feelings. "Like they're going to care," he'd muttered, but continued to stare out of the window.

Three days later, the same fat blond kid who'd spoken to him and offered a ray of hope left St. Joe's with the Wilson's. Paul had watched from his window as the couple ushered the boy into the back seat and drove off, perhaps to a nice house somewhere in the suburbs and a room of his own and kids who wouldn't beat him up every day because they felt like it.

After the car had driven out of sight, the hope of ever being adopted had died. Paul had sat on the edge of his bed and tried not to cry. Not long after, he'd gotten the idea of going through the telephone book in order to find his father. Going through the list of names, he'd found one that matched, but when he'd called, a man with a thick European accent answered. "No, he not here. He move. I rent house from him."

"Can you tell me where he moved to?" Paul had asked, licking his lips and feeling that he'd hit pay dirt. At least he'd found out where his father lived — sort of.

"He don't tell me. Who are you?"

The question had made Paul freeze up as he'd realized his father had been living in the same city all this time and had never bothered coming around. None of this had made any sense. The man had repeated the question.

Without answering, Paul had hung up. Filing away the address, he'd promised himself he'd call again, but never had. However, the feeling of abandonment and the concept of being isolated against his will had never left.

A second later, the memories shifted over to his first escape, then the second and finally the dream segued into the events of the night before. The shouting of the Bangers, the quiet and menacing voices of the henchmen, the smarminess of Simpson...time for a total recall moment.

Then there had been the blood — oh yes, the blood — and it had all come from Angela and out of him. She'd been stabbed and her life's fluids, artificial or not, spurted out and she'd needed them replaced and he'd offered her his blood and his life and he was...

Awake! "Uh, where am...?"

Voice trailing off, he concentrated on focusing his eyes and once sharpened, he recognized this place as his room. A thick bandage was on his right wrist. Every joint felt stiff

and inflamed as he turned over to get a look at the clock —
seven in the morning. It was time to get up.

Even though his limbs felt heavy and unresponsive
and every muscle complained, he had to get out of bed.
Moreover, he needed to see if Angela was all right.

With a massive effort, he swung his legs over the side
of the bed and got up, wavering until his sense of balance
returned. Tottering through the door and over to Angela's
room, he hesitated before knocking.

"Hi, it's me," he said.

His question was answered when he heard a soft voice
call, "Come in."

Angela lay in bed, the covers up to her chin. With her hair
framing her face, she wore a guileless expression and looked
like a little girl, all innocent and pure. Her complexion was
back to its usual porcelain cover and he breathed a sigh of
relief.

"Hi," she said. "Are you doing okay?"

Paul shrugged and decided to try to move as little as
possible. Even breathing hurt. "I'll live to get my ass
trashed another day. What about you? Are you going to be,
uh, you?"

The room spun and in a flash she was at his side, lifting
him off the ground in a firm but gentle grip. As she hauled
him over to the bed, he noticed she was wearing a pair of
dark green pajamas which showcased her slender figure. "I
should go…" he began to say.

With little effort, she tossed him onto the bed. "Get in,"
she commanded. "I took a lot of blood from you and you
need to rest."

Too tired to protest, he got in and she slid in beside him.

Oh…this is intense. He'd never thought of being with her.
"Uh, is this okay? I mean, we just went out once," he said,
feeling embarrassed as well as really stoked by being beside
her.

He attempted to get up, but she gently pushed him down
and hushed him by touching her fingers to his lips. "Lie

down. We're just talking, okay?"

"Okay, I got it."

Paul lay back and took in the details of her room. Initially, he figured it would be as empty as his was, but he noticed an enormous clothes closet in the corner with an assortment of frilly looking outfits hanging up, as well as a diverse number of shoes and boots.

Angela caught his gaze. "My maker wanted me to look like everyone else. I think all of these came from a catalogue."

They looked sort of old-fashioned, but he remembered how she'd dressed before and thought those clothes didn't look so out of place on her. Right now, her body was warmer than the first time he remembered...

"I think your blood did something to me or for me," she began, interrupting his thoughts. "I can't figure out which."

Her hand came up to gently stroke the side of his face. "But you saved me. They could have killed you." After wetting her lips, she added, "They were after me. They were after all of us."

A knock on the door interrupted their discussion. The door opened and Ooze stood there. Once he saw them in bed, he raised his hands and said, "Oh, whoa, wait a second. It seems that I'm interrupting a little *us* time."

Embarrassment, thy name is water, as pink suffused Angela's normally white complexion, and she ducked her head in a moment of supreme shyness. "What is it?" Paul asked, finding his voice.

"I didn't see you in your room," answered Ooze, studiously avoiding looking at the bed. Instead, he focused his watery visage on the ground. "I just wondered if you were all right—uh, I mean, both of you."

"We'll make it," Paul answered.

Ooze backed out without a word and the door closed softly behind him. Angela uttered a nervous giggle, and Paul wondered if this day could get any weirder. Under the covers, he felt her hand grasp his. "What's...uh...what's all this for?" he asked.

"Like I said before, you saved me. Thank you."

Paul shrugged. They would have ripped him open even if she hadn't shown up. "You saved me before a couple of times...and like you said, you can't give up."

She uttered a soft laugh. "Yeah, I did say that, didn't I?" A shudder ran through her. "Not taking my shot made me weak. I'm sorry I didn't come when you called me. I heard your voice and I saw you, but I couldn't move at first."

Her gaze turned inward. "When that fat pig stabbed me, I felt like I was going to die. The electricity made me mortal, the same as you. I guess I have a weakness after all."

"You're fine now, aren't you?" he asked. "I mean, you've got blood in you, right?"

Angela's teeth gleamed in the semi-darkened room. "I'll be fine."

She pulled the collar of her top down just far enough to expose her upper shoulder, the region where she'd been stabbed. Even in the semi-darkened room, he saw the whiteness of her flesh, pure and unmarked. It was as if she'd never been injured at all.

"When we brought you back," she said, pulling her collar back up, "I took my shot right away. As far as I know, I slept through everything. Right now, I feel pretty good."

To prove her point, she leapt out of bed and rolled over and onto the floor. After limbering up by doing some martial arts *katas*, she threw some lightning fast punches and kicks at imaginary opponents, flipped high into the air and spun around then landed gracefully on one foot, like a ballerina. A second later, she slipped back under the covers again. "I can handle it."

Putting her face close to his, she asked, "Are you worried about me taking your blood?"

Her breath, warm and sweet, gave him a measure of peace he'd been lacking as of late. "No, it's cool," he answered. He was actually more worried about blood loss, but it was morning now, he was still here and he'd live. "I just wondered what it would do to you."

She shrugged. "I can't tell the difference, if that's what you're asking. And before you do ask, you're not going to become a vampire," she said. "Don't worry. That's a myth. I'm real."

"Okay, I won't worry."

A note of hesitancy combined with wonder entered her voice. "I'm not sure how I'm supposed to feel about this," she said, still speaking softly. "I've... I haven't figured out what I'm supposed to feel. I don't know what it's like to be like other people. But," her voice grew surer in tone, "you're a really cool person to be with, if that makes any sense. I like having you around."

"I always wanted to be someone's personal blood bank," Paul cracked. "You can feed off me anytime."

This time a cute giggle came from her. "Maybe once is enough? But thanks for the offer. I might just take you up on it." Angela stretched out and sniffed the air. "I think someone needs a shower—and it isn't me."

Paul took a tentative sniff. No doubt about it, he stank. "I got the message."

After slipping out of bed and entering the shower, he stripped down then examined his body. Red welts stood out all over his torso and his whole body felt sore, but on the whole, he felt positive. He'd actually saved someone and for the first time since coming here, he felt like he'd become part of a team.

At the same time, though, he wondered how he could deal with not only the Bangers, but also the team from Rallan. There was no way he could say anything to the authorities. Rallan would simply deny everything.

However, Simpson and his goons couldn't make a move and they were known. So for now, it was more or less a stalemate. At the very least, they didn't know the location of this place.

Shower over, he wrapped the towel around his waist and padded back to his room. Clean clothes sat on the bed, neatly folded. He got dressed then looked in Angela's room, to find it empty. Going downstairs, he found her sitting on the couch dressed in a pair of jeans and a black blouse watching the news with CF and Ooze. Sandstorm didn't make an appearance, but that was his way. Sometimes you had to give up on a person…or a clump of dirt.

Ooze turned around and offered his version of a smile, which meant the water inside his containment suit seemed to harden into upturned lips. If he was feeling any embarrassment over his earlier social gaffe, he didn't show it. Instead, he waved to the sofa. "Hey, we're on the news, bud! Pull up a seat."

Paul took a seat next to Angela. They joined hands and watched the newscast.

An announcer, the same announcer as the other day — bad hairpiece and all — stood outside the abandoned warehouse where it had all gone down the previous night. The bystanders looked familiar. They were the ones who had been at the warehouse the night before.

"Previously I'd given my report about a vampire girl taking on a police officer," the reporter said in breathless tones. *"Now we have reports from some of the individuals behind me that a zombie is loose as well. And everything seems to be masterminded by the same young individual. Citizens aren't sure if this is a prank or the real thing. If it is a prank, then it's the best thing this city has ever seen as crime is down…"*

Ooze changed the channel to a different news report. "Now some people are calling the newest team of the undead, the Nightmare Crew," the announcer said. "Vampires and zombies… We only have to ask, 'What could be next?'"

A third newscast showed one of the homeless people, the toothless guy wearing a pink coat, exclaiming, *"I saw it, man. I saw it! Huge zombie guy was picking up this vampira chick and stuffing her into a van. It was like creature feature. You feel me?"*

The channel changed again, and this time a picture of a hideous vampire appeared with fangs at least a foot long, skinny and diseased-looking. *Do we want this protecting our city?*

That was the caption, and it seemed to set Angela off as she grabbed the remote control and switched off the television. A sour look painted her features. "I don't think I want to be called one of the undead."

Ooze chuckled. "Don't take it so seriously. This is ratings! You looked good out there. You kicked some serious butt, Angela. You did, too, CF my man."

For his part, CF bobbed his head once and got up to go into the kitchen to get his daily feed. Angela sat staring at the television with a more than slightly zoned out expression on her face.

"Is something wrong?" Paul asked.

"They called me undead," she said in a shaky voice. Her confidence seemed to vanish in a split second. "I'm not undead."

Abruptly, she threw the remote down and ran upstairs.

"Better go after her, bud," Ooze advised. "I'll be here."

Paul took the hint and went to her room. He tried the door. It was locked. "Hey," he said, knocking lightly. "Can we talk?"

"Go away."

He rubbed his face. "Angela, let me in...please."

A second later, the door opened. She stood in the doorway with tears streaming down her face. "I'm not human," she said in a voice that wavered between self-pity and self-loathing. "You heard the news report. I'm one of the... undead." She spat out the last word.

Not knowing what else to do, Paul hesitantly put his arms around her. "You're human to me. It's just my opinion, you know, but I wanted to say it."

At first, she stiffened, hard as a block of ice, but a moment later she relaxed and clutched him tightly to her. Her body shook as she wept, and Paul didn't know what to do, but hugging seemed to be the way to go. Finally, she pulled back and wiped her face. "Thank you," she whispered.

He took her hand. "C'mon," he said.

"What...are you doing?" she asked as he led her down the stairs and over to the large dresser. Ooze was on the couch and he watched them as they made their way over, but said nothing.

In a smooth gesture, he put on his jacket and rooted around in one of the drawers for something. "Yeah, that's it," he said, and pulled out another jacket. Designed for a man, it was too large for her, but he tossed it in her direction. "Put that on."

Bewildered, she stared at him. "What are we going to do?"

"Go for a walk."

A mushy hand went up and waved. "I'm going to second what Angela's probably thinking," Ooze said as he formed the letters WTH with his body. "What *are* you doing?"

Paul pointed at the door. "We're going to go for a walk," he repeated. "We won't be out long, just a few minutes, but we can still keep a low profile and have some fun. And I'm getting tired of being stuck in here all the time."

"I need something on my feet," Angela said. "Wait a minute." She ran upstairs and came down a few seconds later wearing a pair of high-heeled black boots. On her they looked more than hot. "I just tried these on. They're comfortable."

"Then let's go," Paul said as a surge of strength went through him and he pulled her out of the door. At roughly eight in the morning, the sun had already come out and they made their way down the silent and cold streets hand in hand.

As they walked along, Angela stared at the houses. "I've never really looked at any of these places before, not in the daytime," she said.

"What do you think?"

She shrugged. "They're houses. People live in them. That's all I know."

"There's a lot more," he said, thinking about the possibilities of what life could be.

Angela glanced at him. "Is this what people who date each other do when they don't go out at night?"

Good question and it was one he didn't have an answer to. "Uh, I guess they walk around, eat something in a restaurant if they have money, go to the park...stuff like that," he answered.

"They do all the human stuff?"

In a moment of ballsiness, he took her hand. "Yeah, we do all the human stuff," he echoed. "And I mean *we*, which includes *you*."

She gave his hand a gentle squeeze and they continued their sojourn to the end of the town then turned around. On the way back, he caught sight of her grinning. "What are you so happy about?" he asked.

The grin faded, but only a little. "It's...nice to be out," she said and gazed in wonder at the various houses and businesses and restaurants that dotted the main street. "I've never... I mean, I didn't think I'd ever do this."

"Well, you're doing it now. And, you know," he added as a thought popped into his head, "If you want, we can do this more..."

"Oh, good morning," a voice said.

Turning around, Mrs. Porter, the old dog lady, stood there with her little pooch straining on the leash. She eyed Angela up and down and her mouth popped open, but she shut it again. Her dog started to whine then it growled. "Down, Peter," she scolded, yanking on the leash.

The dog, however, continued to growl. Its hackles rose while its tail pointed down and its teeth came out in a snarl. Mrs. Porter's eyes widened. "I don't know what's gotten into him," she said in a surprised manner and pulled on the leash. The dog didn't give up any ground. "He usually doesn't act this way around strangers. Have we met before young, er, young lady?"

"I don't think so," answered Angela, backing away from the animal. Her eyes narrowed and her lips curled in an unpleasant sneer. It seemed as if there was no love lost between vampire and canine. "I'm just visiting for the day."

The dog didn't seem to like the reply as it advanced on her, its sounds of anger rising in intensity, and its growls gave way to howls of rage. It only stopped when Mrs. Porter pulled back sharply on his leash and it gave a yelp of surprise and pain. "Dogs...don't like me," Angela muttered.

"What's that?" Mrs. Porter asked, cupping her hand over her ear. "What did you say, young lady?"

"I said," Angela raised her voice, "dogs don't like me."

Peter continued to bay, and Mrs. Porter scooped him up in her arms. "I don't wonder," she remarked in a haughty voice. "With that complexion of yours, you might think about getting out in the sun a little more."

Angela tensed and for a second Paul thought she was going to slap the old woman for her crass remark. Instead, she leaned over and her fangs came out half an inch. "You should see me after dark. I look much better in the moonlight."

She turned on her heel and strode away. Paul followed her, glancing at Mrs. Porter who stood on her little spot of ground, transfixed. This was not a good way to stay hidden, and he nodded politely at the old woman before running off to catch up to Angela.

"Hey, wait," he puffed out as he ran along the street. She kept striding along and didn't deign to look behind her. "Angela, wait...please."

She stopped dead in her tracks. "What is it?"

Rubbing his forehead, he thought of what to say. "Not everyone is like this. I mean, maybe we should try a different place. You have to have hope, right?"

"It'll be the same," said Angela in a voice tinged with acid. A second later, the expression of anger disappeared from her face and her voice held nothing but despair. "Hope is for humans. When you're different, they stare. They don't accept. People just don't like me."

A spear of longing went through Paul. He couldn't understand, not entirely, but he had to run with his feelings and his feelings said *be with her*. "Let me show you that we're not all losers."

They took the van and headed over to a nearby town. She drove with a sure hand and thirty minutes later they ended up in Amity. Mainly rural with large farms, it boasted a number of quaint old-style houses similar in architecture to Angelica's houses, a few restaurants and not much else.

Parking outside a restaurant called The Eatery, a number of trucks sat in a row in the lot. A few large men clad in jeans and lumberjack shirts sat in booths with plates of steak and eggs in front of them, chatting, eating and smoking. The pleasant smell of frying eggs and bacon permeated the air. Sitting at a booth, Paul sniffed the air. Food, he thought, now this was more like it...

"Hi, I'm Paige," a voice said.

He looked up to find that a young slender blonde woman in her early twenties with a pretty face stood next to the table. "Can I get you something...?"

Her voice trailed away to nothing when she saw Angela's complexion...or lack of it thereof. "Uh, get you something to eat?" she said, finally finding her voice.

Angela caught the look and turned her head away. "Nothing for me, thanks," she muttered in a sullen voice.

"I'll have the morning set," Paul said.

The waitress noted it down. "Are you sure you're okay, miss?"

"She's not feeling well," Paul said, trying to find a way out of this situation and going with the obvious excuse.

A nod came from the waitress as if to say she understood and she left to in order to fill another order. "I guess going to restaurants is sort of out of the question," Angela said in a low voice once the waitress was out of earshot. "You saw how she looked at me."

Paul was about to suggest she wear makeup, but then decided against it. Her psyche was fragile enough as it was and he didn't want to set her off. "Um, what happens if you eat?" he asked.

"I toss it up. My body's not made for food."

That settled the question of whether she could eat or not. A few of the truckers were glancing in their direction, but no one had made any moves—yet. Angela stared at the Formica, but picked her head up when a squeal of rage came from a few tables over and her eyes narrowed. "What is it?" Paul asked.

"It's trouble."

Trouble came in the form of a short and very rotund man who had one hand on Paige's butt while the other massaged her shoulder. With a gut that sagged over his belt, he resembled a walking bucket of lard. His girth didn't seem to bother him as he was living his moment—acting like an asshat.

"Stop it," she protested, her voice filled with loathing.

"It's just a love pat, girl," the man replied with a grin on his bearded porcine face. He seemed to think this kind of behavior was acceptable. Paul thought it disgusting. The other patrons either looked on with amusement or contempt, but no one seemed to want to do anything about it.

Apparently, love pats didn't do it for Angela, either, as she slid out of her seat and stalked over the site of the conflict. The fat man was either very sexist or just plain stupid. From his vantage point, it was hard for Paul to tell which. Probably both, he decided. "You've got bad manners," he heard Angela say. "The girl probably said no, didn't she?"

Fat-guy eyed her in the same way a scientist would eye a specimen. "You got a problem? I can see that you do."

"No, it's you who has a problem," responded Angela as her voice dropped an octave. She repeated her earlier statement. "I'm guessing she said no. Am I right?"

Her reply temporarily stopped the man in his tracks and he took his hands away from the waitress' anatomy. His face wore a look of confusion. If he expected her to back down, then he'd just picked the wrong person to bully. "This is between me and her, china-doll, so you can leave any time you want to."

Paul walked over just in time to see Angela smile, but there was no humor behind it. "Make me," she said.

Her teeth started to elongate. The ice in her eyes began to grow so deep the man practically froze and his voice came out fifty shades of terrified. "Sweet mother of God, are you some kind of a freak?"

The waitress scuttled away to safety, and Angela, smile now gone, snatched his forearm in a lightning fast grab and twisted it sharply in a downward motion. The swiftness of the move caused him to bend over. His stomach got in the way and a ripping sound came from his butt. His pants' seat had torn open and no, Paul did *not* want to look.

"Hey…let go," the fat man grunted, and his voice rose to a scream when she twisted it harder. "Let go!"

"How about I grab your butt and you see how you feel?" she asked.

"Get off me, you freak!" he cried.

A few of the larger truckers in the room started to get up, but Angela speared them with a glance and they stayed where they were. As for her prey, he continued to struggle and managed to recover enough to launch a punch straight at her jaw. It connected, but she didn't even blink. "Freak," she spat out. "You molested that girl and you call *me* a freak?"

With a flick of her wrist, she sent the man sailing into the wall. He sagged down and she whirled around, fangs out. "Does anyone else want to add their comments to this conversation?"

No one else did. They were too busy staring then a choking sound came from the fat man. The guy had his hands clasped to his chest and his face had gone from pale to ashen. "He's having a heart attack!" someone cried.

Angela turned to see what was happening and immediately backed off with a look of horror spreading across her face. Her fangs retracted and she waved her hands as if to say it hadn't been her fault.

"No," she whispered, "no…no…"

Two other patrons rushed to the fallen man's side while a third pulled out his cellphone and started dialing. "We have to go," Paul said as his sense of urgency went from worried into full-scale panic mode. "We have to go *now!*"

He grabbed Angela's hand and pulled her outside. Inside the van, she sat like a rock behind the wheel staring blindly through the windshield. "We have to go!" he yelled and banged on the dashboard.

His plea seemed to take effect as she started the van and gunned the motor. They took off, the van fishtailing out of the parking lot. Snatching a look behind them, no one seemed to be following. He leaned back in his seat and breathed a sigh of relief.

"I told you," she said between gritted teeth as they zoomed down the highway. Tears — perhaps of rage or shame and probably both — coursed down her cheeks. "I told you this would happen. You said people were nice." She shot him a look that made him feel more than insignificant. "You lied…then this happened. I caused him to have his heart attack."

"No, you didn't," Paul protested over the roar of the engine. "The guy's probably been eating bacon since he was two."

Angela shook her head in dismay. "He's a porker, but maybe he was right. I am a freak."

Back at the house, she stormed inside. Ooze and CF sat in their familiar positions on the couch. "Have a good time?" asked Ooze. He was in the middle of searching for a program and flicked the remote from channel to channel until he found what he was looking for. "Ah, pro wrestling, that's my kind of sport. Are you interested, CF? You'd be a winner."

"I'm hungry," replied the zombie as he got off the couch and lumbered over to the kitchen.

"That figures." Ooze swiveled around. "So, are we on for tonight?"

Her mouth set in a straight line and she burst out with, "Screw this monster mash. I'm tired of being the star. If this is what it means to be human, then forget it." She shook off Paul's arm and ran upstairs.

With a sigh, Ooze shut off the television. "I guess that's a no."

* * * *

Two days passed with no surprises and no outdoor excursions, except at night. Paul caught the news of their outing on the afternoon report with Ooze. A shot on television indicated the restaurant and the reporter interviewed the witnesses.

"It was like she had some kind of super strength or something," one man said. *"She lifted Jim up like he was nothing, and he ain't light."*

Paige offered her testimony. *"I'm grateful this woman helped me out,"* she said. *"That customer was sexually harassing me. I'm sorry he had a heart attack, but he…"* She broke down then, wiping her eyes, and ran off-camera.

The reporter went on to add the victim, one James Matthews, had been hospitalized. *"And we have learned that Mr. Matthews had been suffering from heart disease for a number of years,"* he said.

"While fear undoubtedly played a role, it is more important to note Mr. Matthews' condition was a severe one. It is also important to note that he was sexually harassing the waitress, Ms. Paige Waters, who, in light of his illness, is refusing to press charges."

"Let's hear it for decency," Ooze offered as an aside.

"Authorities are more worried as to what kind of person was in the restaurant," the reporter continued. *"Reportedly, she was the same individual that was seen in New York the previous week, and if so, the authorities are anxious to contact her…"*

Clicking off the television, Ooze offered, "Well, look on the bright side. You're in the clear. I'm just glad I don't eat.

Trans-fats will kill you."

Sarcasm was so not needed right now, Paul considered. "Try telling that to Angela," he replied. "She thinks she's responsible."

"You should tell her."

Paul tried, but her door remained locked and she didn't come out except to go downstairs twice a day to take her shot. She said nothing to anyone during that time. At night she went out on her own, came back early in the morning and went straight to her room. Sandstorm practiced his shape shifting in all corners of the house.

Ooze busied himself at the computer, trying to work the kinks out. When not working on the computer, he went about performing analyses of various chemicals and studied the 'effects of various combinations of amino acids and proteins on the building blocks of life' as he put it.

With nothing better to do, Paul spent most of the daytime reading, but at night he went out with CF, as the zombie was into cleaning mode. He figured it best to keep an eye on the big guy, just in case. "I like a pretty river," CF said as he effortlessly yanked out the garbage and molded it into small cubes of metal and plastic.

Life went on and the news reports continued. Various accounts had The Nightmare Crew — the name seemed to be official — heading due east after their accounts. This was partially true, as Angela was the only one on the job.

Images of her flying over the city were enough to scare the would-be crooks from committing any misdemeanors. When the reporters asked the people on the street for their opinions, they cautiously approved of the new arrivals, even though they weren't sure who or what they were.

On the other hand, the police took a more jaundiced view. "Whoever or whatever these people are," said the Chief of Police, "while we applaud them taking care of our streets, that is our responsibility. We do not condone vigilantism in any way, shape or form. If these individuals are really on the side of the law, then they should come into police headquarters and talk to us. We promise to listen."

BS was more like it, Paul thought. However, keeping the concept of a low profile in mind, he did nothing. While he wanted to work things out with Angela, she kept her door locked. Discussion was out for now.

Bored and frustrated, he went down to the lab on the third day and found Ooze peering at the computer. "Have you found anything?" he asked.

Ooze turned around, a troubled expression on his face. "Yeah, I found a couple of files, but they were incomplete. The first said something about an additional member, but our maker never got around to doing anything about it. He had another chamber, but it's an experimental model."

Paul looked around, but saw nothing. "Where is it?"

"In the garage," Ooze replied. "After you mentioned the door to me, I went outside, picked the lock and found a spare chamber. I don't know why he never brought it in here, but whatever."

Turning around, he searched on the table for something and found it, picking up a notebook and waving it in the air. "I wrote down the equations, just in case."

"What about the second file?" Paul asked.

Ooze's look of concern deepened and he shook his head. "Read it and you'll get the picture," he said as he got off the chair and waved his hand at the computer.

Paul sat down and began to read through the data. The file was only a couple of pages long, but the first two paragraphs made him gasp.

The file was marked Longevity. His heart began to pound as the awful truth hit home. It couldn't be true. He didn't want it to be true, but the facts were right there in front of him.

Subjects Angela and Cannon Fodder will exhibit evidence of cell decay. Molecular instability in subjects is irreversible. No possibility of regeneration.

"Damn," he muttered. The truth hurt sometimes. They'd

been engineered to die. It seemed as though the scientist had built in an expiration date to his subjects. "No...no..." he mumbled, and nothing else came out.

No, it couldn't be possible...but it was. They—meaning Angela and CF—had a very short shelf life. Their cells were unstable and...

A sudden fizzling sound jerked him back to reality. The files abruptly vanished and then the screen went black. "Oh crap," he said, and turned off the computer. After turning it on, he tried to reboot it, but while the power worked, the screen remained black.

"Move." Ooze waved him off.

Paul got off the chair, speechless as the moving bag of water tried to reboot the computer. He muttered something dire under his breath, slid a disc into the side port and shook his head. "Well, it's out again...but you saw it, didn't you?"

"Yeah, I did."

A sense of grief overwhelmed Paul. "So what are we going to do now?" he managed to choke out. He was worried sick over what might and probably would occur. He bit his lip so hard that blood ran out and spilled onto the table.

Ooze's face wore a placid expression and he briefly gazed at the drops of blood. "You understand what the term molecular instability means, right? You understand they're on a time limit."

Sick at heart, Paul nodded dumbly. "I know enough. Just fix the computer if you can. I have to know more."

The water-bag turned around, and this time his face held an expression Paul had never seen before. It was one of loss. "It doesn't matter. I read through the file. I know all about it."

Chapter Nine
"What do we do now?"

Adrenaline overload time and Paul thought his heart would explode from the influx of the hormone. A million thoughts ran through his mind at light speed, yet he couldn't find the proper words and transfer them from his brain to his tongue. Only after a massive effort did he come out with, "You knew?"

Ooze swept his hand at the chemicals and slides and beakers on one of the worktables. "Yeah, I knew and that's why I've been down here so much. I've been trying to find a cure or at least, a stopgap," he replied then added, "I tried telling myself if I didn't say anything, then no one would be the wiser." For a change the sarcasm was absent in his voice. Instead, it sounded altogether sad.

"Try keeping that kind of secret and it does a number on your mind," he continued. Turning back to the computer, he continued to tinker with it. Heavy as his oversized hands appeared he manipulated them in such a manner as to delicately tap each key lightly, almost reverently.

Paul licked suddenly dry lips. "I thought Bolson transferred his, um, knowledge to you."

"He did, most of it," Ooze said and pointed to what would have been the top of his head. "Like I said earlier on, I got most of the smarts and most of the background, but there are gaps. I think Bolson didn't want us finding out the truth."

It seemed like an extremely cruel thing to do, to give life then have it end just as suddenly. Perhaps that had been the scientist's intention all along, to create life and see what would happen. They were the experiment, and right now Paul didn't know what to say, except, "That's pretty harsh."

Ooze shrugged, and the movement sent water inside him rolling around in a gentle wave. "Yeah, but it's sort of practical when you think about it."

The notion of practicality made Paul's blood boil. He'd just had his first date a few days ago with someone he really liked. At the time, he figured he and Angela had made some kind of connection that would lead to something further. Now it seemed as though the object of his affection was going to expire. "How do you figure?"

Ooze stopped tinkering and swung around in the chair. "Think about it. We were created for reasons, right? You read the file. I'm supposed to go in via some kind of waterway and spy on people. Sandstorm was designed to go in by land and spy on people. Angela and CF are supposed to raise hell."

He didn't wait for an answer, just plowed ahead. "If you had superpowers and you knew that you were going to die, what would you do? Hang on 'til the end or go out and take the bad guys with you?"

Paul had no way to answer the question. He'd never been in either situation. Finally, he said, "I don't know."

"Huh," the watery man responded. "Well, from what I figured out, either Bolson or the people who ran Rallan were afraid their creations—us—would go rogue. You read about that all the time in the comics, right? Well, welcome to reality show number one. If anyone did decide to switch sides, Bolson took that into account. He built in a safety program. He tinkered with the genetic makeup, and basically, he gave us a limited lifespan. After a time, cellular breakdown occurs and that's all she wrote."

His thick fingers danced over the keyboard. A few seconds later, he leaned back and gave what sounded like a sigh of supreme sadness. "According to the info, if I'm reading it right, the subjects decay really fast, like in ten seconds fast. He also figured if people like us had nothing to lose, they'd do something really crazy, like go out and kill the President or someone just as famous."

"Did he say when, exactly?"

Ooze threw up his arms in frustration. "No, and that's what's driving me crazy. I tried searching my memory, but all I come up with are gaps. That means maybe Bolson didn't know or maybe he didn't want anyone else copying his research. Either he did it or the owners did it.

"But from what I read, whoever did it? They seem to have built in these stopgaps for Angela and CF. I couldn't find anything about a time limit for me and Sandstorm. So maybe we're safe and maybe not. If we don't have an expiration period, I guess… I guess we're not important enough to matter."

A certain quality of dullness had entered his voice as if he were calculating the odds and coming up short each time. "Would you…" Paul began. He was afraid to ask the question of how long, not just out of curiosity but also because of an overwhelming sadness that threatened to engulf him.

Ooze's expression never changed. "If you're going to ask me how long my buddies have got, I figure six months or so for Angela and a lot less for CF. I based that number on the cell decay rate mentioned in the file, but it wasn't complete there, either. In my case or Sandstorm's case, if we do have a time limit" — he shivered — "I couldn't tell you."

"Would it hurt?" It sounded like the dumbest question around, but it had to be asked. Cells rotting at light speed would have to hurt, sort of like a fire spreading out of control in your body and consuming you. The very thought made him shiver.

If Ooze was angry at the question, he didn't show it. He spoke in a very calm and somewhat subdued voice. "I don't know. I guess it might, but I don't have any pain receptors. I don't feel anything except the water and air around me."

Angela had received a shock and she'd been stabbed. She could be hurt and therefore she could also feel pain. As for

CF, would he even know? Ooze interrupted his thoughts by saying, "The files don't say anything about pain. They don't say when it will happen or even talk about the symptoms. I can't even guess what they might be. If it happens fast, then, well..."

In a stabbing motion, he shut off the computer. "I've been trying to figure out how to counteract the process. I'm good, but I'm not that good—not yet. Maybe some of the doctor's download will click in later, but I'm not counting on it. From here on in, it's all guesswork. I'm doing what I can to figure out a solution, but I'm not sure if I can get it right."

Ooze fiddled with his oversized fingers, a pensive look on his face. "If it ever happens to me, I'll..." His voice caught. "I'll break down in water. So if you can, get me to a nice lake or river before it does. I don't want to go in my suit. I want to end up in nature somewhere. If you dump me in a river, maybe I'll wind up in an ocean."

He turned away, but not before muttering, "I've never seen the ocean, just pictures." A second later, he swiveled around with a haunted look in his eyes. The expression made Paul feel even worse than he did. "If you want me to tell her, I will. It's not like we were ever alive to begin with."

What was life, anyway? If it was thought and movement, then this was life, as far as Paul was concerned. He nodded and walked over to the door. "I'll tell her. And you're alive to me."

Going upstairs to his room, along the way he passed by Angela's room and after knocking gently, whispered, "Angela, are you up?"

No answer came, so he tried the door and found it unlocked. She was asleep in bed, the covers drawn up around her chin. She'd been so angry before, *so* angry. Now, a half-smile was on her face and she looked at peace, as innocent as a baby.

Tears started from his eyes. He couldn't do this. He

couldn't tell her. Gently, he closed the door and went to his own room, sat on the bed, and the outflow began in earnest. He couldn't stop crying and didn't want to.

* * * *

A knock came at his door a few hours later. It was night time, and he'd been lying in bed trying to think of some way to tell Angela about her condition and more importantly, how he felt about her. Endless combinations of words swirled in his head and a million excuses swirled along with them. None of them made any sense and none of them would make her feel better about what was going to happen.

The knock came again, more insistently this time.

"Who is it?" he asked.

"Me," Angela's voice answered. "Can I come in?"

Opening the door, she stood in front of him wearing a jeans-blouse combo. She'd also put on makeup, a kind of flesh-colored tan, and it made her look almost like him, fair-skinned, but not overly white. Her eyes shone out a soft and mild blue, and she wore a tentative smile.

"Uh, you look great," he said and immediately clammed up not wishing to ruin the moment.

"I thought we could go down to the creek," she said in a hopeful manner. "CF is already down there, and we should keep an eye on him, don't you think?"

"What about the city?"

Angela shook her head. "I don't feel like going to the city tonight. I, um... I wanted to talk to you."

Talking was a positive sign, he felt. "Okay, we can go wherever you want."

"It's pretty dark now," she continued, her fingers twisting her hair, "and...not so many people will be out. I don't think anyone will recognize me."

In his admittedly biased opinion, Angela looked better than great, but he realized that what was important wasn't what he thought but what she did. "You look fine," he finally managed to say. "Let me get my jacket."

A cold winter air blew against their faces as they made their way down the road. For a change, Angela wore a coat and they walked down the main street arms brushing against one another. The few people they did meet hurried by without anyone so much as giving them a second glance. "See," Paul whispered, "no one's staring at you and no one is interested. You're just like everyone else."

Angela nodded, but said nothing until they reached the bottom of the hill and stood at the edge of the creek. CF was busy hauling out garbage and neatly stacking it by the side of the bank. He took no notice of them and continued to work with a single-minded purpose that Paul envied.

With another stab of envy, he viewed the rushing water. It flowed by in a seemingly endless cycle of going downstream to be circulated upstream again and follow gravity. It brought consistency and he wanted that kind of that consistency. At the same time, though, the concept of shelf life came to the forefront of his mind. With it came the terrible decision whether to tell Angela or not.

Two seconds later, he checked his thoughts as she asked, "What's it like to be human? I know that sounds dumb, but I haven't been around very long and download or not, I really don't know."

Paul bit his lip and stared out at the moving water. He'd only been alive for seventeen years, and in all that time, he'd never really thought about what life consisted of. This wasn't Philosophy 101. He hadn't experienced much in his life and what he had experienced was only misery.

"I don't know," he said after a time. "We're born and we grow up and meet people..." He didn't know what else to say except, "We get married—at least, most people do—then we die someday."

Angela turned her head toward the water. "I don't know what it's like to grow up. I was made like this." She swept her hands down her body. "I was never a kid. I'm supposed to be around eighteen. All I am is a cell turned into something different."

She started to shake, and Paul clumsily put his arms around her. She stiffened against him, but he held her close and whispered, "You're not so different. You can learn and make friends and do what everyone else can't. I can't fly. I'm not strong, but I'm here — with you."

Her shaking stopped and she rubbed her eyes. "So you like me, even though I can't eat and I look like a china plate and…"

"All of those things," he said, hoping he didn't sound too sappy.

Angela put her forehead against his. In spite of the weather, it was warm and her skin was soft. "You asked me before if you could kiss me. Do you want to kiss me now?"

Paul looked into her eyes and saw a certain kind of moistness in them he'd never seen before, the want and the need. "Yeah, I do."

Hesitantly, he leaned over and planted one on her lips, feeling their warmth. Angela's eyes closed in a lazy, almost sensual, manner, and with a move too fast for him to follow, she wound her arms around him in a steely embrace.

Immediately the air rushed out of his lungs. "You're crushing me," he gasped.

Angela opened her eyes and released him. "Sorry," she said and hurriedly put up her hands. A nervous giggle came out. "I didn't know."

There's always something new to learn. "It's supposed to be gentle," he said, slowing his breathing and hoping she hadn't broken a rib.

"Let me try it again."

This time, they held onto each other, but softly, almost reverently, and Paul felt tonight had to be the most perfect night in the history of the world. However, he suddenly shivered and figured they should go back. Breaking the clinch, he inclined his head in the direction of the path they'd taken. "Maybe we should, uh, get going."

"Okay."

At the house, Angela ran upstairs to divest herself of her boots, and Paul went down to the laboratory to see if Ooze had made any progress. From the doleful look on the water-bag's face, it seemed as though he hadn't. "I don't know what it is," he said, the frustration evident in his voice.

Paul felt as though his heart would stop. "Isn't there anything you can do?" he asked. "Angela's cool, and—"

"You couldn't tell her, could you?"

"No."

How could you tell someone you were into they wouldn't be around too much longer? He tried to think of a logical, plausible excuse…and came up with less than nothing.

An "ahem" broke his train of thought. Turning around, he saw Angela standing in the doorway, tears streaming down her face. "You heard?" he asked. "How long were you there?"

With a few strides over to their position, she choked out, "Long enough to hear everything."

Tears laced every word she uttered with an ineffable sadness and Paul felt as if he were the one about to expire.

Chapter Ten
Lockdown

An eternity passed in the few seconds between Ooze's confession of imminent death, Paul feeling like his heart had been broken and Angela's entrance. No one spoke. No one breathed. It was as if anyone had spoken, they'd have made the situation worse. How much worse could it get?

The sound of dripping made everyone turn around. CF stood in the doorway, blank-eyed as usual. A swamp would have been cleaner. Water dripped from his body and reeds entangled his enormous legs. Mud caked his boots and hands. In his dim-witted state, he hadn't realized his condition walking into the house. The vacuum cleaner he held looked tiny in his monstrous paws. "Can I clean in here?" he asked.

"Not now!" Ooze snapped and pointed upward. "Man, not now. Get out and clean yourself off first."

A hurt look formed on the zombie's face. He looked down at his filth-encrusted form and a spark briefly flared in his eyes. "I guess I'll clean up. I'll come back later."

Paul looked closely at him. His skin seemed to be rotting away faster than usual, especially on his hands, as shreds of flesh were peeling off and hung precariously from his fingertips. Maybe this was the precursor to the cell decay. A second later, the pinky finger on his right hand dropped off.

Along with the flesh came the smell of rotting moss and it permeated the air. Usually it didn't bother him too much, but right now it seemed more than a little noxious.

"You'd better eat," Paul suggested.

The zombie looked down at his hands then at the floor. Something seemed to click as he picked up his fallen digit and placed it in his pocket.

"I need something," he agreed.

After he lumbered off, Angela swiveled around with a look of fury on her face. Her makeup came off in her hand when she swiped at her face, leaving streaks of tan color painting her face like a Plains Indian. "That's what's probably going to happen to me, too. When were you going to tell me? Or *were* you going to tell me?"

"I..." Paul began. A second later his throat closed up.

Her hand chopped the air. "No, don't say anything. You don't have to be nice. You're not the one who's going to quick-rot. You're not the one who's going to die." Her voice began to quiver. "You're alive. I'm not. So it doesn't matter, does it?"

Tears streamed down her face as her eyes, now the coldest blue around, caught and held Ooze in a vise so intense he actually winced. "And *you* knew all along and didn't tell me, either. How long have I got?" When he didn't respond immediately, she shouted, "How long?"

"I don't know," he finally said. "Bolson's downloaded information in me didn't account for this. He left a lot of things out. Maybe he didn't know at the time. I've been trying to find a way to stabilize things..."

"You stink," she cut him off. "I trusted you, because we were made at the same time."

Lashing Paul with her eyes, she spoke sharper than a knife and sliced through his psyche. "And after what you told me, I trusted you, too. You said you liked me. You kissed me. And now..."

She choked up and fled the lab, running upstairs. Ooze motioned at the door with his head. "I'll see what I can do here," he said, flicking his finger at the computer. "She needs you. Go."

Silently, Paul exited and tried to coax Angela out of her room. He knocked on her door and offered to talk things over, but after hearing her yell "Go away!" more times than he could count, he finally gave up.

In frustration, he kicked the door — gently — and went downstairs, only to find Ooze sitting in front of the television. "I'm running a program on the computer," he said. "It's going to take some time."

CF had cleaned up although a few bits of mud still dotted his arms and shoulders. Four empty packets of food stuck out between his fingers, and his skin had begun to heal. The smell had also vanished and his pinky had regenerated... most of it.

Making his way over, vacuum cleaner in hand, he asked in a childlike way, "Is it okay if I clean downstairs now?"

"Yeah, go ahead," Ooze answered. "Just be careful around the computer, will you?"

The zombie turned to leave but twisted around long enough to ask, "Angela...is she mad at me?"

Of all things, he'd have to ask that now, Paul thought, and realized CF meant well. "No, she's not mad at you," he said, forcing out a smile. He hated lying to anyone, particularly the only people he thought of as his friends. "She's, uh... She's having a bad day is all."

The massive zombie looked at the mud tracks, his shoes and he blinked, his mind seemingly making the connection. "We all have bad days sometimes."

Not long afterward, he left the room and Paul stared after him, realizing there were bad days and *really* bad days. This was a case of the latter. Things had gotten ultra-complicated and there was no easy answer to anything. He sat down on the couch, blowing out a deep breath. "What do I do now?"

No answer came his way for a few moments. "I don't know," Ooze finally said, shaking his head. "I've been trying to figure things out and I..."

Suddenly he put his hands to his head as if to shut out the noise and rocked back and forth on the sofa. "Oh...this is bad. This is *really* bad."

Increasing the volume, the sounds of a news flash came

through. The New York City Police Commissioner, a middle-aged fat man with a florid complexion, stood in front of a bank of microphones at City Hall in downtown Manhattan.

"This city is effectively in a state of lockdown," he announced in an angry, strident tone. "I have just been informed that James Matthews who was attacked by this... *creature*...has passed away. Furthermore, I've been informed the gang members who were attacked by this same creature have all been hospitalized with severe, although not life-threatening, injuries."

Breathless, Paul spat out, "It wasn't her fault! The guy was a whale. He had a bad heart. And the other scumbags were asking for it, too. Tell me I'm right."

"You are...but try telling *him*," Ooze said while pointing a stubby finger at the television.

The commissioner continued, "We will not tolerate any interference by anyone or anything. There will be patrols on the street, and we will not put up with flagrant abuses of the law. Whether the citizens of the city like it or not, we are imposing a curfew of eleven p.m. until such time as the perpetrators of this foul crime are caught. We are also putting more uniformed officers on the street in order to provide a strong police presence..."

In disgust, Paul switched to another channel. A reporter stood in the middle of Times Square, interviewing people. "We got vampires. We got zombies, and the city's doin' nothing!" one person complained. She wore a shapeless dress and threadbare coat along with a floppy hat that barely concealed a head of unruly blonde hair. "I don't feel safe anymore."

"I feel scared," said a little girl, no older than six, as she clung to her mother's arm.

A young man in his twenties, large and powerfully built, stared at the camera and intoned, "This is why we should have more guns. We have a right to protect ourselves. No one needs vigilantes." He hefted a baseball bat studded with nails. "I got this. If they come after me, I'm going down swinging…"

Paul clicked off the television. "What about the rights of that girl?" he asked. "That jerk was practically raping her in front of everyone. Angela stopped him. What else was she supposed to do?"

The sound of rustling dust interrupted his musings and a trail of sand wove its way downstairs from the second floor. A sand-hand formed out of the shapeless mass and pointed to the kitchen.

Silently, Paul followed the shifting grains. Inside, away from the roar of the vacuum cleaner, Sandstorm gave his views. *I was watching the news from the staircase. People are scared. They want protection. We can't give it to them.*

"So what are we supposed to do?" Indecision and anger ruled Paul's universe and at this moment in time he was so pissed he could hardly think straight. "Angela was doing her job. Now the cops think we're guilty?"

The lump of sand shifted into a variety of patterns, but finally threw up a series of words, spelling things out clearly. *We were created to help. We should help…but only within the law.*

Since the law decided to do something else, Sandstorm's argument seemed pretty pointless. In fact, it pissed Paul off even more. "Yeah, you're telling me all this, but what have *you* done? Every time we went out, you decided to wait here. You've got superpowers. What's the problem, because I'm not seeing it?"

'I'm afraid.' Sandstorm shifted back and forth in a shapeless mass. *'I'm afraid. I know I shouldn't be, but I was created to observe and report, not to interfere. That's the way my maker made me.'*

If there was ever a time for a WTH response, this was it. However, Paul bit his tongue and simply said, "You've got powers to help. Sitting here and working on your shapes isn't helping. I'm a weak loser and I know it, but I want to do the right thing."

More words of rage, mainly of the four-letter variety, filled his head, but instead of responding, he walked out and went to his room. There didn't seem to be any point in talking to anyone—not now. He sat on the edge of his bed for a long time in the darkness, not feeling the cold, not feeling anything except a sense of impending loss.

* * * *

Early the next morning, Paul got up and went to Angela's room. The door was unlocked and she sat on the edge of her bed, staring at the floor. When he walked in, she turned to look at him, eyes puffy. "What do you want?" she asked in a voice that wavered between anger and hopelessness.

Confounded as to what to say, he sat beside her. "I wanted to see you."

"Get a good look because I probably won't be here much longer."

Her words sent a shaft of fear down his spine, but he fought it off and held her hand. She leaned against him, her voice trembling as she spoke. "I don't know what it's like to be like you. I think about things, but I don't know how I'm supposed to feel. All I know is I'm scared."

Bolson had downloaded emotions and feelings into her. If there was ever a time for saying something to soothe her ravaged psyche, this was it, but he didn't know how to phrase things.

Fumbling for the right response, Angela repeated her question from the other night. "What is being human?"

Her question gave him the answer and he cursed himself for not thinking of it earlier on. Putting his mouth to her ear, he whispered, "Caring."

Angela's eyes grew round and she asked, "Is that all there is?"

"Yeah," he said, and his thoughts came thick and fast. "I mean, we're all going to die one day. It doesn't matter if it happens in a week or a year or more. But if we care about each other, to me that makes a big difference. We care and…" He stopped as another thought occurred to him. "We stay together, like a team…and like a family. That's what it's all about."

A brief smile flitted over her face. "And you care about me?"

With a sense of certainty knowing what the outcome of their relationship would be, he nodded, anyway. "Yeah, I do."

Angela hung her head. "Before, I didn't know what it was like to care for someone. I just know, now I mean" — she bit her lip — "that I like being around you and the others."

"Then you're sort of stuck with me, er, us…me."

A wan smile came from her. "That's not such a bad thing." In a burst of emotion, she hugged him tightly and whispered, "And I want to be around you and stay around you."

Throat clearing sounds interrupted their embrace. CF stood in the doorway. He blinked a few times then nodded, as if remembering what to say. "Ooze wants to speak to you guys."

Down in the laboratory, four members — one human and three synthetic — gathered around the computer. The sound of the vacuum cleaner reverberated through the wood from the upstairs. Once everyone was ready, Ooze pointed at the screen with a stubby finger. "Take a look at this."

A grainy video clip of Bolson flickered on the screen. The time on the tape showed it had been filmed around six months ago. The scientist's face was a sickly yellow, his features drawn and gaunt and his eyes hollow from lack of sleep combined with illness. His voice, shaky and weak, cut in and out, but Paul caught most of the words.

"To my children, if you see this video, then it means I am no longer here to see your birth and your entrance into the world of mankind. My name is Doctor Morton Bolson, and I am a scientist, a genetic researcher. More importantly, I am your father and I would like you to think of me as such. I have been

engaged in this work for many years and now, I am pleased that you will be among the living."

He stopped to wipe his mouth and took a glass of water from off-camera to drink. Finishing it, a look of pain crossed his face. After swallowing repeatedly, he took a number of deep breaths before continuing.

"You may wonder why I created you. I did so to prove that different forms of life could exist among that which we know. I did it as I never married and never had children of my own. And I did it because I felt I owed the scientific community the chance to see life in a different manner. I am just sorry I will not be here long enough to personally usher you into this world."

Paul snuck at peak at Angela. Her body was shaking and hesitantly, he put out his hand. She took it and held it tightly as if to draw strength from him. Right now, if he could have given her all of his strength, he would have.

"For your birth, I take full responsibility," said Bolson as the tape continued. *"You were all created from a single stem cell — from me. I did my research under the aegis of Rallan Incorporated, and it is to my eternal damnation that I agreed to work for them. Rallan is owned by a very evil man, someone named Andres Peterson.*

"Like me, he is a scientist. He was the one who initially recruited me and funded my research. He wished to take what I knew and turn it into something vile and cruel. His subordinate, Thurmond Simpson is just as twisted and just as evil. They both wished to pervert my work and use my creations as living weapons in order to bring chaos to the world then to impose their own brand of stability.

"I could not allow such a thing to happen, so I reprogrammed you from gestation, unbeknownst to them. I gave you all a new purpose, that being to help those who could not help themselves. With the science that I knew and the technology made available, I endowed you all with certain genetic gifts.

"Angela, you will have the power of flight, strength above norm

and speed. Sandstorm and Ooze, you will be able to control the elements.
"*CF —* " *He paused to shake his head ever so slightly.* "*You will have the strength to endure. I am sorry some of you will not live long enough, but if there is any consolation, your basic cells can be…*"

The tape cut off at the point and the screen went dark. No one said anything for a time. Only Angela's body moved in a series of small tremors, her shoulders shaking as she wept. Her father — their father — had died, yet from the way he spoke and the words he used, it was very clear that he loved them all.

Angela clung to Paul and he felt her warm tears splash upon his shoulder. "What's going on?" he asked.

"He loved us," she whispered. "He made us and loved us."

Upon hearing those words, he realized that she meant more to him than anyone or anything else. Something else, though, filled him besides an emotional attachment. He now felt a sense of purpose.

A tap on his leg made him look around. Sandstorm whipped up a series of words. *I'm not human and I know it, but I can think. I can move and I can help out.*

"You want to help?" Paul asked.

Now I do.

Angela pushed away from Paul long enough to view the message and a brief smile flickered across her face. "It was a good message. We may not be human, but we're alive. I can…" Her voice caught, but only for a moment. "I can live with that."

In a quick motion, she spun on her heel and exited the room with sure and confident strides. Paul followed her out and up into the living room. There, she sat on the couch watching television, her eyes blinking rapidly as she flicked through channel after channel. "What are you doing?" he asked after taking a seat next to her.

"Learning," she said. "I don't know how much time I've got, but I might as well learn something outside of what I already know."

The channel-surfing continued, but a few minutes later, she got up and went to the cabinet. Pulling open a drawer, she took out a thick telephone book and tossed it at Paul. "What's this for?" he asked as he caught it.

"I have a family," she said with a hopeful note in her voice. Her eyes were bright and she added, "I just found out who my father is. It's time you found yours."

Chapter Eleven
Family Reunion

The telephone book, yellow and heavy, stared Paul in the face. It wasn't as if he hadn't already thought of calling the address he'd memorized years back. He had...but now it was time for a gut check. The only question that remained was whether he wanted to go through with it or not.

He flipped open the book, went to the appropriate section then ran his finger down the list to find the name he remembered calling before. The number was the same, but there was also no guarantee his father would be living at that address. For all he knew, the same European dude owned the house and his father could be residing in Hong Kong or Monaco.

He shut the book and went over to the couch where Angela sat watching some blow-'em-up flick. After telling his housemates what he intended to do, Paul saw Ooze's reaction was less than positive. His watery eyebrows arched so high they almost receded to the middle of his liquid head.

"Are you sure you want to do this?" he asked and his sarcasm started in. "Not that I'm going to nix the deal or anything. I mean, from what I know, your father dumped you, right?"

"We know who our father is," Angela chimed in. "I may not be around too much longer, but at least I know who made me—"

"And I have to know who made me," interrupted Paul, aching at the possibility of losing someone he cared for. However, there wasn't a trace of pity in Angela's voice. She simply wanted to do the right thing for everyone.

Apparently, someone had parted the drapes a few inches, as a friendly stream of light poured in along with the sun. Spring was still a long way off, but if this semi-warm spell continued, then the cold days wouldn't be so hard to bear.

Angela took his hand in his and held it. Her touch gave him a sense of solidity, something he'd been lacking as of late. "If you're sure about this," she said, "then I can drive you over. I'll go with you, to see him. I mean, if you want."

"I'll be fine on my own," Paul said. Maybe he would, he reflected, but not knowing for sure had been eating at his soul for a long time. Whatever truth he found out, it would have to be enough.

Ooze still didn't seem to be convinced. He shifted his position on the sofa, his body flowing from side to side as he did so. Peevishness entered his voice. "What's all this supposed to do? What's it going to prove? That you got dumped? That you got abandoned? Same thing happened to us, you know — "

"We didn't get abandoned," Angela cut in with a touch of anger. "You saw the tape. You know the truth. Our maker died. It was his time. That's all. Paul's problem is different."

Ooze shrugged. The movement sent his inner water flowing around his transparent body. His attitude didn't change, though. "So his problem's different. My question stands. What good will it do?" he asked in a biting tone. "You got dumped. You weren't accepted...just like us. So what's the point of finding out you're not wanted?"

The words stung, but Paul felt a streak of pride surface. He had to know, one way or the other. "I need to find out, is all I'm saying. It's not that I don't like you guys, but this is for me, okay? I'm not going to tell anyone about you, if that's what you're worried about."

A clumping sound made everyone turn their heads. CF stood at the bottom of the stairs. "I'm hungry," he said, breaking the tension. "I need to eat."

"You know where the food is." Ooze pointed with a long,

slender arm in the general direction of the kitchen. "Why can't you get it for yourself once in a while?"

"I'm hungry. I'm not very smart, but I know you're supposed to feed me when I get hungry," CF replied in the tone of a more than slightly spoiled child. "You promised."

Ooze sighed and it was the sound of someone who found the vagaries of life more than a little vexing. His pseudo-hands quivered and right now he seemed on the verge of erupting. "Just because we have a download doesn't mean you can't think for yourself. Get a clue, CF. Think for yourself."

The sharply delivered speech caused a sad look to creep into CF's eyes which contrasted sharply with the rotting, yellowish-green skin. It made him appear almost human. A mossy smell clung to him and yet managed to diffuse itself through the air, and his skin began to sag around his forehead. It seemed the only thing keeping him alive was a constant intake of edibles. "You promised," he whined in the manner of a child wanting its favorite toy. "You promised."

With a furious motion, Ooze rubbed the area that would have been his nose had he been a person. "Yeah." He nodded and his voice switched from sarcastic to resigned, "Yeah, I promised. Hang on and I'll get you something from the fridge."

He slid down the sofa and made for the kitchen. Angela caressed Paul's face. "You do what you have to do," she said in her soft voice. "I'll be there for you."

With a warning note in her voice, she cautioned the trio not to get into trouble. "We're not going to be gone very long, but you guys stay here. Eat something. Watch television. But don't you dare go outside."

Sandstorm flowed upstairs after saying he wanted to practice some more. Ooze formed an okay sign with pseudo-thumb and forefinger. CF tried to do the same, but the movement proved to be too complex for his mind to make the necessary synaptic connections, so he stuck his thumb up instead. Angela sighed. "Let's go," she said, motioning to the door.

Outside the city limits, Angela pulled over to a phone booth, and Paul called the number. The same man he'd spoken to years ago answered the phone.

"Mr. Wiseman doesn't live here now," the man said. "He is in a nursing home, I hear. He sell me house about a year ago. Sorry, I cannot help."

Nursing homes…that could wait for a moment. Paul hung up, and returning to the van, said, "I need to see the house."

"Is there a reason why?"

"I want to see where I first grew up."

Wordlessly, she motioned to the car and they motored off. Neither of them said a word during the trip, but finally they pulled up outside a small, old but well-kept two-story house on the outskirts of Manhattan. A residential neighborhood, cars lined the streets, but only a few people were walking around in the bitter cold and no one bothered glancing in their direction.

Gazing at the front yard, Paul tried to recall what kind of tree sat there. It was withered and sere, and stood in the center of the snow-covered grass. Bushes covered in white lined the front wall. A large, twelve-paned window stood out.

Blinking rapidly, in a flash of total recall, the memories poured in. He sat in the window playing with his toys and waiting for his father to drive up after a hard day on the job. The house had smelled of cinnamon. His room had had yellow wallpaper, stuffed toys in the corners…he'd had a bed to sleep in and not a cot.

At that age, he didn't recall what his father did, but he'd known that he usually came home at night. All those thoughts ran through his mind at light speed…but try as he might, no memories of his mother surfaced.

After sliding out of the car, Paul took a step toward the house, but then shied back. He remained rooted to his spot until he felt Angela's presence beside him. The proximity to her made him feel more reassured. "I'm here," she said. "Are you going to go over and talk to the owner?"

He didn't answer. Blinking, he recalled the tree in the front yard. It had been a cherry tree once. Now it was dead. Its branches sagged and its trunk had been eaten away by insects.

Glancing up at the second floor, another flash of memory intruded. He sat spread-legged on the floor looking at picture books, the brightly colored drawings making him laugh with delight at the antics of bears and cats and other animals. He remembered his father's laugh, a high-pitched sound, the hiss of the radiator and the sound of the television playing...

"Paul?"

Angela's voice startled him. "What is it?"

She gestured toward the house. "We can go over and say hello if you want."

A short and stocky man came out of the front door wearing a pair of long johns and boots, cursing the cold. He kicked some snow off his walk and went back inside, slamming the door behind him. "No," Paul said, suddenly feeling this trip was a waste of his time as well as hers. "Let's get going."

They drove off and stopped at a nearby service station. "I'll just be a few minutes," he said.

Inside the booth, he went through the list of nursing homes and began to make the calls. Thirty minutes later, he found what he thought he was looking for. Angela, who'd been waiting patiently outside the booth and feeding him quarters every so often, kept her head down to avoid the stares of the passersby.

After the tenth call, Paul hung up and slipped out of the booth. "Can you drive me over to a place on Lexington Avenue?" he asked.

She gave him a look of concern, but said nothing. Forty minutes later, they stopped outside Mount Nebo Nursing Home. The sign outside read *Palliative Care Center* and as had been the case at his old house, Paul pulled up short.

Her voice came like a whisper of reassurance in his ear. "If this makes you feel bad, you don't have to go inside," she urged. "I don't have much experience with people, but I know what it's like to lose someone. You know what kind of place this is, don't you?"

Paul nodded and swallowed. His throat had suddenly gone dry. "I'll be fine on my own," he said. Half of him said to go inside while the other half told him to stay in the car. He ended up at the reception desk where he asked the nurse on duty if there was a Paul Wiseman, Senior, as a patient.

The nurse looked at him carefully, nodded, and gave him the room number. A minute later, Paul sat on a decrepit wooden chair next to the bed where a sallow-skinned and shriveled up man lay on the sheets, a breathing tube up his nose. A small birthmark on his cheek stood out. Paul began to breathe faster.

Although the man appeared to be asleep, after a moment, he opened his eyes as if sensing the presence of someone. Seconds later, a look of recognition crept in and he nodded.

"I thought...I thought I'd never see you again," Paul Wiseman, Senior, said with difficulty.

"I'm here," said Paul and as he listened to the man rasp and heard the oncoming rattle in his throat, he wondered how long this person had to live. He really didn't want to know. Finally, he asked, "Are you my father? I mean, my real father. Are you?"

With a slight grunt coupled with a moan of pain, the man in the bed pulled out the tube from his nose. His eyes, formerly rheumy and half-closed, grew clear. "I see the birthmark on your face," he wheezed out. "When I first held you, that's all I noticed. Your mother did, too." He pointed at his own birthmark.

His father's admission of the truth caused Paul's heart to jump in his chest. He sat back in his chair and tried to stem the flood of tears that threatened to flow at any moment.

After heaving in a deep breath to calm down, he pressed on. "What's wrong with you?" It may have sounded rude, but he had to find out as much as he could.

"Lung cancer," the man replied. "Funny thing is, I never smoked. I never drank, either. That's what you get for having bad genes. We look the same. Your voice even sounds like mine did when I was your age…" His voice died away as a coughing fit overcame him.

With an effort, he turned over and grabbed a box of tissues from the nightstand. He pulled out a handful then spat out a wad of phlegm. He balled up the tissue then tossed it into a trash basket at the side of the bed. "Chemotherapy only delays the inevitable. I'd been…been feeling bad, coughing…and the doctors gave me the verdict three months back. I'd come back from…from California… over two years ago." He heaved in a deep, rattling breath. "I rented out my house here while I was living on the West Coast, but…I wanted to come back. It's where I was born, so…only right that it ends here."

Listening to the explanation of impending death didn't matter, but he did ask, "Are you going to get better?"

His father shook his head. "The doctors say…there's a chance of remission. They're full of it."

He wheezed again, a painful inhalation and exhalation of breath. "Some days I feel like choking and don't want to breathe, just let it all end," he said between puffs of air. "Other days, I want to live so badly it hurts. I don't have very much time left, if that's of any use to you."

Paul wasn't startled by the news, yet it still hit him hard. This man, however much a stranger he was, was still his father. He couldn't have been more than forty-five at most, but he looked seventy. His body was rapidly wasting away, eaten up by the illness. Used, spent and dying, his father deserved pity, but at the same time angst ruled and Paul cried out, "Why did you get rid of me? What did I do to you?"

His father started to say something, coughed and

hurriedly ripped out some more tissues. Paul started to go over to help, but the older man waved him off. "I can do this."

Once again, he went through the ritual of spitting out his bodily waste. When he recovered his breath, a whisper of his voice emerged from a throat ravaged by his disease and it was a cry of agony and of fading life. "You didn't do anything wrong, son. It was me and your mother, and even then, it wasn't her fault."

He sank back into the sheets, his withered and sunken chest rising and falling in a series of rapid pants. "We got married young. I was…twenty and she was a year younger. We thought we were doing the right thing at the time." He softened his gaze, perhaps reflecting on his past. "Hell… we were too young. She got pregnant and you came along about a year later."

He rubbed his eyes. "We raised you until you were about four years old. Your mother got sick—ovarian cancer. She died six weeks later. I spent everything I had on treatment. It wasn't enough. She died, anyway. Then my company downsized me and I had no choice. I couldn't make payments on the house we'd bought. The bank said they understood, but…" He paused to draw in a rattling breath. "They also wanted their money. I had to make a choice and so I rented it out in order to pay for things. I had to make a fresh start, so when the offer of a job came up in California, I took it."

Paul heard the words, digested their meaning, then asked, "What did you do in California?"

"I was an insurance adjuster, a paper pusher," the reply came. "It was a desk job, but it was okay."

Hearing the word "okay" sounded like his father had done well financially, and the contempt came out loud and clear. "You gave me away," Paul said, barely able to keep the anger in check. "You got your job, but you couldn't take me along. People always tell young kids to be responsible. You made me with my mother then you decided to dump

166

me, just like everyone else."

The desiccated and dried-up semi-corpse in the bed nodded, now teary-eyed. His lips trembled as he spoke. "I never wanted to, but I had to make a choice. I had no money, no future...nothing. It was the hardest and worst decision I ever made."

Paul lost it then and rivulets of water burst from his eyes and blurred his vision. No matter how much he wiped them, the tears kept coming. "So once you got set out west, why didn't you come back for me?"

When his father didn't answer, he repeated the question, but just as quickly his voice dried up. He wanted to continue berating his father, wanted to tell him what kind of rotten life he'd had — the beatings, the hazing and the misery associated with the foster and orphanage life — but decided it wasn't worth it. In an abrupt reality check, he realized this man had ceased to be his father long ago.

"I don't know," the senior Wiseman answered after a few seconds of erratic breathing. "Once I got out there, I started working and told myself that when things were better, when I had money, I'd come back and find you. I'd bring you home."

A sigh emerged from his damaged lungs. It was a wet sound, one laden with chemicals and blood and impending death. "One day turned into the next, then a week, then a month...then longer."

Another ratchety cough burst from his decaying body. "Finally, I got enough money to come back here. I moved into my old house, the one you might remember when you were a child. Then...I got sick and had to sell it in order to pay for this place." He waved his hand weakly at the wall.

That explained the flip-flop on the house deal, but it didn't explain the most important thing. "Why didn't you come back for me?" asked Paul and tried very hard to keep his voice from cracking.

It didn't work, but the man in the bed didn't notice. Instead, he stared at his fingers. The skin on the backs of his hands was black and his fingertips were turning the same color. "It became easy to convince myself someone else was doing a better job of parenting than me," he finally said.

"Yeah, you were a wonderful parent."

Sarcasm combined with anger ruled as Paul spit out his response. He wanted to say something worse, but couldn't bring himself to utter the filthy and vicious words that churned in his mind. He got up to leave. "Don't worry. I didn't come to ask you for money or anything. I just wanted to come back and find out why you got rid of me. Now I know."

As he reached the door, his father's voice stopped him. "For what it's worth...you're still my son. I wasn't there for you and I'm sorry, but...to me...you're still my son. I want you to know that."

Paul hesitated, but only for a moment. "You're my father," he managed to get out. As hard as this was to say, it had to be said. "But you're not my family. I have a different one now."

He didn't bother turning around. Instead, he slid the door open and walked out. In the hallway, he leaned against the wall and the tears began to fall once more.

A few people shuffled by and Paul hid his face as he ran into the washroom to clean up. After he'd washed his face, he took out the picture of his father from his pocket and stared at it until the tears started to fall once again and blinded him. With shaky hands, he tore the picture up into little pieces and dumped them into the trash can. It was time for him to leave this place of death and begin living again.

Wiping his eyes, he walked outside only to find Angela waiting for him. More patients shuffled by on their way to nowhere, and they didn't bother looking in his direction. Paul was grateful for the anonymity.

"What's going on?" he asked.

"I, uh, got tired of waiting in the car," she said, her voice soft and caring. "I thought you might want to talk about things."

Shrugging, he took a seat on a nearby bench. "I found out what I needed to know," he said after a time. "I found out why people leave and why they don't come back." He looked at her. "I guess you know all about that, don't you?"

Angela offered a sad smile. "Our maker was very ill. When I came out of the chamber, because of the information he'd downloaded into me, I knew about his condition. Ooze and Sandstorm did as well. CF, well" — she shrugged — "he's not so bad. He doesn't know and maybe it's better that way."

"He *is* sort of dense," Paul agreed, "but I like the guy."

"Yeah, he's sort of likeable."

They fell silent, and Paul began to cry once more. He hated himself for being weak, hated the fact he'd come to this place of misery and death only to be turned away by the person who'd helped to give him life, and hated admitting that he needed help. Angela reached over and pulled him to her, rocked him gently, and whispered things would be okay.

"You know, I was thinking about what you told me, that we all die someday," she said in a voice laden with introspection. "I mean, I don't know when I will or not and Ooze...I'm not sure, unless someone turns a heating lamp on him or something. CF...he will, but he doesn't know it, yet." Her eyes began to moisten. "I'll be sad when that happens. I'm sad now, for you."

Paul lifted his head and saw a single tear trace its way from her right eye down to her mouth. He wiped it away and in a move, impulsive and strange for him, he kissed her on the lips. They were warm and supple, and her eyes widened with surprise. "Why...why did you do that?" she asked after touching her hand to her mouth. "This isn't a date. I mean, I thought people only did that on dates."

"Uh, well, humans kiss whenever and wherever they want," he answered, feeling foolish yet not feeling so alone anymore. "And if I'm going to teach you about being a human, then this is part of it. If you like it, that is," he added hastily, wondering if he'd messed up.

"I do," she answered, and got up holding his hand. "Do you want to go home now?"

He nodded. He had a home to go to. "Yeah, let's go. CF has probably eaten all the synthetic brains in the fridge and Ooze won't be able to handle it."

They walked outside hand in hand, and Paul considered that whatever came his way, he'd be able to deal with it. He had a family now, unconventional as they might have seemed to anyone else.

His notion, though, of having a happy ending faded when two black vans shot over to their position from up the street and screeched to a halt in front of them. Men in black suits piled out on the sidewalk, ten in all. The last three people to exit were Mr. Finger and Mr. Hand, with Simpson in the lead. "Fan out," he ordered his men.

They immediately took up positions on either side of Simpson, their guns drawn and ready, and they kept the crowd back. Someone called for the police and in the distance, the wail of sirens began to sound. "Hurry it up," Simpson shouted.

"Get out of here, Angela," Paul whispered fiercely. "Just take off."

She shook her head. "I won't leave you. And I can't fly in daylight, remember?"

Damn it, her loyalty was infuriating and he tried pushing her away. "So run. I'll be okay. You have to leave."

She didn't budge an inch, and Simpson called out, "I hate to break up your romantic interlude, but the girl belongs to us. You can leave. I'll give you your chance right now and you've got five seconds to decide."

Angela hissed and her skin went even whiter. Her fangs came out, and when one man ran over, she quickly seized him, bit his face, and hurled him into the crowd. Mass panic ensued and the onlookers ran off screaming in every direction. The guards pushed the frantic pedestrians aside, but kept their guns down. "No shooting!" Simpson yelled.

"Take her down. Use the Tasers!"

The men surged forward like a tidal wave. Angela met the surge head-on, and took on the lackeys by evading their grasp, smacking them around and generally causing mass bodily damage.

It all looked good, but their plans of escape went out of the window when Mr. Hand, a huge grin on his face, fired something at Angela. A field of blue electricity surrounded her and she writhed for a moment before falling to the ground in a heap. Paul ran over to her, but Simpson moved quickly for a fat man and clubbed him on the back of his neck.

As Paul hit the ground, he caught a glimpse of the older man's face. Simpson's eyes, cold and green, held nothing but emptiness. However, he wore a grin. It was a sly and malicious grin that said he could take them down anytime and he wanted nothing more than to do it in front of a crowd. In fact, he already had.

"Did you miss me?" he asked.

Chapter Twelve
A Little Talk

Two of Simpson's men loaded Angela's unconscious form into one of the vans. Hand, Finger and five others went with them. Simpson grabbed Paul's arm and heaved him inside a second van and got in with him along with two other faceless drones. They drove off at high speed through the startled crowd.

"Floor it," said Simpson, looking out of the window. "The authorities are here. Head for Angelica."

Three police cruisers had pulled up to the scene, sirens wailing, but in a movement resembling a wave cresting on the shore, the crowd surged in and around the cars and made it impossible for them to move. Simpson laughed as if to underscore the moment. "Our vans aren't carrying any plates. Forget about the cavalry, kid."

The van sped up, the miles passed, and Paul finally got up the nerve to ask "Why are you doing this?"

A tight smile emerged from the fat man's lips. "You don't know what this program is for, do you?"

"I know enough," Paul replied, still steamed at being caught and doubly steamed at his inability to do anything about it. "I know Dr. Bolson created them. I know he made them people. That's it."

Simpson didn't appear to be impressed. Instead, he gave a snort of what had to be contempt. "You're only a kid, so I'll cut you some slack. Y'see, Bolson was one of our own. Our organization gave him a lot of leeway in creating what he did. We're a private company attached to the armed forces—all very hush-hush, you understand."

As if reading his mind, he snapped his fingers. "My guess is right now you're probably wondering why we're going to all this trouble for these *things*."

Things, they weren't *things*. They were people. Well…at least one of them was. Paul saw red, but he kept a lid on his temper. "Yeah, I was, sort of." Maybe this tool would spill a few more details. The bad guys usually did when they felt they were in control.

In a gesture of total nonchalance, Simpson leaned back against the wall of the van and allowed his belly to sag. "Kid, these days armed combat is too impersonal. They use drones. They use bombs, but the problem is intelligence can only go on what they know at the moment they get the information. They don't know what can change in a few minutes, who can walk in, who's innocent and who isn't. Every presidential administration has struggled with this."

He rubbed his chin, pulled out a pack of gum, and after peeling off the wrappers of three sticks, popped them into his mouth and chewed noisily, blowing a bubble here and there and wearing a smirk a mile wide.

"So you make weapons to go where the army can't," replied Paul, not bothering to hide his contempt for someone who thought of war as a game and discussed death so casually.

"Basically, yeah." Simpson nodded as he spit out the used wad of gum onto the floor. Taking a few more sticks, he stuffed them in his mouth and proceeded to masticate them. "You're a pretty bright kid. And to answer your question, I'm going to say 'can't or won't'. Like I said, the bad thing about a bomb is that it takes out too many people and collateral damage is something no president wants. So, the government—that is, Homeland Security—arranged to have the army develop a program to counteract public opinion on drone usage."

In a leisurely movement, he leaned back to blow out another large bubble the size of an oversized melon, popped it and folded the wad with his enormous tongue back into his mouth. "In turn, the army made a deal with us to create super-soldiers, people who could go in, spot the enemy and inform us of their whereabouts, take the hits if necessary then take out specific targets if ordered to."

It would certainly be easy enough. Ooze could seep into a water supply. No one would know. Someone like CF would be the shield and kill as many of the enemy as possible, and a vampiric assassin like Angela would murder whoever she was programmed to kill.

However, somewhere along the way, a hitch had developed. Bolson hadn't wanted that. The files and his personal thoughts made it very clear he'd been against the idea from the start. "I guess your doctor didn't want to go along with the plan," Paul offered.

Apparently in dismay at the scientist's lack of team play, his captor shook his head. "Bolson was old. He was sick, and he knew that he was dying. At the beginning, we put him in charge of the program and let him do what he wanted."

"And he got results."

Simpson's eyes shone with a kind of manic glee, the kind that knew a secret and wanted so very much to impart it. "Oh, he got more than just results. The man was brilliant. You have no idea what ideas he had! Everyone said it was impossible to create life — not just cells, but different *people* — from stem cells. He proved them wrong."

With a grunt he shifted his bulk and scratched his jaw. A note of respect combined with awe entered his voice. "It was his idea to create beings based on nightmares. He said they'd be more terrifying to the enemy and he achieved just that. All *we* wanted were results and we let him do what he wanted, provided he came through for us. Well, he did — big time."

After he noisily cleared his throat, Simpson's voice took on an introspective air. "But, like a lot of the bleeding hearts out there, over time he grew a conscience. Bolson told us he didn't want to play along. We told him he was under contract. This was a matter of national security, and if he didn't do as ordered...pfft." He made a slitting gesture across his fat throat.

"Bolson got the message. What we didn't know was that he'd altered the programming of what he created. And no one caught on. His work was so top-level and so secret only two people knew about it, me and the owner of the company. As head of security, I knew every little detail of what Bolson had access to. And he had access to everything — shipping manifests, contractors...everything.

"And he was clever, too. He got the parts from about twenty different suppliers. It was like stealing wheelbarrows from the company."

Paul didn't get the wheelbarrow analogy, but he recalled Mrs. Porter's words about different crews of workmen coming at all times and from different towns. It all made sense now. "So how did you find out where we were?" he asked.

A harsh chuckle followed along with a knowing smile playing around Simpson's fleshy lips. "We figured out from the girl's flight patterns where she was going. That, and we got a call from a concerned citizen who saw your girlfriend hiss at her dog a couple of days ago."

"Mrs. Porter," Paul said softly, recalling the old lady's nosy nature and realizing that he'd been under the microscope all along. His anger then grew at her betrayal. "She would rat me out."

Simpson shrugged and recited, "I can neither confirm nor deny the identity of the informant." A snort followed his by-the-book statement. "She was just worried. So being the good citizen that she is, she called the FBI and told them what happened. I still have a couple of contacts on the force and they came through for us."

As Paul stewed, Simpson made a dismissive gesture with his hand. "You can't blame her for that," he said. "Anyway, as I was saying, Bolson did some cutting-edge stuff. He didn't just make creatures. He made those things people, gave them feelings and emotions and made them almost...

human."

With that last word, a note of venom entered his voice. Shifting his position briefly in order to scratch his huge rump, he resembled a water buffalo about to dump its morning breakfast.

"Is that so bad?" Paul asked.

"For you, maybe not," Simpson said, "but for us, it was. We wanted weapons, controllable weapons. We never knew what Bolson was thinking. Then one day, he decided to cut and run. And the little bastard managed to escape us with the most important data for almost two years."

"It doesn't say much for your spying ability," stated Paul, unable to contain his sarcasm. "I thought you used to work for the FBI. Didn't they train you guys well enough?"

His remark earned him a swat across the face. For a big man, Simpson moved fast. "You got a big mouth, kid, and a big nose, too. Keep yapping and we'll close one and cut the other. You figure out which."

An immense glower settled over his features, but he eventually nodded as if admitting defeat. "Yeah, we fouled up. I admit that. We never thought he'd actually run, but he did. It took us all this time to track him down. Who figured he'd set up shop in the countryside? We spent millions trying to track him down. We sent agents to Europe, Asia, and the Middle East. At first, we thought he turned traitor and wanted to sell his secrets to the highest bidder, but no, he wanted to create a nice group of monsters."

The van made a right turn and sped up. Simpson turned around and asked the driver how long until they arrived at their destination. He got the reply of "soon" and turned back again.

"In a way, we're lucky you happened along. We were searching for the girl, but you happened to be with her and we figured on getting all of you in one fell swoop." He snapped his fingers. "It's as simple as that."

"You want what's yours."

Simpson leaned forward as if to impart some confidential

information. "It's all about property. We're just reclaiming it. Bolson's gone, but now that we have his knowledge in our hands, we're going to create our own private army. This is something no country will ever be able to match. Even if one of our own gets killed, we can always make another. That's the beauty of the program. Unlimited soldiers and unlimited potential — think about it, kid."

"You've got killers at your fingertips."

Simpson's eyes started to shine with the zeal of a true nut. "Welcome to the twenty-first century. This isn't myth anymore. It's not science-fiction or fantasy novel time. It's science."

Paul caught the look. "And you think the government is going to let you get away with it? They'll —"

"They'll…what?" Simpson interrupted. "They'll stop us?" As he leaned back, he spit out a giggle which sounded somewhat incongruous, considering his size. "They *paid* for it. They'll never admit it and it's all off the books — plausible deniability and all that — but they knew damn well what we were doing and they allowed it. So don't try any morality games on me, kid. There are no morals here, only business."

Money and big business, they worked together. "Business," Paul said, "You mean business like your guys contacting the Bangers."

In a split second, the gleam in Simpson's eyes changed to a dead-fish glaze. Practicality had to be this man's middle name. "The Bangers serve a purpose. They're target practice. They're just too stupid to notice. So we made a deal with them. They stir up the people and then the nightmare group practices taking the thugs down."

The dead-fish glaze disappeared as the zealous gleam resurfaced. "And it's worked perfectly. We've been watching you through our operatives. We could have picked you up at any time, but we let you run free because you were helping us in the long run."

Paul gasped when he heard that. "But your guys — Hand and Finger — they attacked me —"

"They did it under orders," Simpson interrupted in a flat, businesslike tone. "I told them to whack you around and see if the vampire girl and the zombie would help out. They did. It usually sucks for someone to grow a conscience, but in their case, we made an exception once. It was nothing personal."

Paul still remembered the skinny operative kicking him and grinning while he did so. If the chance ever arose, there would be payback.

Simpson snapped his fingers again and pointed at his chest. "Pay attention, boy. Your mind must be wandering. I'm about to give you a compliment. You've done great things with the group. You've helped to train them in urban pacification, whether you know it or not."

The notion that he'd done their dirty work made Paul feel ill, but Simpson seemed to relish uttering every word. "Once we get them reconditioned—a little torture here, a little mind-reprogramming there—they'll be fit for combat," he said. "Somalia, Afghanistan, the Middle East... Anyone messes with us, we send in our team and make their nightmares real, but they won't last. Our enemies will be history."

The way the compliments were piled on in an insincere and smarmy voice made Paul want to heave. Instead, he turned the kiss-butt session in another direction. "How did you manage to solve the decay factor?" he asked. "I read about that in one of the files."

As he spoke, remorse hit him hard. CF wasn't the sharpest knife in the drawer, but he was decent and he'd done nothing but good. He didn't even know that he was going to expire.

He also deliberately left out the idea of the cell decay in Angela, for the thought made him sick with worry. How would a person feel if they knew they might fall apart at any moment? That had to be the cruelest joke of all.

Simpson rubbed his fleshy jaw as if decided whether to impart the information or not. Finally, he offered a shrug.

"We knew about it, but only insofar that Bolson built in certain stopgaps, just in case the experiments decided to rebel. Those stopgaps make the creatures controllable."

He ticked off the points on his fingers. "See, they all have weaknesses. The water guy, all you have to do is to burn or freeze him. Then he's history. Same deal with the sand thing. Just spray enough glue in the air and pfft" — he made a spitting noise — "he's history, too.

"As for the zombie, it'll take the hits. If it gets shot enough times, it dies and its body instantly decays, so there's no chance the enemy will ever be able to clone it. I don't know if Bolson ever managed to resolve that problem, but even if he didn't, it's of no consequence. The best thing about zombies is their expendability. Even if those things don't get blown up in combat, they've got a life span of only a month at best."

Paul focused his attention on the floor. He'd heard the words, but they hadn't registered, and he only looked up when he felt a sharp smack on his cheek. Simpson stared at him, his eyes like green stones of death. "You're zoning out on me again, kid. I was talking. The least that you could do is to listen.

"Like I was saying, as for the girl, the only thing capable of killing her is electricity. That's it. She can take enough punishment to kill a thousand soldiers and still keep moving forward. A girl like her will live forever."

"What about the decay factor?" Paul repeated as he rubbed the soreness from his face.

Simpson shook his head. "What about it?" he retorted. "It applies only to zombies — or didn't you get the memo?"

Cutting though the reply was, it sent a shock through Paul and only in the most positive way. She'd live. She would live...

As if reading his thoughts, Simpson let out another giggle as if amused by the idea of a human and a stem-cell creation finding romance. A second later, his good humor disappeared. "So you like the girl after all," he remarked in a matter-of-fact tone. "Well, lucky you, kid, you got to be with the frontline soldier of the future." This time, wonder mixed with sarcasm laced every word.

"And because she's going to be the frontline soldier of the future, we can't have our best killers dying on us, now can we? That's why she was engineered to live a long time. It's just amazing, and we've got her. Soon, we'll have fifty more like her."

"Sir," the voice came from the front. "We're about twenty minutes away."

"Good," Simpson said as he took out his pistol. He checked the load, but kept the safety on. "Sorry about this, but lights out, kid."

Paul never saw the blow coming.

Minutes or hours later, he swam up from a sea of pain into consciousness and consciousness hurt. He found himself lying on the front walk of the Bolson home. Simpson stood in front of him. The area was empty and where were the neighbors when you needed them?

"We're he-e-e-re," Simpson sang out with terrible glee. "Oh, and just in case you're wondering what happened to everyone, we already told them this is a matter of national security. They've been confined to their homes. We told them you were a runaway and that you're leaving today, so if you think anyone's going to help you, then you can forget about it."

Vicious thoughts ran through Paul's mind, but all he came out with was, "Screw you."

The fat man chuckled. "Yeah, I figured you'd say something like that. My men are searching the place now. We have the zombie in one of the vans. Electricity is also his weakness, and he's so stupid he couldn't figure out why we were there. He just asked us to feed him." A chuckle escaped his lips, nasty and cutting. There was absolutely nothing likeable about this man at all.

A shout came their way as two men ran out of the house and over to their position. "What is it?" Simpson wanted to know. "Did you find the water guy or the sand thing?"

"No, sir," answered one of the men. He held up a containment suit. "When we entered the premises and subdued the zombie, the water-man ran upstairs to the bathroom. He disappeared, and we couldn't find the sand creature, either."

Upon hearing that news, Paul inwardly breathed a sigh of relief. At least Ooze and Sandstorm had escaped. As for Simpson, he took the news without moving a muscle in his face. Finally, he gave a brief nod. "Did you secure the lab?"

"Yes, sir," the second agent said. "We have the computer. The chambers don't look operable, though. What do we do?"

The fat man rubbed his hands together. "Torch the place. Leave no traces. By the time the fire trucks get here, there won't be anything left to examine."

"But what do we do about the water guy or the sand thing?"

Simpson laughed and his belly shook. "Nothing, do nothing. Neither of those creatures can stop us. Without his containment suit, the water-man is powerless. If he does manage to turn up, we'll freeze or fry him. And we have aerosol glue to stop the other monster. Now hop to it, men."

The agents left, and a few minutes later, Paul heard a whoosh and the house exploded into flames. He stared at the conflagration and cursed the fat man who was now grinning like a cat that had swallowed ten canaries. "You're a real jerk, you know that?" he ground out.

Simpson stared at him with a bland expression. "You've been out of school for too long, kid. Your friends must be missing you."

He took out a small T-shaped device from his pocket and before Paul could react, Simpson jabbed him with it.

Taser, it's a Taser. Paul convulsed as the electrical current ran through him and he fell to the ground, every nerve ending on fire. He still heard the man's oily voice, though.

Simpson knelt down next to him. "A mind is a terrible

thing to waste, so I'm going to do you a favor. I'm bringing you back to that jail you call a home. You won't tell anyone what happened because there's no evidence. No one will believe you. So I'd suggest you get over it and move on with your useless little life."

Paul felt another charge run through him then blackness swallowed him up.

* * * *

The voice cut through the darkness. "Paul, are you okay?"

With an effort, Paul forced his eyes open. Gray walls, cracked floorboards...this was St. Joe's. He looked up into the eyes of Brother Max. The large man helped him to stand up.

"We were very worried about you," the big man said. "You were gone almost two weeks, and we thought something bad had happened. Thank goodness you're all right."

Paul said nothing. When there wasn't anything to say, what was the point? Simpson had him right where he wanted him. Angela was gone. There was no way of knowing where she was. He had no superpowers, no friends, and right now he was in a hellhole that he hated.

The big man shepherded him down the hallway and back to his room. There, he sat Paul down on one bed and took a seat on a chair. The look on his face was kindly. "Son, I know this isn't the ideal place for you. I know you've had a hard time here. Many of the boys have. But you have to realize that running away won't solve your problems."

When there was nothing to say, say nothing. Paul remained mute, ran through all the options in his mind, and right now he couldn't think of a thing. "Sorry," he finally managed.

"That's it?" Max's face wore a disappointed look. "You've run away twice, we've gotten the police to look for you, and all you can say is you're sorry?"

There was a time to keep it and a time to let it all out. Paul decided this was the time to let it all out and he shouted, "Yeah, that's all I got. I took off because this place stinks, because I got tired of being beat on and because no one cared if I lived or died. You know what happens here. You know when someone ages out they have to leave. Who cared about me before? No one did. So you caught me. Fine...do whatever you want."

Explosion over, he sat back and waited for the inevitable scolding. For a change, though, it didn't come. Instead, the older man simply looked disconcerted. He rubbed his chin in a slow, measured fashion and said, "I want to help you, Paul. This is what I volunteered for. Where were you?"

Taken aback at this sudden burst of decency, it was time to improvise. "I stayed with some friends, but, uh, they moved on and...I'm here now."

From the dubious expression on the older man's face, clearly he didn't believe the story, but he nodded, anyway. "They must have been good people to have taken care of you so well. You're wearing good clothes and you look healthy."

Paul wanted to tell him they were they best people he'd ever known. He wanted to tell him that for the first time in his life he felt he'd been part of something. He wanted to say those things and more...but couldn't. Instead, he choked out, "I guess I'll do some studying or something. Sorry I yelled at you."

Max offered a tiny smile. "It's understandable." He blew out a deep breath. "I'm glad you're back. In your absence, Social Services contacted us. We have a family coming in the day after tomorrow and you're going to meet with them. I'd call that good news, wouldn't you?"

Paul forced out a smile although he felt like crying. "Yes sir, that's good news."

He didn't cry then. Only after Brother Max left did Paul let his feelings show and the tears flowed unchecked. Sobs racking his body, he cried for his lost years, cried for his friends, and most of all, cried for the girl he'd met and whose life was in the hands of monsters and there was nothing he could do about it.

Chapter Thirteen
Breakout and Broken Dreams

The maps, they held the key. Paul had been sitting in the library since lunch ended, going over some maps of the city. It was late afternoon, the day after his return to the orphanage, and the sunlight streamed in through the dirty windows, illuminating the aged library in a cheery glow.

It may have been cheery for someone else, but for him, it was simply a reminder his friends weren't around anymore. He didn't want to think about what Simpson was doing to Angela, but he had a pretty good idea, and it made him sick. He wanted…no, *needed* to find her in the worst way, but since he had no frame of reference, he couldn't do a damn thing.

As for how the other kids reacted when he'd come back, say hello to Ignore Mode. His teachers had welcomed him back, all had been forgiven, but as for the rest of the student populace, they had gone about their business with their cliques. For once, he'd actually been grateful for the anonymity.

Beginning his search where it all started, he found Angelica well enough, but New York State was large, and Simpson and his goons could be anywhere. Struggling to put the pieces together and using his city smarts, he wondered where a person would take someone like Angela. Neither she nor CF could stand up to electricity, so where would someone be able to get all that power?

Then it hit him. Power stations — there were a lot of them. The goons at Rallan wouldn't risk going to one of the major power stations, but maybe there were some inactive ones.

No, how could they be using all that electricity and have no one notice? It didn't make sense. The power drain would probably show up on a power grid somewhere in the city, unless they were hiding it somehow.

The possibilities of where to go and which authority to talk to were endless, but at the same time, all of this had to be kept secret. Would anyone take the word of a teen runaway? Moreover, would they care? In a burst of cynicism and despair, Paul heaved a tremendous sigh. Simpson had been right. No one would listen…

"Hey, nerd, you're back."

When he swiveled around on his chair, he saw that two of his classmates stood three feet away. Big for their age, tough looking, they had the appearance of future gangsters.

"What do you want?" he asked, and clicked off the computer. Rage flowed through him, and he got up, balled his fists, and prepared for war. "If you're here to smack me around, go ahead."

For a change, the other kids held their ground. Perhaps it was the anger in Paul's voice or perhaps the look in his eyes that said he wouldn't be put down, not this time and not ever.

After glancing at each other, the larger of the two boys, dark haired with a face full of pimples, held up his hands as a gesture of peace. "No man, we just want to ask you how you did it. I mean, you were gone for almost two weeks. It's friggin' rough out there. How'd you make it?" His voice held a measure of respect, which was something new.

What could Paul say? No way in the world would anyone believe him, so what else to do but to lie? He wove a story of skulking around during the day, hiding out in abandoned buildings and movie theaters at night, always on the run and stealing when he had to. It was total BS, but the two boys bought into it.

"Man, that is just too hardcore," the bigger kid said with admiration. "Too many Bangers around, and did you ever see that vampire chick? We were watching it on the news.

Her and some zombie, that was totally sick!"

"Uh, well, I didn't see anything except people out there," Paul added, trying to change the course of the conversation. "I mean, I was on the run and inside half the time, so — "

"I think it's all bogus," the other kid put in. "It had to be some kind of movie stunt." He pulled on his friend's arm. "C'mon, Joey. Everyone's waiting downstairs."

He left, but Joey lingered long enough to say, "Hey, I heard some family's coming by tomorrow to talk to you. You think you'll get lucky?"

Luck was only an opportunity, and right now Paul figured his luck had already run out. "I don't know," he finally said. "Either way, I'm out of here in six months."

"Yeah," Joey affirmed, nodding, "me, too. Anyway, see ya."

He took off, and Paul sat in the library until it was closing time, not seeing or hearing anything. Once the librarian told him that he was closing up, Paul went back to his room. He now had an idea of what to look for. What he needed was someone who knew where it was.

* * * *

"I'm pleased to meet you," Mrs. Collins said.

It was late in the afternoon the next day, roughly five-thirty, and Paul sat in the administration's office, dressed in his only suit. Actually, it was a suit that the orphanage provided, as he possessed nothing outside of a few pairs of jeans, some T-shirts and socks that needed darning. Black with worn elbows and knees, the suit was two sizes too large and hung from his frame.

Brother Max welcomed Mrs. Collins in and asked her to sit alongside him. She was a short and slender blonde woman in her mid-forties. In a pleasant voice, she introduced herself, talked a bit about where she lived and apologized for her husband's absence, but he'd been called away on a sudden business trip and couldn't make it.

"My husband's a professor at Rutgers University," she said. "That's in New Jersey. He specializes in computer science. I also work part-time in a boutique and do home schooling in my spare time. We, er, couldn't have children, so we devoted ourselves to our jobs. However, we discussed the matter about raising a teenager and we'd welcome the challenge."

Their talk continued. Mrs. Collins asked all the right questions, nodded at his answers, and seemed more than kind. To his surprise, she seemed concerned for his welfare and in fact, Paul began to like her...but a sudden dripping sound made him lose his concentration.

It came from the sink behind Mrs. Collins and Brother Max. A few drops fell from the tap. Max turned around, muttered something about calling the plumber, and swiveled around in his seat again. The drip continued, and a few seconds later, a tiny hand formed from the drops. The hand waved, and it took everything Paul had not to lose it in front of his temporary guardian and his potential future foster mother. With a massive effort to calm his thundering heart, he took in a few deep breaths and bit his lip to keep from yelling out.

"Is something wrong?" Max enquired.

"Uh, no, sir," Paul stammered out. "This is all happening really fast. I mean, I was just thinking, um, I've never been to New Jersey. It sounds like a fun place."

"It is," Mrs. Collins affirmed. She rummaged around in her purse. "I have some pictures here of our house... Please wait a moment..."

While she searched, Paul affixed his gaze on the water coming from the tap. The hand then changed to letters. *I got away. Sandstorm is with me.*

"Yes!" Paul exclaimed as he started out of his seat. Hastily, he clamped his lips shut.

"Yes, what?" asked Max.

What to say? Taking his seat again, Paul fumbled for an answer then came up with, "I meant, yes, this is a very good meeting and I'm very happy." Abruptly he stopped speaking when he realized his answer made him sound like he was on drugs.

"Well, it seems as though he's enthusiastic," Mrs. Collins said, and handed over the pictures. "Do you like the house?"

Quickly leafing through the photos, Paul had to admit that the house was everything he'd ever hoped for. It looked like a mansion with a garden in front, at least ten rooms, and a pool in the backyard. It looked perfect...but the one person who mattered most wasn't in these pictures.

"I think it's a great place, Mrs. Collins," he answered truthfully, and knew in his heart he'd have to say no. It also meant throwing away his future, but someone out there needed him and he couldn't let her down. "I'm, uh, just a little snowed by all the attention. I mean, I've been here a long time, and —"

"I understand," she interrupted in a kindly manner. "If you want to think about it, take your time. My husband and I will talk it over tonight when he comes back, but we're very open to having you."

The meeting concluded with the usual handshakes, the tour of the facility and the promise to call at the end of the week. "It was wonderful to meet you, Paul," she said. "I hope you'll be able to come out to our house one day. Please stay in touch."

She nodded and left, and with her car's departure it was a sure bet no one else would ever come close to being his adopted mother. Even if no other chances came his way, he couldn't go through with this adoption process. He said nothing, though, except to offer a goodbye.

Brother Max turned to him and gestured toward the door to signal the meeting was over. "That seemed to go very well. I'm sure she'll call us and I'll be only too happy to make the arrangements."

Once back in his room, Paul locked the door and turned on the faucet. Ooze poured out and spoke to him in the shape of a bar of soap. "You have *zero* idea of how nasty the sewers are," he began, sounding more than a little testy. "They have alien life forms down there! I almost got swallowed by something worse than what CF looks like."

"Keep your voice down, man," Paul answered, nervously glancing around. He wasn't sure if someone wouldn't walk in and how could a person explain that they'd been talking to water? "How'd you know where to find me?"

Ooze proceeded to explain. When Simpson's men had torched the farmhouse, he'd returned from hiding in the drain and doused the flames. He'd also overheard one of the men mentioning St. Joe's and knew the location, courtesy of his download. "You saw a fire, right?"

"Yes."

"That was just on the first floor," Ooze said. "It's pretty much history, but the basement where the doctor had his chambers and files? I pulled out the water from the pipes and managed to douse the fire. The chambers used to make us are inoperable, but there's one left. It's in the garage, remember? They didn't look there.

"I also found another file before those morons took everything else away. It had all the instructions on it. I figure Bolson decided to keep it as insurance, just in case he decided to go straight. I got it stashed under the floorboards in the basement, so don't worry."

It wouldn't help things if they had the computer. As if reading his mind, Ooze added, "I trashed the hard drive on the computer. They'll never get it to work again."

That was a bit of good news. Paul thought hard and a plan began to form in his mind. It was weird — probably a suicide mission — but he didn't have any other ideas. After explaining the logistics, Ooze chuckled softly. "You know," he said, "that's so insane it just might work. What do you need?"

"I need a map."

After Ooze formed a map on his body, he twisted his neck around to gaze at it and then resumed his normal shape. "Yeah, this is doable," he stated. "The cops didn't take the van. I can drive."

"Where's Sandstorm?"

A knock came at the window. Outside, a sand-fist stood out in contrast to the dusk and rapped on the window. After opening up, Sandstorm swirled around and formed a question mark with his body. "I need you to find a place," said Paul, ignoring the cold.

Giving him directions, Sandstorm shifted his form to say, *I can find this place. Wait a few minutes.*

He slithered off and Paul paced back and forth impatiently like an expectant father. A number of agonizing minutes later, a tap on the window alerted him to the sand being's return. *He's there.*

Paul felt an evil smile begin to spread across his face. "Then let's go talk to the hand."

* * * *

That same night, once his roommates passed out, Paul got dressed in a warm pair of jeans, two T-shirts and his reliable hoodie. Carefully, he crept down the corridor wearing only socks. He skirted the places where he knew the Brothers would patrol and snuck down to the basement. There, he found a flashlight and some rope. Now he was ready.

Making as little noise as possible, he took off his hoodie then placed it against the window. With a sharp elbow smash, he opened a hole then snuck out onto the street. A cold, sharp wind blew and threw up swirls of snow. His feet instantly felt chilled, but he wasn't thinking about the temperature. He was thinking about a certain sorry-ass henchman who was about to get his butt kicked.

The streets were practically empty with only a few stragglers moving quickly to get out of the frigid weather. No one noticed him as he made his way to the corner. There, the van waited. Ooze opened the door. "Get in," he called out.

Sandstorm sat in the front seat in a shapeless pile, quiet

and ready.

They drove to the Donut Hole. Ooze got out of the van and walked over to a grate near the sidewalk. In a quick twisting motion, he opened a valve on his suit and poured himself into the grate. Paul took up a position across the street, next to the shop and tried not to shiver.

Sneaking a peek, sure enough, the tall, skinny henchman sat inside at a booth sucking down sweet after sweet and swilling enough coffee to keep a city awake. When Hand came out, Paul whispered, "Hey, moron," and took off around the corner and into the alleyway. The henchman gave chase and once he rounded the corner, Paul whirled around and brained him with the flashlight. Hand pitched forward and sagged to his knees.

Quickly, Paul searched him, took his gun and tied his hands up behind his back. Grabbing onto the rope, he proceeded to drag the skinny man deeper into the alleyway and over to a manhole grating.

With no crowbar to lift the cover off, he wondered what to do, but took a chance and called down, "Ooze, are you there?"

"Yeah," a voice answered. "Hang on."

The manhole cover blew off and went straight up in the air, only to come clanging right back down. "Way to keep a low profile," Paul muttered. "I got a visitor."

Hand stirred, his mouth making semi-coherent noises. "What? Who? It's you!"

"Shut up," Paul replied and smashed him in the mouth with the flashlight. He took the sock he'd stored in his pocket and stuffed it in the man's mouth. Muffled noises came from the downed man as he struggled against his bonds, but he wasn't going anywhere, not now.

"Yeah, it's me," Paul ground out. He felt the heft of the gun in his hand, wondered briefly if he'd have the balls to use it…but anger drove him to make the decision. He'd use it if he had to. "Now, we need a little information. Where are you keeping Angela and CF?"

He pulled out the sock and it was accompanied by a river of blood. "Screw you, kid," Hand uttered with hatred lacing every word.

"Wrong answer," Paul said and pushed him headfirst down the hole. "Try again."

A scream came from the hapless henchman as he plummeted, but a geyser shot out of the sewer with him encased in a bubble. He started to thrash around, his eyes wide with panic.

"This guy smells worse than the sewer," Ooze burbled out. "Should I keep drowning him?"

"Just a few more seconds," Paul said, and focused his attention on the slowly suffocating scumbag. "I'm not going to ask you again. Where are they keeping her?"

Hand nodded, his eyes bulging. Ooze released him and he fell to the hard concrete, gasping for breath. Water trickled from his mouth and he heaved in great gasps of air before groaning and turning over onto his back.

While he was recovering, Paul kept the gun trained on him. Ooze went back into the sewer, but poked a humanoid head out to listen in.

The henchmen kept coughing out water and other unmentionables. "It's... She's at Yonkers Power Station. It's an old station...abandoned long ago. Rallan bought it. We're using it as a base of operations."

"If you're lying to me, get ready for a bullet you know where." Paul's hand moved down a few inches.

Under the harsh lights of the city lamps, the henchman's face turned white. "I swear it's the truth! We've been...been siphoning off electricity from the New York power grid. No one knows. We don't need that much, but if we want to kill those monsters..."

Paul shoved the barrel of the gun in his mouth, cutting off all speech. This was a matter of life and death and seconds counted. "They're my friends. You got that?" Hand nodded, eyes bulging in fear. He pulled the gun out but kept it trained on the henchman.

"I got it! I got it!" yelled Hand as he spat out a river of blood along with three teeth and he sneered, "You're just a punk."

Some guys just don't understand.

Paul waved the gun in the henchman's face. "Yeah, you're right, but I've got the gun and you don't. Let's go." He turned to Ooze. "You got all that?"

The water-being nodded. "I do, but what's the plan once we get there?"

"We improvise."

A smile formed on Ooze's face. "I can do that. Bring him over to the van." A second later, he disappeared down the manhole.

Keeping Hand tied up, Paul laid down one warning. "No false moves. You do, and I'm not going to care."

Hand eyed him with a sullen expression, but nodded. They went to the van. Ooze had already re-entered his containment suit and gotten into the driver's seat. Firing up the engine, he took off and kept the vehicle moving steadily. The trip passed in silence until they reached the station. It was located on the waterfront and while old, the lights were on inside.

"We're here," Hand said and nodded in the direction of a massive wrought iron gate.

After getting out, Sandstorm slithered quickly away. He had another mission to complete. Ooze got out of the van and searched for a manhole. Finding one, he once more opened up the valve to his suit and his essence went down the hole. Hand watched them go with a stoned look on his face then spoke up, triumph in his voice, "The gate uses a retinal eye scanner. You won't be able to get in."

"Not unless we take your eye first," Paul said.

Hand started to quiver and his face turned white. "You're not going to do that."

If it came to matching their evil, so be it, Paul thought. "I might," he said, "but I just got a better idea. We're going to walk up to the gate and you're going to let us in. After that, you can go."

Disbelief crossed the henchman's face. "Just like that—I can go?"

"Yeah, just like that."

Hand told him all he knew. Second floor down, last door on the right, he'd find the engine room. The turbines were there, so were the captives. "How many men?" Paul asked.

"At least ten," replied Hand, his words coming out slowly and indistinctly. "Did you have to hit me so hard before?"

Maybe he was going into shock or maybe he was faking. Paul figured it had to be the latter and pistol-whipped him again, this time across the cheek, which elicited another scream of pain. "Keep talking. Do they have guns?"

The answer was a frantic "yes", so it was time to improvise a little more. He got out and pulled out the henchman with him, and they marched over to the scanner. Paul reached over to open a lid and a mini-camera popped out. Hand leaned into the camera and a second later, the gate swung open.

"Move," Paul said, and with the gun in the small of his prisoner's back, he marched the man over to the front door.

Two other men opened up and immediately stuck their hands in the air when they saw the pistol pointed at them.

"Get down on the ground," Paul ordered.

They did, and he used the remainder of the rope to tie them up. Stuffing their ties in their mouths, he whacked them hard enough across their temples to knock them out. After checking on their breathing—yep, still alive—he ran down to the second level.

Just as Hand had said, the engine room was located at the end of the hallway. It was enormous, holding three large electrical turbines. The walls were solid brick, easily a century old. Places like this had been built to last.

The turbines had also been built to last, although these looked totally refurbished. Three large square boxes the side of restaurant freezers sat beside the turbines with cables connecting them—the power sources.

Paul's thoughts of power changed to rage when he saw Angela and CF chained to the turbines. Blue electricity danced over their bodies, making them writhe in torment. The noise was incredible, a high, ear-shattering whine.

Creeping forward, he got his bearings. Five other men in black suits, including Mr. Finger, lounged against a far wall, smoking and drinking coffee. Two others stood at one of the far turbines, taking readings. Simpson stood in front of the captives scarfing down a candy bar and watching with a smile on his face.

As he saw Paul, the smile faded. "I really have to hand it to you, son. You found us out. Good for you."

Paul pointed the gun at him. "Tell your men not to shoot, no matter what."

A smirk flitted across Simpson's face, but after a moment's hesitation, he lifted his hand and gave the order. "Okay, what's next?" he asked.

Indicating the turbines with a wave, Paul ordered, "Turn off the power."

"What if I don't?"

Squeezing the trigger was a no-brainer. A bullet came from the gun and it missed Simpson's leg by an inch. "Next time it's your knee," Paul warned, sick it had come to this, but determined to finish things. "Do it."

After a second's hesitation, Simpson moved over to the control panel then shut down the power. The turbines gradually ground to a stop. "If you're wondering how we got all the power, take a look at our mini-nuclear generators," he said. "Perfectly safe, I assure you."

Right now it didn't matter where the power came from. It was all about Angela and her safety. Her head lolled, but her chest was moving. As for CF, he seemed to be rotting away at an incredible speed as bits of pieces of skin were raining from his face and hands, but he picked his head up long enough to ask, "Do you have any food?"

"You probably have some more candy in your pocket, fat guy," said Paul. "Take it out."

An insolent smirk formed on the fat man's face. "Make me."

This time a single bullet went into Simpson's right knee and the fat man went down howling. "All right, all right," he screamed. "I've got something!"

With a trembling hand, he reached into his pocket and pulled out two chocolate bars. Paul snatched them from his hands, tore off the wrappers and fed them to the large zombie. CF chomped and chewed and his skin began to knit, but very slowly. He was in the last stages of decay. However, he still had enough power to snap the chains. "I feel better," he rumbled.

"Can you get Angela out of there?" Paul asked.

CF lumbered over and tore the chains away from the turbines. Angela sank to the floor and opened her eyes. She smiled when she saw Paul. "Hey," she said. "You made it."

"I wouldn't go anywhere else…" he started to say, but stopped when a shot rang out. He looked at the right side of his chest. It was leaking blood. "How'd that happen?" he muttered, and dropped to the ground, the gun falling out of his suddenly nerveless hand.

Simpson leveraged himself up by holding onto the console. In his free hand, he held a pistol. "That makes us even, you little twerp," he said, sweat pouring down his fleshy jowls. "I can't kill your friends, but I can kill you."

He fired again, and Paul screamed as the bullet entered his left leg. Immediately, blood spewed out, staining the floor. Angela went over to help him, but Simpson and his men started toward her, Taser weapons at the ready.

"Don't make a move, girl," he said. "You too, big man," he said to CF who now had a wary look in his eyes. "You both know what these weapons are. And I've got a gun pointed at the bleeding punk on the floor, so if you're smart, you'll stay back."

"He'll die," Angela pleaded.

"Ask me if I care," Simpson responded.

Paul laid quietly watching, breathing slowly in an effort

to control the pain.

Mr. Finger came forward to support his boss by putting his arm around the fat man's waist. Simpson looked at the trio. "So what do we do now?" he asked. "I can't let any of you go. Too many witnesses, you know."

He reached into this pocket and took out a cell phone. "Everyone, get down here on the double," he yelled. "Get your weapons hot!"

A minute later, ten more men poured into the room, Tasers at the ready. Among them was Mr. Hand. Somehow, he and the others had managed to work their way out of their bonds. An evil grin shone through his bloody face. As Paul looked at him through rapidly dimming eyes, the thought of payback reverberated through his mind. He knew who was going to be on the receiving end.

"Are you ready, punk?" Hand asked with sadism coating every word.

Steeling himself for the inevitable punishment, Paul waited for the first blow. "Go ahead and do it," he said.

Hand worked quickly and efficiently, and as the seconds ticked by, Paul heard his ribs snap, his right wrist break, felt tendons being wrenched and his heart thundered in his ears. Taking in a breath…he almost choked and had to breathe shallowly.

A cough erupted from his chest and blood jetted into the air. It was getting harder and harder to take in enough oxygen. Shallow breathing didn't cut it, but if he inhaled more deeply then he'd choke on the blood…

"Stop it!" Angela screamed. "You've got us. What more do you want?"

"His death," Simpson replied in the coldest voice imaginable and kept his weapons ready to repel any attempts at aid. "I want his death then yours. Keep working, Hand. Keep…"

His voice trailed off when a cloud of dust smashed through the windows. "Sandstorm," Paul whispered.

He watched in awe as the stinging bits of sand swirled

around the henchmen and blinded them. They fired wildly into the air, but they couldn't hit sand. It abruptly withdrew, but not before making a sign like that of an upraised middle finger and forming the words *no fear.*

Another sound came, that of rushing water. One of the brick walls began to crumble, then it collapsed as a wall of water entered and surrounded the henchmen. Numerous liquid hands plucked the Tasers and pistols from their grasp and tossed them far away. The men shifted their position and looked to Simpson for support. He hung onto Finger, a sudden bath of fear-sweat covering his face.

"Guess who's been practicing?" Ooze's voice sounded from inside the mass of swirling liquid. "Should I drown them?" he asked.

Paul stared at the zombie who had a look of something totally unholy beginning to form in his eyes. "Go back to the house and take Sandstorm with you," he croaked. "We'll meet you there." He didn't know how long he'd last, but there was one more job that had to be done. "CF, I need…a favor."

The zombie gazed at him. "What is it?"

By now, Simpson was trembling like a paper house in the middle of an earthquake and he swung his head back and forth between Paul and the zombie. "He…he shouldn't even be able to think."

"Sugar," Paul told him while forcing out a grin. It hurt to move his face, but this was worth it. "The brain…it runs on sugar." He winked at CF. "Hey, clean up, will you?"

A tiny smile, one of rotting teeth and blackened tongue, emerged from the zombie. The smile spoke of wreaking havoc on an almost apocalyptic scale. CF proceeded to smash and crush every human being in the room, save Simpson, into the same kind of small packages he'd made on the river bank.

The horror was so great that Paul wanted to close his eyes, but he couldn't shut out the screams of terror, nor could he shut out the smell of blood, heavy and thick as it painted the air.

Finally, only Simpson remained, sitting on his blobby butt. He looked up in terror as CF hauled him off the floor. "Clean him, too?" he asked.

"No," Angela said as she made her way over. "He's mine."

She plucked the fat man from CF's grasp and pulled his ugly, terrified face to an inch away from hers. "I once swore I'd always protect people, that I'd never kill anyone who didn't deserve it. You wanted to kill me for not being human. You're way less than that."

Her fangs came out and they sank into the folds of his neck. He let out a frightened scream, but it soon burbled away to nothing as she tore his throat out. Spitting out a lump of flesh, she let his corpse drop to the ground. "He was O-negative," she said with distaste. "Not my type."

Running over to Paul, she put her hand on his wounds, trying to staunch the flow of blood. "It's done," she said.

Blood stained the floor and the air was thick with the smell of smashed flesh and organs. Shallow breaths didn't cut it anymore. Paul's vision began to blur from a lack of oxygen. *You have to focus.*

Abruptly, CF groaned and sank to his knees. Then he fell flat on his face. He didn't move, and seconds later his body dissolved into a kind of synthetic yet organic mess. He was gone.

Paul wanted to wipe the tears that had suddenly sprung from his eyes, but he had no strength. "Oh, man, he saved us. They all did…"

His voice cut out and his eyesight began to fail as well. Through dimmed eyes, he saw Angela go over to the remains of CF and stoop down. She then straightened up and returned to his side.

"Time to go," she said.

He felt powerful hands lift him up. Then they were airborne, and she flew swiftly upon the winds. Part of him knew he was flying alongside her, while the other part concentrated on the cold air, the whiteness of the landscape below him and his breathing.

His girlfriend whispered into his ear, "Paul, stay with me." Her voice took on a pleading quality. "Please…stay with me."

"Want to," he managed to utter. "Want to, but…"

Blackness, like dark water, swirled around him. Is this what it's like to die, he wondered. They always said that the last thing to go was the hearing. Angela's words kept repeating themselves in his mind. *Paul, stay with me… Stay with me…*

Epilogue
Life on the Other Side

Paul wondered how long it would take to die. Strange how that thought went through his mind during their departure from Yonkers back to Angelica. In spite of the below zero temperature, he felt no pain. The frigid night air caressed him and he welcomed its embrace. Blurry though his eyesight was, he made out the familiar sight of the Genesee River then the houses that comprised the town.

His flight path took an abrupt downturn and the impact of Angela's boots on the hard ground sent a vibration through him. A smell, the after-stench of scorched wood, drifted into his nostrils. They'd arrived, and his vision cleared a little more as he saw numerous yellow strips lacing every wall of his temporary yet oh-so-beloved home. *Do not enter,* the message said.

Angela carried him in a different direction and he heard a door swing up. A second later, he heard her call for help.

Help – yeah, I'm gonna need it. The cold air had temporarily subdued the pain, but now as his mind woke up, agony stabbed at his body like a series of knives. Part of him wanted to see what would happen while the other part simply wanted to sink into the well of unconsciousness and enter the realm known as death. "It's okay," he murmured. "It's okay...you can leave me."

Abruptly his voice failed. The experts always said that hearing was the last sense to go. It seemed as though they had been rights, as he could no longer see or feel his body. However, through it all, he clearly heard the sound of what seemed like a door being torn off its hinges, followed by people speaking. "Get the chamber ready."

"You don't know what it could do to him."

"He'll die in seconds if we don't do something!"

The last voice he heard had been Angela's. He felt her strong yet gentle hands pull him over to some place, heard the sound of ripping cloth and felt the jab of needles in his arms, legs and back. His legs hit...glass. Where was he?

Before he could get a word out, a surge of energy hit him between the eyes. It filled his entire being, and his mind traveled outside his body to witness a miracle of science combined with a revolutionary process unknown to the outside world.

A gasp escaped his lips as bones began to crack—his. They cracked and reformed, lengthened and somehow grew thicker. While doing his disembodied mind-dance, he swam back to his body and swore he felt the muscle fibers in his body begin to swell, a pop-popping sound that he knew was impossible, yet he thought real.

A second later, he heard screaming—and realized he was the one doing the screaming. Then he saw blackness and nothing more...

* * * *

"Hey, are you feeling better?"

Paul blinked and opened his eyes. He found himself lying on a makeshift cot of boxes covered by a blanket. It was dim and he recognized the garage, the garage of their house. Focusing his vision, Angela stood in front of him, Ooze at her side. Both of them wore expectant looks on their faces. Silence hung in the air until the bag of water snuffled out a laugh.

"Well, he made it," Ooze cracked, and trundled over to a table to retrieve a pair of pants and a long-sleeved shirt. He tossed them in Paul's direction and they landed on his stomach. "Put those on. You're bare-ass naked."

Peeking under the sheet, Paul saw that he was, indeed,

naked, but something else caught his attention. His hands were covered in a light coating of fur, dark brown fur, and it covered his whole body all the way down to his feet. "What's...what's going on here?"

In a rapid movement, he snatched the pants, twisted over on his side and struggled into them. The shirt came next and it fit tightly over his upper body. Job complete, he got up feeling no pain and barely felt the cold. Barefoot, he should have felt chilled, but wonder of wonders, no. Walking over to gaze in wonder at the chamber, it was black. Swinging around, he asked, "What happened?"

Angela walked over and held out a small pocket mirror. "See for yourself."

Taking it, he examined his face. With higher, sharper cheekbones, it had the same light coating of fur, but his nose had become smaller, his eyes had changed from their usual brown to yellow, and his mouth...he had long canines, similar to Angela's, but much sharper looking. Frightened, his first instinct was to retract them, and he was even more surprised when they did. "Oh man, I'm..."

His hand fell to his side, and he dropped the mirror. It bounced on the ground, but didn't break. Ooze stooped over to pick it up. "Well, at least you won't have seven years of bad luck," he said.

There was a time for humor and a time not to have it. Paul decided this fell into the *not* category. "What did you do to me?"

"It was the only way to save your life," said Angela as she laid a friendly hand on his shoulder. "You were shot, remember?"

Instantly, the memory flooded back. The crack the gun had made when it went off, the impact he'd felt from the bullets slamming into and through his flesh and the accompanying agony...

"I was bleeding — " he began.

"And you were dying," Ooze chimed in and pointed to the chamber. "When those guys from Rallan came, they torched the place, but I put the fire out, remember?"

Paul nodded. "Yeah, I remember. So—"

"So, I told you Bolson had a spare chamber in his garage. Those bozos from Rallan completely forgot about this place and didn't know there was an extra chamber here," continued Ooze. "They took the computer, but they didn't take the chemicals, and I had Bolson's file, along with his knowledge."

He tapped the side of his head. "Well, I have most of it, anyway. The rest, Bolson wrote down what I needed to know. How much and what type of chemical to put in, how to set the chamber up…it's all there." He held up the file as proof.

"You would have died without the treatment," Angela cut in and squeezed Paul's shoulder. Her fingers lingered on his arm for a few seconds before she withdrew her hand. The very touch of her hand imparted a sense of solidity, but all the same, the idea of being different, made him wonder just what he'd become.

"I'm a werewolf?" he asked.

A state of disbelief swept over him, but he couldn't discount his improved senses. Everything from sounds and smells came through in a whirl that was almost three-dimensional. It was as if he could discern the layers and gradations within each sound, smell—even color.

Aside from feeling better than he had in a long time, he felt much stronger. Focusing on his aural skills, he heard Angela's heartbeat, rapid yet steady. The fluttering of a moth's wings and the scratch-scratch sound of an ant crawling across the floor came through clearly.

The smell of the water inside Ooze's suit, a kind of brackish, marshy odor, filtered through. It was different, yet not unpleasant. A double-dozen more sensations came at once, yet he was somehow able to differentiate between them and place them in order and they did not bother him. "So," he asked again after contemplating what he'd seen in the mirror, "I'm a werewolf?"

With a tiny giggle accompanied by a shrug, she said, "You are. That was the last creature Bolson managed to create on paper, but he never synthesized one. And," she hesitated, "he'd never tried it on a human before—"

"It was a prototype, designed for humans," Ooze cut in. "It has nothing to do with stem cells. Congrats, man, you're the first recipient." He formed his hand into the shape of a microphone and held it out. "Tell us how you feel."

Sarcasm was *so* not needed at this point, and Angela slapped the hand away. With a somber expression, she said, "I guess you're feeling sort of how I feel. I was created from my maker's cells, so I guess I'm human in a way like you said, but I've n-never..." Her voice caught. "I've never known what it's like to *be* human."

While she'd come to terms with being what she was, a sense of disorientation made Paul's knees go weak. In a daze, he tottered over to the box-bed and sat down. "So... what am I now?"

Ooze moved over and slid his squishy rump onto the boxes beside him. His voice came out somber. "Sorry for the wisecrack before. From what I can figure out, you're a hybrid. Bolson's notes didn't account for this because he'd never had a human subject before and I don't have a download. Still, since you are human, there's no chance of decay, so you're all set."

Decay...a five–letter word meaning death. Then again, death also had five letters. Looking at Angela, Paul said, "Simpson told me about you. He said they'd solved the decay factor."

Ooze chuckled and a series of bubbles danced in his suit. "It turns out Simpson was only partially right. The decay factor in Angela's case meant normal decay, like any other person. By person, I mean human, and that means aging naturally. It seems that when she drank your blood, it somehow helped to enhance her condition. I've got a lot of data to go over, so maybe one day I'll figure it all out."

As he spoke, Paul's sense of wonder returned. "So..." he

said slowly, "all of this means she'll—"

"Live a normal life," Ooze interrupted. "Like you will… only neither of you is exactly normal. Me, too, or Sandstorm, for that matter," he added.

He reached over to a small table then he held up a test tube. Inside it was a smear of pinkish material. "See this?" he asked. "Angela took that from CF's remains. I'm not sure, but I think we can reconstitute him. I mean, it's going to take some time to get the proper materials, mix the correct amount of chemical compounds and all that. Then we have to think about building another chamber, but I think we can bring him back. I might even be able to upgrade him."

Upgrade him or keep him dense—that was the question. A smile broke over Paul's face. "I want him back just as he was."

"I thought you'd say that," said Angela, grinning now, and she pointed at the exit. "Door's over there. It's night, so there's no chance of you meeting anyone. Just…stick to the forests."

Feeling a sense of possibility, Paul lifted the garage door and cautiously peered outside. Fortunately, the streets were empty. It was cold, but he didn't feel it. Having warm fur helped guard against the cold.

Instead, he took a deep breath and inhaled the smells, faint as they were, of a winter's night. The rabbit droppings ten feet to his left, the smell of the water—clean now—and the musky and somewhat oily smell of an owl's feathers… they all came to his nose and he reveled in the sensation. "So this is what being enhanced means," he said softly, wonder in every word.

He began to run. His muscles bunched and swelled under his clothes, and it came as both a thrill as well as distinct relief that he didn't have to bend over and lope as a true wolf would. Instead, he ran upright down the road and he ran fast, very fast. The houses soon gave way to trees and they whizzed by him. His steps were quick and sure and he hit no branches and made very little noise as he made his way through the forest.

An immense pile of logs perhaps twenty feet high stood in his way, and in what had to be the most immediate revelation, he realized that he could not only jump over this pile but also jump way over it.

His muscles worked in concert, and with a powerful spring from his legs, he leapt up and caught hold of a tree's trunk perhaps thirty feet off the ground. "Oh yeah," he breathed. "I *like* it!"

With another spring, he launched himself at another tree and yet another, hanging onto the trunks with powerful hands. He didn't have claws, though, just abnormally strong fingers.

Perhaps a minute later, much faster than any normal person would, he emerged on the other side of the forest and felt his heart rate slow down. A lonely road lay in front of him and he started down it, only to halt in his tracks as he heard the sound of an approaching vehicle. Cautiously, he crept to the side of the road and hid until the car passed by.

As the sounds of the car faded, so did his previous air of confidence. "What am I doing out here?" he asked, but only heard the whisper of the wind. "What if someone sees me?"

He pivoted on the ball of his foot then raced back to the house. Walking into the garage, he found Ooze and Angela waiting expectantly. Ooze held Bolson's file and was flipping through it, murmuring at a few things. Angela's face wore a questioning look as if to ask, *Well, is it everything you thought it would be?*

For his part, Paul was surprised to find he wasn't even out of breath. Not even a bead of sweat dripped from his forehead. This was...

"Pretty radical for you, isn't it?" Angela interrupted his thoughts. "So how was your first run?"

"Decent," he responded, still at a loss over what else to say. "I, uh, just don't know how to handle this. I mean, look at me."

"I am," said Angela as she went over to him. "And I see someone cute and special—just like Ooze and Sandstorm and just like me."

Mind whirling with the possibilities, Paul sat down on the cot. "I, um…what do we do now?"

Ooze got up, waving the diary in front of him. "Let's total up the scorecard on you, shall we? You just went for your test drive. You can run fast, yes?"

"Yeah…and I can jump pretty high, too."

A smile formed in the watery mixture. "You'll be able to do more than that." He pointed to the diary. "This is cutting edge stuff. If I'm reading this right, you'll have enhanced speed, strength and regenerative abilities. What more could you want?"

Thinking about it, nothing immediately came to mind. "So…I'm going to live a long time…and that's cool," Paul said. The implications of an enhanced life span hadn't hit home yet, but the powers thing…very different. And now *he* was different. "So what do we do?"

"While you were gone," Ooze said, "I took a little inventory. You know the dresser where the cash was?"

"Yeah, I do, and so what?"

"It didn't get burned. Apparently, the guys from Rallan were in such a hurry to take me and CF down the first time, they never bothered to look and the fire didn't touch it. There's about five hundred thousand dollars there. It isn't a fortune, but it should be enough to start you and your girlfriend off."

Paul felt his own face grow hot. "Well, yeah, that's cool, but…you didn't answer me before. What do we do now?"

Angela took up the slack and linked her arm with his. "You remember the guy who owned Rallan?"

Peterson—Andres Peterson… "Yeah, I do," Paul replied, his mind working overtime. "You think that we should pay him a visit?"

Ooze chuckled. "Hey, he's not so clued out after all."

Angela flipped her hair back. Her voice held a confidence

it hadn't had before. "I'll second that. I'm down with what I am — now. I don't know what it's like to be human, not entirely, but I can learn. Even if I'm different, it doesn't matter."

"No?" Paul asked.

A broad and beautiful smile shone out and lit up the room. "No, it doesn't. Because you're with me and that's all that counts. I still want to find out more about this Peterson guy and what he's really up to. Besides, I don't care for snow. I'd like to try swimming for a change."

That settled it. It was time to pack up the van and head for warmer climes. "When do we move?" he asked.

"Just as soon as I get the materials I need," Ooze answered. "Once we're ready, we go out and do what others can't."

* * * *

Los Angeles, Hollywood and Vine
Midnight, Six Months Later

The alleyway was dark and Paul saw the young woman cower in fear. She was obviously unaware of the kind of area of town she'd wandered into. This was one of the worst sections of the downtown area. Who cared about how famous this place was during the day? By night, it became a grid of terror.

Call it bad luck. She'd gone down the wrong alley. A fence lay at the far end of the alley, twenty feet away. When she'd turned to leave, Paul had seen the men come to block off her escape.

"You shouldn't be out at night," one of the men said. Dressed in a pair of jeans and a bright orange shirt that denoted him as a Scummer, he nodded at his six friends. "It could get dangerous."

The man who'd spoken chuckled. This kind of thing would usually be easy for them, he knew. As Los Angeles' premiere take-'em-out experts, they had a code, Paul had learned — turn no potential member away. Black, white,

Asian or mixed, they did not discriminate and asked only loyalty and respect.

He also knew that because of the recent activities, strength in numbers was the way they'd decided to go. It had to be that way, as the past ten days had been pretty dire for them. In that time period, a number of their men had been smacked around and subsequently arrested.

However, the smackdowns hadn't come from the cops, but from Paul's crew. Some of their members had sworn they'd seen a zombie, while others said something about fast-moving water or shifting sand or monsters.

Monsters… Paul had heard their speculation that it had to be a BS story. The gang had heard about them showing up in New York, but here? No way did they believe that was going to happen.

Snapping back to the moment at hand, Paul saw the leader turn his attention to the victim. "So I'm going to ask you," he said in an almost friendly tone. "What should we do with you?"

Crawling on her hands and knees, the woman scurried toward the exit, but the Scummers tossed her back. In desperation, she looked around and naturally the streets were devoid of anything resembling law and order.

"Why are you doing this to me?" she cried. "I didn't do anything to you. I just want to go home."

With a sigh that transitioned into a chortle, the leader took another step toward her. "But you *did* do something, girlie," he said as a malicious grin crossed his worse than ugly features. "You were walking on the streets. That makes you scum in my book. So we're going to clean the streets, and…"

Paul decided he'd seen and heard enough, so he gave the signal.

The leader suddenly stopped as a whisper of wind rushed by him, formed a barrier and pushed him and his men back. He tapped the switchblade in his left pocket and the gun in his waistband.

The wind grew in intensity, and Paul could see the leader's feelings change. "Guys, we should leave now," he said.

"You're not leaving yet," Paul said, growling from the entrance.

The leader whirled around, watching as Paul dropped in from around twenty feet off the ground. He wore a pair of jeans and a long-sleeved shirt over his now taut, well-muscled frame.

The leader smirked and brought out his pistol. With a snap of his fingers, his minions did the same. "If you're trying to scare me, buddy, you're not doing a very good job of it. You're a little short to be bustin' heads…"

His voice trailed off when Paul stepped forward into the alleyway and rolled up his sleeves to expose hairy, muscular forearms. He lowered his fangs — practice helped, and now he could control them at will — but he adopted a more relaxed stance. "Maybe I'm not," he said and made a come-here gesture. "But if you think I'm not so tough, then you can deal with my friend."

CF stepped into the alleyway behind him and let out a grunt. "Do I clean now?"

Paul shook his head and said in a conversational manner, "Wait for it. You can do it later."

"Oh…holy crap," the gang leader uttered as his eyes bugged out. The gun fell from his hand and he began to shiver. "You're…you're…"

"Monsters," CF grated, and his response made the gang leader practically keel over from sheer fright. Seeing a wolf-man and a zombie, both of whom looked very capable of doing major damage, could do that to a person.

As for the other gang members, they dropped their weapons and did a U-turn, heading for the fence, only to stop when they saw Angela, who'd landed lightly behind them. Her being there cut off all possibility of escape.

"So which one of us do you want to take on first," she asked in a tone most pleasant as she sauntered over to the leader in order to grab him by his shoulder and shake him.

"Me or my boyfriend?"

A stain appeared on the front of the leader's trousers and he gibbered, "He's your... He's your boyfriend?"

Angela tossed him to the wall where he hit hard and slid down, arms and legs splayed out like a broken Raggedy Andy doll. Her grin, fangs out and white teeth shining, made him cower, but she roughly grabbed his chin and forced his head up.

"Yeah, he's my boyfriend," she said in a voice softer than silk. "And you heard about New York, didn't you?"

"I don't think they watch much television," Paul supplied as he dispatched two of the punks with lightning fast punches. That left four others, and they fell to their knees without a peep. "But these guys look pretty smart."

Shaking like a leaf caught in the eye of a storm, the Scummer leader whipped out his switchblade and brandished it. Angela smirked, and in a lightning quick movement, she plucked it from his grasp. "A new toy," she said, just before snapping it in two. "You got anything else?"

Fear-sweat sparkled on the leader's brow and his voice shook with dread. "What are you guys?"

"I'll tell you just this once," Angela answered in a sweet tone laced with iron. She bent over and shoved her face an inch away from his. "We're your nightmares come true, the ones you don't talk about. Only this time, I want you to give everyone a message. We're here and we're staying."

"But you're leaving," Paul added. "Right now, so get out!"

The four remaining men plus their leader did as ordered, scrambling all over themselves in a frantic attempt to escape. CF stood to the side in order to let them pass, and they escaped into the night.

After they'd gone, Paul turned his attention to the young woman who was staring at them with wide eyes and he slowly raised his hands in a gesture of peace. "Hey, don't worry about us," he said. "We're here to help you...as in, you know, everyone?"

"Help us?" she squeaked.

Angela offered a cool and collected smile that spoke of future crime-fighting efforts. "Yeah, help you. You and everyone else, like he said." She indicated Paul and CF with a wave of her hand. "So go home. Be safe."

With an uncertain look on her face, the woman got to her feet and ran out. A van pulled up to the edge of the alley. The window rolled down to reveal Ooze at the wheel. "Hey, CF," he called out. "Climb aboard. You're hungry, right?"

CF nodded and silently got in. As the van drove off in a whirl of dust, Angela soared to the top of the building, and Paul clambered up the wall using his fingers and toes to dig into the brick and find a hold. Once on top, they joined hands and stared up at the moon. "You're not going to howl, are you?" she asked.

Miffed at her sense of humor, he gently shoved her. "Well, I don't know. The moon's sort of nice looking. Are you going to hang upside down after we go home?"

"There's a first time for everything." She grinned and waved her arm at the sprawling city before them. "C'mon. I don't want to go home yet." She fingered something on her belt. A small black box pulsed out a tiny red light. "These are clever little trackers, aren't they?"

Paul dug into his pocket and came out with the same device. "Ooze is pretty inventive."

Angela put her arms around his waist. She took his tracker and turned it off then turned hers off as well. "I'd say we've done our good deed for tonight, but the rest of the evening is still up for grabs," she said, her voice soft and heading toward the realm of something more than a kiss. "The question is what you're up for."

Paul felt the heat rush to his face and he reluctantly broke the embrace. "Um, we still have a few hours before daylight. I was thinking…uh, we could, you know, take care of the city." Actually, he wanted to take her out on a date, but he didn't think that the movie theaters were ready for him yet.

Angela nodded with a knowing smile on her face. "I kind

of thought you'd say that." She kissed him fondly on the lips. "Catch me if you can."

With a graceful leap from the roof's edge, she soared away. Paul lingered a moment before jumping the twenty-foot gap to the next building. He couldn't fly, but he could jump up to sixty feet or more and ran approximately three times as fast as a normal human. His powers were growing daily, and he wondered just how much he would change.

Right now it was all fun and games, but as he scanned the empty streets, he made a silent vow. The nightmares for the crooks were just beginning and the horror would be all theirs. With that thought in mind, he ran to join up with Angela, who was winging her way over the city.

Law and Order

Excerpt

Chapter One

Los Angeles, warehouse district, five minutes shy of midnight

Paul Wiseman scanned the area, inhaled a breath of foul night air, wrinkled his nose at the various smells abounding — car exhaust fumes, sweat and the nasty stench of beer and vomit — then exhaled softly. Odors on a hot summer night, he reflected. What else did one get when patrolling a large city?

Turning to the matter at hand, he touched the tiny com-link inside his left ear. It gave a small beep, and he whispered into the intercom that hung around his neck, "Is everyone ready?"

From his position in an alleyway across from the target, he made sure to keep in the shadows. Nothing save a few rats looking for food disturbed the quiet of the night.

Still, he kept an eye out for anyone who might happen by. This wasn't the friendliest of all places to walk, but some homeless people occasionally turned up and he didn't want their lives endangered.

Keeping the idea of a low profile in mind, he flattened his back against the wall, surveyed the area and stayed as motionless as possible. Night was his friend, his ally, and hiding in the shadows, crouching on rooftops and even taking to the sewers all had their merits, although the stench of the last hideaway nauseated him.

Tonight's target sat on the surface and lay at the edge of town. It was a warehouse, large and aged, sandwiched between two other abandoned ones. Everyone knew it manufactured illegal drugs.

From preliminary reports, he knew it to be heavily guarded. Ironically, even though the police acknowledged its existence, they never went near it. They knew who ran the show, so did everyone else. It was a just a matter of who wanted to cross the line and take on the syndicate first.

Since coming from the Bronx five months ago to live in the mountains of Sierra Madre near Los Angeles, Paul had studied the topography, learned every street name, scouted the hotspots and knew as much about the area as any native Los Angelino. From researching files on America's Most Wanted, he also knew the police wanted to take down this particular manufacturer of death. He was also after the same target, a kingpin, the drug lord known only as 'Azuras'.

Little was known about this man. He might have come from Colombia or from Canada. Paul had seen one picture of him. In his forties, he stood around six-four, weighed in the neighborhood of four hundred pounds, and always traveled in a limousine with bodyguards—lots of them. If the chance came, then he'd—

His earpiece crackled.

"Ready." The reply came from Angela.

Casting his gaze upward, he saw her lounged against

the brick railing of a building opposite the warehouse, six stories up. Even in the darkness, he saw her costume—a black leather outfit, leather boots, and a long cape the color of the night that she'd tricked out with an edge that glowed in the dark and illuminated her slender figure as she flew along. In contrast, he wore jeans and a T-shirt and felt positively underdressed for the occasion. Superheroes had capes and creative costumes. He used Target throwaways.

For any ordinary person, to see someone from so far away would have been impossible, yet Paul could not be considered ordinary in any way. A hybrid of a teenager and a wolf, he had enhanced night vision, among his other assets of speed and strength.

Right now, he wasn't thinking about what he could do. Instead, he focused his gaze on Angela. A slow, shy—yet sexy—smile spread across her face, and it never failed to give him confidence in whatever assignment they'd decided to tackle. "I'm good here," she added.

He waved his hand in a quick, sharp motion. She gave him the thumbs-up sign and went back to her patrolling duties.

Another voice came through Paul's intercom. It was Ooze, and he also gave a one word reply—"Ready."

Ooze always sounded as if he were underwater. Though, considering Ooze was made of water and lived in a containment suit, how else would he speak? Positioned in a van about two blocks away, he'd parked in a place where he could observe, yet still be out of harm's way. "I'm watching things. Haven't seen any movement yet."

From that distance, Ooze had his eye on everything, courtesy of some heat-imaging equipment that could track anything within a thousand meters. He also had a radio transmitter, removable license plates on the van so the authorities wouldn't be able to trace them and other assorted goodies that he'd dreamed up in his spare time.

"I'm hungry."

The voice, gravelly and low, came from CF. Dressed in

dark pants, heavy workman's boots and a shirt barely able to contain his bulk, he lurked in the shadows of another alleyway a block away to the right. "When aren't you hungry?" muttered Paul into his intercom, as he got himself into position for the strike.

The intercom he wore was indeed a marvelous device. No larger than a pin, it was capable of picking up and transmitting the faintest sounds within a five-hundred-meter radius — very useful for when the group had to be on the move.

"Always," came the answer.

"Did you bring enough food?" Paul whispered.

"I'm out."

That's just wonderful… Paul shook his head in frustration, as well as with a tinge of respect for the zombie's size, strength and willingness to get hit. CF stood for cannon fodder. It was amazing, another medical miracle, in fact, that something so large — in the realm of seven feet high and around three hundred pounds — could eat so much, never get rid of it and still ask for more.

"Hang on. We'll be finished soon," he whispered.

"Okay."

Turning his eyes back to the warehouse, Paul took note of the location, the time and other sundry details. Checking for movement up and down the street, he found none. Previous reconnaissance had revealed that no one inhabited those abandoned warehouses, and that was an added bonus. Good thing, as there was likely to be gunfire, and he didn't want anyone hurt. Civilians were innocent. They needed to be protected.

In the quiet before the upcoming storm, he reflected on the name the press had given them — the Nightmare Crew. He didn't think of himself as some kind of superhero or his friends as being anything but people with extraordinary powers. All the same, though, they were different and special. The media? They liked to stick monikers on everyone.

Since they had a moniker, the Nightmare Crew had also adopted a mantra. 'Protect the innocent. Take down the guilty. Leave no traces.' He thought the nickname was cool and the mantra even cooler. Who cared if it sounded corny? To him, it totally rocked, and the people along with the mass media seemed to groove to it as well.

More books from
J.S. Frankel

Facing off against an old enemy isn't without repercussions. Paul and the Nightmare Crew take on not only their most dangerous adversary but also the establishment.

THE MENAGERIE

BEING A NANNY TO A GROUP
OF INTERGALACTIC CRITTERS
WASN'T HIGH ON KAREN'S LIST
OF SUMMERTIME ACTIVITIES

J.S. FRANKEL

*Taking care of a pet is one thing, but when orphaned
teenager Karen Fox is kidnapped to service an interstellar
zoo, she gets more than she bargained for.*

About the Author

J.S. Frankel

J.S. Frankel was born in Toronto, Canada, a good number of years ago and managed to scrape through the University of Toronto with a BA in English Literature. In 1988 he moved to Japan and started teaching ESL to anyone who would listen to him. In 1997, he married the charming Akiko Koike and their union produced two sons, Kai and Ray. J.S. Frankel makes his home in Osaka where he teaches English by day and writes by night until the wee hours of the morning.

J.S. Frankel loves to hear from readers. You can find contact information, website details and an author profile page at https://www.finch-books.com/